Her Majesty

Her Majesty

21 stories by women

edited by
Jackie Gay and Emma Hargrave

TINDAL STREET PRESS

First published in 2002 by
Tindal Street Press Ltd
217 The Custard Factory, Gibb Street, Birmingham B9 4AA
www.tindalstreet.org.uk

Typesetting: Tindal Street Press Ltd

The front cover fire drawing is from a project with Walsall Community Arts Team
in conjunction with Walk the Plank and The New Art Gallery Walsall, to mark the
50th year of the Walsall Illuminations. This image was created by artist Sabine
Gollner working with Barbara Walker, Rob Hill, Helen Anthony and young people
from the West Midlands. The project was a collaboration with Public Art West
Midlands and the Campaign for Drawing. The fire drawing is after an original
painting, *The Blue Girl* by Theodore Garman. The designer would like to thank
Walsall Leisure and Community Services for their assistance.

Ali Smith's 'End of Story', originally commissioned as a short story premier
by Ilkley Literature Festival in 2001, is reprinted here with thanks.

ISBN 0 9535895 7 9

Printed and bound in Great Britain by
Biddles Ltd, Woodbridge Park Estate, Guildford.

Contents

Short stories are some of the best things to find between the covers of a book. A short story offers the chance to enter and return from a fictional world in one uninterrupted sitting. And a good anthology has it all: its stories are short enough to welcome brief encounters and passing trysts, but the book itself is long enough to invite a lengthy relationship.

Enter the fictional worlds created by *Her Majesty*'s twenty-one women writers and share in their tales. Get a new take on this world we think we know so well until we read fiction that leads us to hidden corners and confronts us with other views. Many of *Her Majesty*'s characters are exploring the limits and the possibilities of lives for which there are few precedents or maps. There are no guidebooks to such uncertain times, but there are plenty of fine fictions.

Sadie Plant
December 2001

Introduction

When should we live, if not now? asks Seneca, and Rachel Bentham in her elemental story: hard decisions on a soft day in Ireland. And how to live is a question fiction has always posed, as important as ever now, in the twenty-first century, when the patterns of our lives are transient and indistinct.

Here are twenty-one majestic stories in which women writers examine this question from many different perspectives. From a static caravan on the North Wales coast, to two African sisters displaced into a 'little England' boarding school, to bohemian Birmingham in the 'liberated' 1960s. These are stories peopled by characters who graft hard to make sense of their own existences, take risks and become heroic in unexpected ways. Stories of human interaction: between men, women, children, dogs; across villages, cities, continents. The characters might 'fail like common people' – Jarvis Cocker even makes an appearance in Amy Prior's story – but fictional attention reveals the courage of ordinary people, the everyday splendour to which our title refers. Majesty shines through: an illiterate woman sharing peaches on a roadside with an African refugee; a schoolgirl, more tart than sophisticate, escaping to sit in the sun with her maths teacher's baby; a teenage boy catching sight of love while tending his grandmother's garden. And in Myra Connell's 'The Skirt', a glorious feeling of freedom: 'High clouds and sunshine and wind and clear air, and the shadows of the clouds sudden on the buildings of Manhattan. Howard was glad to be alive.'

The stories in *Her Majesty* are adventures of the spirit; characters don't set out to conquer the earth but they do dare to open up worlds that might otherwise remain closed to them. These characters show dignity and emotional bravery, forge relationships with others in an unsettling world: Ju sits up 'straight like a queen' when she finds herself 'out on the wire'; peeling onions is like 'unwrapping jewels'; Beverley is seen as 'a priestess from a Pocomania church'; Christine dusts herself down 'to walk out with her head up, have nobody ask what's wrong'. A sister cooks up her own solution in a Saturday soup where 'islands of yellow-green pumpkin pieces float like speckled frogs'. Whatever the horror – the 'vicious, evil bastards' and the damage of 'always saying yes' – there endures an inextinguishable, transformative sense of self. We *will* live now.

So, why short stories and why women's writing? In Birmingham we know that there's an audience for collections such as this one. Tindal Street Press's success with *Hard Shoulder* and *Whispers in the Walls* continues a fine tradition of short-story writing in the city. *Her Majesty* began with an event that showcased the talent of women short-story writers; the audience's spirited response to the range of voices and perspectives they heard inspired us as editors. But this audience is not evident from the bestseller lists: do women only like to read books with pink covers and fancy fonts, about working in the media and finding a date? We think not, and are keen to offer more. Confessional journalism is another popular choice: 'real life' is sometimes viewed as closer to women's true voices. Many of these powerful memoirs, however, use fictional techniques; the love of language and emotional insight typical of imagined representations of life. Does this suggest that women's writing is more acceptable if it is 'real'? Is it more of a risk to write fiction rather than remembered fact about poverty, abuse, insanity? Perhaps the popularity of confessional narratives marks a retreat from contemporary uncertainties.

We think that one purpose of fiction is to tackle these uncertainties, to try to make sense of lives by fictionalizing them. The authors in this anthology observe their worlds closely – giving their stories an appealing, intimate quality – but also step back to take a wider angle, spotlighting brutalities we would rather ignore. They pin down detail, root out inconsistencies. As Ali Smith says, 'We need to know what happens,' and we can't turn away from the truth of what's happening because without that clarity we are powerless.

We hope *Her Majesty* reinforces women's voices in fiction by imagining and reflecting on who we are and who we might be. Thus continuing the feminist practice of reclaiming the past by fictionalizing it – telling hidden stories – but also daring to tackle the hazy present and the unknown future. *Her Majesty*'s men and women feel the comfortless weight of history – cruel traditions, economic migrations, gender inequalities – and know that they must make brave choices in order to determine their individual futures.

The possibilities of the here-and-now are well expressed by the short-story form. A single overarching narrative might not be representative of contemporary existence; we live episodic, fragmented lives – no maps, no predetermined routes to guide us. By focusing sharply on moments of change in such lives, these narratives illuminate the tensive web of politics, economics, families and relationships upon which we are all poised.

The first story, 'Indian Throw', highlights the shifts in attitudes towards seemliness across three generations. Is the narrator's shock at pornographic images of her daughter-in-law any different from her own mother-in-law's disgust at the sight of bare legs? Throughout *Her Majesty*, modern dilemmas jostle with ancient themes: fertility, loneliness, survival. Gemma Blackshaw's 'Girlfriend' desires her man so strongly that she blanks out his violence, yet she's utterly modern: glossy, upfront, invincible. The socially excluded, despite authority's distrust, find ways to survive, love, be hopeful, make money. 'Smell the Cheese' is how Siddy lets fawning Nick know who's top of a pecking order where the 'KLF survivalist vibe' gets you more respect than being 'successful and creative'.

Even worlds where the routes are mapped out can be thrown into turmoil by something as universal as having a baby. In 'SeaSky' Annie Murray's Sam wades 'across dark, flooded fields . . . back to the mainland', but obstacles are submerged; the paths individual and shifting. The women in 'Tutto Bene?', Polly Wright's engaging comedy of holiday manners, accept with good humour the consequences of those decisions that are 'gone in a flash'. And it takes courage for men to live in the moment too. The most appealing ones in *Her Majesty* are not like Ben with his 'new corporate web design' conversation, nor are they professional techies carefully guarding their 'mouse-clicking world of logical responses' from the 'anarchy' of fatherhood. They've strayed much further. Are strong-willed enough in their search for 'singularity and acceptance' to break through the clouds of loneliness and low expectation: a jaunty refugee saxophonist, a rough sleeper winning love with the 'long sad notes' of his harmonica, council house Clint with his head full of songs. After everything the twenty-first century can throw at them, these characters are optimistic, energetic, vital.

Jackie Gay and Emma Hargrave
December 2001

Indian Throw
Liza Cody

Am I the last woman left on earth who thinks that sex is dirty? Here I am, washing the Indian throw, angry. Sex *is* dirty. If it wasn't, the Indian throw wouldn't need washing, would it? The spare room wouldn't need airing, the scented candle wouldn't be lit and mysteriously licking the apple-green walls with ambiguous, moving shadows.

By day I deal with shadows, bruises, yes – the rubric of domestic violence. By night I wash the bedspread. Team leader, laundress. I am confused.

At work I have two clients, Maya and Mira, who need places of safety from abusive relationships. But at home my very own daughter-in-law, Sherrilyn, needed my exotic fabric as the background for her audition. A girl-on-girl sex video requires more than plain white sheets, it seems.

Last week Sherrilyn said, 'Our bedroom's too small. Craig wants to be able to walk all round the bed with his camcorder.'

'No,' I said. I looked at my son, astounded. He stirred his tea and scratched his ear. 'Sanjay?' I said.

'I'll be there,' he said. 'We won't break anything.'

'Oh yes,' Sherrilyn said, 'I want Sanj here. Then he can see there's nothing wrong, so he won't worry.'

'Sanjay!' I said.

'For fucksake,' he exploded. 'It's a career move. What *is* your problem, Mama?'

My daughter-in-law thinks that girl-on-girl sex for a porno

video is a career move. My lovely, out-of-work, deluded son agrees with her.

'Why're you staring at me like that?' Sherrilyn complained. 'I'm not doing anything wrong.'

'Not in my spare room, you're not,' I said.

'It's the fastest growing industry in the world,' Sanjay said. '*You* are denying us entry.'

I was denying them entry to my spare room for the specific purpose of making a porn video. What they do in their own room is their own affair. Or should be. A mother, a mother-in-law, should not be involved in such matters, and I can only be awestruck that she is. So this is the shift in family values I've been reading about in the journals at work. I'm staggering in the earthquake, the ground is opening beneath my feet.

Maya has the scars of cigarette burns on the soles of her feet and the insides of her thighs. In Mira's file, the glossy prints taken by a police photographer show clouds of purple bruising all over her back, stomach and chest. It's my business to look at intimate shots of women, to witness the details of their personal relationships.

Sherrilyn and Sanjay have a portfolio of images too, mainly of Sherrilyn, but some of the two of them together. They sent copies to Craig Gattes, MD of Shh!girlfrenz.com. They showed them to me too. Oddly, my first impression was that they were harsher, more forensic than the police photographs. They certainly weren't the snaps you used to share with your family in that other century, the one I was born in.

I thought the pair had come round to tell me that Sherrilyn was pregnant, that I was to be a grandmother. Well, silly me.

'I shouldn't be seeing this,' I said.

'Why not? Don't you think Sherri has a beautiful body?' my son asked.

She has indeed, but that wasn't my point.

'Why shouldn't I show my body? It's mine – I can do what I want. There's nothing wrong with showing it.'

But not to me. Why? Because *I* don't want to see it,

especially not with her legs up here and her fingers down there.

Obviously Craig Gattes, MD of Shh!girlfrenz.com, thought otherwise. He set up the audition for which my Indian throw was necessary. He would supply the camcorder and the co-star.

'Baybeebelle?' I said. 'What sort of name is that?'

'I'm going to call myself Licka Laine,' Sherrilyn informed me.

'How about Lacka Brain?' I said, because I thought ridicule might make her change her mind.

'I never took you for a prude,' Sanjay said, disappointed. 'Have you got any idea how much porn stars earn these days? A lot more than interpersonal counsellors, I can tell you.'

'Even so, you're not using my spare room,' I told him.

But that was last week and they ignored my prohibition. My son Sanjay is nineteen and thinks that what's mine is his. He still has his collection of football memorabilia under the bed in said spare room, so clearly he felt that he didn't need my permission for whatever Sherrilyn did on top of it. I thought he would go to college and be the first of my family to come home with a degree. Instead, he got married and came home with Sherrilyn.

Twenty-two years ago, Sanjay's father, call-me-Vik-dammit, came home with me, and possibly I was as big a shock to his mother as Sherrilyn is to me. Surely she was as unwilling to see my English-born, English-educated legs as I am to see Sherrilyn's private parts. Certainly call-me-Vik-dammit thought she was a prude. But as I stand here with suds up to my elbows, washing a bedspread, I wonder: is history repeating itself or am I being swamped by a tidal flow of alien moral values? 'No difference,' Sanjay insists, 'between legs and private parts. Both are good to look at; both can get you where you want to go.'

In Maya's case, both were burned with the glowing end of a cigarette, and my job is to look at them with clinical detachment and professional compassion. I don't feel like I'm turning into my own mother-in-law. And I don't think Sanjay and Sherrilyn have the right to make me feel as old and depressed and *traditional* as she was.

I drape the dripping throw over the clothes horse in the utility room and phone my best friend, Joanie.

'I'm so mad with them,' I say. 'I got home an hour ago and found they'd totally ignored me. The spare room's a mess and I had to wash the bedspread.'

Joanie says, 'I don't understand. How do you get stains from girl-on-girl stuff? I thought it was boys who did the staining.'

There's a minute's silence while we contemplate our ignorance of stains, then Joanie says, 'Itching powder. If I were you I'd sprinkle itching powder on the bed and make them regret it if they ever did it again.'

'Good idea,' I say, although I am thinking that the reason I had to wash the throw by hand was because it is a work of love, covered with much intricate appliqué and embroidery. It's the only piece I have left after call-me-Vik-dammit went back home. His mother gave it to me. I used to think it was horribly old-fashioned.

Joanie says, 'Come for a drink. There's a blues band playing live at the Bell. It'll cheer you up.'

'I'm not blue,' I say. 'I'm mad as a thistle.'

But blues, like a good strong cup of tea, is a cure for whatever ails you, and I will take whatever I can get. The pub is warm, the band is hot, and I do feel better, in spite of seeing an old client sitting on the knee of the man who broke her arm, her jaw and her china. A DIY tattoo on his forearm reads, Shit happens. There's truth in tattoos.

The next day, I answer the door and take delivery of an ugly bunch of pink carnations. There is no apology, no explanation: simply a card saying, 'Happy Mother's Day, love, Sanjay.' He used to make me cards when he was in primary school. Since then, nothing. There's no truth in Mother's Day cards. But I put the carnations in water and stand them on the spare-room windowsill. The flowers can't help it if they're the colour of cheap toilet paper and nobody wants them.

Downstairs, I fold and carefully wrap the Indian throw in tissue and brown paper. I lay it like a sleeping child on the back seat of my car and drive to Sanjay's flat.

Sherrilyn opens the door and starts immediately.

'The trouble with you is that you don't know the difference between sex and a real relationship. I'll have you know that Craig Gattes' wife Bestia is dead famous. She's been in hundreds of vids and they've been married for more than five years.'

'Five years, wow!' I say, in spite of having promised myself to be non-judgemental. Maya has been married fifteen years.

'Yes, and they make pots of money. They're a business partnership. You think, because you're Sanjie's mother, you have the right to criticize. Well, I got news for you, Sanj is my biggest fan.'

She has a little pale face with no more chin than a gerbil. I wonder how much makeup it will take to transform her into a porn star. It's true that she has a lovely body, but her face is pure girl-at-the-bus-stop.

'I haven't come to criticize,' I say, sighing at her extreme youth.

'Yeah, well you better not. There's nothing wrong with what I'm doing.'

'I've brought something for you and Sanjay,' I tell her.

'What? Some kind of peace offering? Sanj is very angry with you, you know. He says you're trying to make us feel bad about ourselves.'

But she relents enough to make a cup of weak, milky tea. I'm sure she's too impatient to let the water boil properly. The kitchen is cramped, and crammed with white goods. We sit with our knees almost touching. No room for Craig and his camcorder in here.

Sherrilyn comes straight back to the point. 'You've spent your whole life in those women's refuges and it's warped you. Sanj says you should change jobs, change your attitude. Like, women aren't all victims any more. Some of us have got girl power now.'

I wonder what Maya and Mira would say to that.

'Sanj grew up in those women's shelters. He says it practically ruined his life.'

'It practically saved his life.'

'Bad things only happen if you let them happen. I can't understand why you didn't take control, make something more of yourself.'

'I thought I did.'

'Look at me,' Sherrilyn says. 'When I left school they said I'd never be good for anything but stacking shelves. They didn't know *shit*. Look at that microwave. We bought it with Craig's cheque. I'm going to get a boob job next. Sanj sent away for a catalogue.'

It's Saturday, and I say, 'Is Sanjay at the match?'

She sniffs, and we smile at each other for the first time.

I think about last night in the Bell when my old client pretended she didn't recognize me. I pretended I hadn't seen her with her jaw wired because her man with the tattoo whacked all the beauty out of her when he thought other men were looking at her.

Sherrilyn picks at the string around the brown paper parcel on the kitchen table. Her long fingernails are the colour of blackberries. 'Oh,' she says. 'The Indian throw. Why are you giving it to us?'

'Well,' I say carefully, 'Sanjay's grandmother gave it to me. She made it with the help of her sisters – Sanjay's great-aunties. So it should stay in the family. You like it, don't you? And I thought it was time you and Sanjay inherited some family tradition.'

'It'll need dry cleaning,' she says without thinking or looking. And maybe, just maybe, I can see her beginning to blush.

The Skirt

Myra Connell

High clouds and sunshine and wind and clear air, and the shadows of the clouds sudden on the buildings of Manhattan. Howard was glad to be alive. Spring was coming, at last, after all the rain and cold. His body felt strong and well: the Saturday morning run, from his apartment as far as the end of Brooklyn Bridge and back again, was easy; and it was exhilarating running across over the water: seeing the sky and the water and the clouds, the expansiveness of it all. Even on dull days it was a pleasure: today even more so.

It was on the way back that he saw the skirt. It was displayed in the window of a little shop that was a favourite of his, which he passed often on his way to the art supply store. It was run by a stylish Jewish woman who picked up and sold out-of-the-way things: jewellery, hats, dresses from the forties with shoulder-pads and nipped-in waists and knife-sharp kick-pleats at the back.

The skirt was a long one, black and rather full, slightly Japanese-looking. Howard stopped outside the window and looked at it. He hesitated only for a second over going in in his vest and running shoes, sweaty and no doubt smelling a bit. He'd struck up quite a friendship with Arlene – even though he used the shop like a museum, to feed his pleasure in looking at nice things, and never bought anything. She was an eccentric and she wouldn't care how he was dressed.

She smiled when she saw him. 'You been running?'

'Yes. Just over the bridge and back. Great day.'

'Fabulous.' Her favourite word of praise, for everything – a ring, a dress, the look of the seam on some stockings, the day.

'Too nice to be indoors.'

She shrugged. She was tightly dressed for work, in one of her own suits. A smart gabardine in a tasteful grey-green colour to go with the particular shade of blond that she dyed her hair. Short bob. Lipstick, court shoes, glasses. She looked business-like, as ever.

'Can I see that skirt in the window?'

'The black one?' She started to take it off the display. 'It's great, isn't it? It's Japanese.'

'Is it old?'

'Not particularly. It's one that was left over at the end of a season, I suppose. Or it could have been that somebody bought it and wore it a couple of times and then decided she didn't like it.'

He looked at the price tag. 'But it's expensive.'

'Yes. It happens.'

He looked at the skirt carefully, while Arlene turned to another customer. He liked it. He liked it a lot. It was wonderfully well made. The fabric was a fine but densely woven wool. It had long darts from the waist, front and back, and a side zip with a simple hook and eye at the top, no waistband. It was lined with black satin, and it was heavy; he felt the tug of the yards of fabric as he held the hanger in his hand.

He loved it. There was something about it – the weight of it, the incredible cleanness of the cut, the heavy satin lining. It would be floor-length on anyone who wore it. A floor-length, simple, sweeping black skirt.

He wanted to buy it. He didn't know who he would give it to. But he didn't want to let it go. He didn't have his wallet on him; but Arlene would keep it for him if he asked her to.

The customer had left, and Arlene came over to him.

'I love it. I just don't know who I'd buy it for.'

'Cinderella. You'd have to look for the girl who would wear it.'

He suddenly felt embarrassed. 'No. I won't get it.' He handed it back to her abruptly. 'I'll see you later.'

'Have a nice day.'

But the skirt stayed on his mind. He imagined all sorts of things that might happen to him – not exactly a confirmed bachelor, he wouldn't say that of himself, but definitely single, and for a long time – if he bought it. An observer could watch him for six months and never see him with a woman: there was never more than an occasional date to go with him to opening nights or dinners, to come home afterwards. Nothing more ever developed. People probably wondered if he was homosexual: living alone in his mid-forties. He wasn't, as far as he knew. He didn't want the skirt for himself. Even if he let himself imagine being a man who liked wearing women's clothes, this wasn't something that would excite him. It wasn't feminine enough: no lace, no clinging to the bottom or thighs, nothing revealing of a smoothed-down crotch. He just loved it for its fine quality: as he loved his simple, well-made furniture, or the heavy old woollen blankets, woven in strips because that was the width of the loom, that he had on his bed.

He imagined having it hanging in his closet and then being out somewhere – at an exhibition, say – and seeing a girl who would be the right size for it, tall and long-legged and slim-waisted, and somehow finding a way to go up to her and say, 'I have something at home that I think you might like.' But you can't say that. 'Something I'd like to give you.' Even worse – not even a chat-up line, that just sounded like the sort of thing that a flasher might say before exposing himself.

He'd have to take it with him. No good bundled up in a bag. He'd need a suit carrier, the kind that businessmen take on aeroplanes, so that it would still look beautiful when he took it out. *Took it out*: it was beginning to seem that his unconscious mind was making a symbol – a fetish perhaps – out of this skirt.

He shut it down. Got on with his day. Took a different route to the bridge in the mornings.

But the next time he passed the shop, the skirt had been reduced. Now it was not only beautiful and desirable, it was a bargain too. He went in again, this time with his wallet.

Arlene laughed. 'Can't keep away from it?'

'No,' he admitted. 'You've reduced it.'

'I have. I don't want it around all summer, I haven't the space.'

She got it out for him again and again he held it; so heavy. Falling so gracefully. He looked inside, between the lining and the skirt itself. It was finished immaculately, not a single loose thread, the seams neatly overstitched. There had been no haste in the making of it, no expense spared. No underpaid and careless machinist had rushed through the stitching in order to get on to the next one as fast as possible. You just didn't see things made like this.

'OK,' he said. 'I'll take it.' He gave her his credit card. 'What for I have no idea.'

'Time will tell,' said Arlene. 'Something will happen. If you go with your heart, things happen.' She interleaved the skirt with pink tissue paper as she folded it, so that the fabric didn't touch itself, and then placed it neatly in one of her bags and sealed the top with tape.

'Enjoy,' she said, as she handed it to him. She smiled. 'You get to be Prince Charming now.'

At home, Howard hung it from a hook on the wall opposite his bed. People did buy clothes to hang on their walls. Kimonos, for example. If he wanted, he could display this like one of those, with the skirt pinned out to show the semicircle of dark fabric against the white wall.

But that wasn't it. He wanted it to be used and worn. Actually, he wanted it to be used and worn by somebody who would then become part of his life. Someone who had in herself the same fineness as the skirt; someone who would wear it with smooth bare legs underneath; who would climb with him out of the window on to the deck that he had built on the flat roof of the next building and sit with the skirt hitched above her knees sunning herself; and who knew him in such a way that she would let him put his hand on one smooth, rounded knee and then slide it up the inside of the thigh under the skirt's satin lining.

That thought moved him, in his heart and in his groin, and suddenly his pants were too tight. He fell asleep that night holding himself and thinking of the girl under the skirt and her silent desire for him.

Nothing got achieved. Howard's fantasies remained fantasies, and he couldn't think of any way to make them into reality. He went to Arlene's a couple of times, chatted, looked at her stuff. She asked him every time how he was doing as Prince Charming, and he told her that the skirt was still hanging on his wall and he was no more Prince Charming than she was. She raised an eyebrow at that, in the knowing way that she had, and then they burst out laughing.

'What are you going to do about it, Howard?' she asked.

'God knows.' He fingered a thick shiny plastic bracelet on the corner of the table. 'I can't do anything about it, it's in the hands of fate.'

That day he was buoyant about it. But sometimes, and more and more as the weeks passed, he felt low, and a little ashamed. He looked at himself with a critical, hostile eye, and berated himself for being a failure, weird: sick even. The truth was that he was lonely, and he was angry with himself for not being able to find a girl in the ways that other men did. He stopped going to see Arlene and he made himself stop thinking about the skirt. He ignored it, and it lost its special charge; blended in with the other objects in his place. He left town for a few weeks, stayed with a friend upstate; and then the summer had gone by and he was back. His work going better.

Routines taking him through the days into the fall; darker days, still an occasional warm one, and the rain coming, whipping the sad trees in the little park where the Chinese women did Tai Chi in the mornings. The daily run less exhilarating, more of an effort.

Howard's friend Steve had been placing ads in the lonely hearts columns; and when they met for a beer as they did every couple of weeks, Steve was full of the dates he'd been on.

'You should do it. You're going to be a sad old man if you don't watch out,' he told Howard. 'Look at the state of you. You're scruffy. You don't shave often enough. You ought to make an effort.'

He was walking home from one of these sessions, a little tipsy from the beers, about eight-thirty on an October evening, already dark, when a woman stopped him. She wanted to know the way to the subway.

'I'm going past it, it's just along here,' he said. She was from out of town, here on a visit. She had come to Chinatown to look round, had got caught up in looking in the shops. He knew what they sold: cooking utensils; huge woks and vat-like pans for cooking rice in restaurant quantities; silk embroidered jackets and purses; dishes of all shapes and sizes with blue fishes painted on them.

As they walked the couple of blocks to the subway entrance, the rain suddenly came down again, as it had been doing on and off all day, pelting and fierce, and they took shelter in a doorway to wait for it to stop.

'It's wild, this weather. Does it often rain like this in New York?' she asked.

'Lately.'

He noticed that she had no coat. It had been warm in the morning, the sort of morning that looks as if it's going to stay fine all day. There wasn't enough room in the doorway for him to stand away from her and see her. Glancing sideways, he saw wet hair and dark eyebrows, rain running down her forehead.

She had a small leather rucksack, the straps neat over her shoulders. He imagined standing sheltering like this with her if he knew her better, and how they would stand close and he would pull her to him and in the dark, with the street emptied by the rain, he would kiss her and slip his hand into her wet jeans.

Maybe this was the chemistry that people talked about. He hadn't seen her at all really, he didn't know her, not even her name, he was just standing beside her in the doorway: but he seemed to be aroused by her. The beer had done it perhaps. Not Steve's talking about his conquests, that had left Howard cold. The months of being alone, going into years now.

'I'd better be going,' she said. 'I said I'd be back by ten.'

'You'll get soaked.' The rain was no less than it'd been before.

'I know. I already am. I'm like a kid – if it's sunny when I leave home I think it's going to be sunny all day, and so I don't take a coat. But I'm staying with people and they'll worry if I'm not back.'

'Couldn't you call them?' A broken gutter was flushing water, in great whooshes, across the sidewalk in front of them, and the plastic sheeting over the last of the noodle stalls was bulging with water. The owner took a broom handle to it and poked it, so that the whole two, three gallons deluged over the ground.

'I live near by. You could call from there, and I could lend you an umbrella.' A skirt, he thought. This is it, this is the moment.

She looked at him now for the first time. Her eyes were brown and steady. In spite of the unsuitable clothes, she looked like a woman who could take care of herself. Not someone you could mess with. She reminded him of the Tai Chi teacher, out there every morning with her strong quiet body, teaching the fan form in the park, each student with her own bright scarlet fan. She had that same quiet, unarguable strength: she didn't need to insist on it or make a fuss about it;

but it was unquestionably there. She was probably about the same age too, somewhere in her mid-forties.

He felt himself being looked at and appraised. And for a moment he wished he hadn't had that fantasy about enticing women off the street and asking them to try the skirt on for him. But as he met her eyes, he expanded himself to include that too, and somehow to include all of it, all of himself, and Arlene and the skirt and the beauty of it and the fantasies and the loneliness, and to let all of it be there. It was very simple, no point in trying to hide or pretend. He stood there letting her look at him, and he felt naked and accepted and not ashamed, and his heart opened and he smiled and she smiled back.

'OK,' she said lightly; and now his heart sang.

'OK. Let's just go for it then. Follow me.' And he set off running with her beside him and the rain still hammering down and both of them getting soaked through. Lights going out in the shops now, the stalls emptied of vegetables, street vendors with their heavy barrows leaning into them doggedly as they pushed them home for the night. Past the subway station entrance, and round the corner to his block and then his doorway and then up the stairs. He slowed down now, calmed down, though his heart was beating fast from the running. He opened the doors for her and was happy that her face showed no sign of regret for having said yes to this. Water was dripping off both of them; it had seeped through his coat. He took it off and hung it behind the door.

'Do you want to make that call?' he said.

'I'd better.' She took off the rucksack, sodden and stiff, and rummaged in it, brought out an address book. He gave her the handset of the phone and went into the kitchen to let her be private.

He felt quiet, very calm: happy, he realized. Peaceful. He put away a few things, tidied a bit. He heard her say a few words and then, 'OK, see you later. Yep. OK. Bye.'

He went out to her again. 'Is that OK?'

She gave him back the phone. 'It's fine.'

He could see her now: tallish, slim, face flushed after the cold and wet. The jeans dark with water, the jacket and shirt bedraggled. Shoulder-length hair, black and wet, steady eyes. There was something oriental about the width of her cheekbones.

'If you wanted you could take a bath and I'll give you some dry things. Or I'll give you the umbrella if you want to go straight away.' He wanted to keep every bit of excitement, hope and desire out of his voice and his face. He wanted to be for her; for her not to be afraid, for her to have what she needed. It was reassuring to him that he had seen that strength in her; it meant he could trust that she would look after herself, make her own choice.

'A hot bath would be great. If that's OK.'

'It's fine. Would you like tea? I have brandy too.'

'Tea! And brandy in it!' Her face lit up. 'That would be wonderful. I'm really cold.'

He went to run the bath, took a clean towel from the drawer, put rosemary oil and ginger in the water to keep her from catching cold.

When he came back out, she was standing by the heater. He made ginger tea and added brandy, just a little; gave it to her. Found a dry T-shirt – one of the ones that had shrunk and that he'd kept in case it fitted somebody sometime. And then reached up and lifted the skirt off its hook.

'A skirt?' she said. 'A beautiful one.'

'Yes,' he said.

He handed it to her, with the towel and the T-shirt, and she took them over her arm, the tea in her free hand, into the bathroom.

Smell the Cheese
Tina Jackson

At the age of thirty-seven, Eleanor is chazzed up for the first time.

– Politically, I can't agree with what taking drugs means in terms of maintaining dependent economies in the third world, she argues. But seeing as Nick doesn't seem to have the same objections, and neither do the others, she bows to social pressure and gingerly sniffs the fourth line off the mirror.

Niamh fingers a sleek blond strand of hair. Put a sock in it, she thinks. Political correctness is boring. So the wrong kind of eighties retro. Like Eleanor's dress, with that polo neck, and the skirt clinging to her shanks like mould. Black's really not attractive when it fades to a vaguely green tint.

The charlie doesn't seem to have any effect, decides Eleanor after waiting anxiously for five scared minutes. All that fuss for nothing, she thinks. Worrying that it was going to give me a heart attack. What a waste of money. I'm dying for a drink.

She looks at Nick. Not quite handsome, but reassuring and attractive as well as successful and creative. She feels her fanny twitch at the thought of him, and also a great desire to tell him about how stressed she is that, existentially speaking, she's been terribly mistaken about her lifestyle choices. Even the back of his head looks sympathetic. She cranes forward, nearer to it.

– Do you think I've taken the wrong direction for my life, Nick? she implores. – Because I made the decision to fulfil my intellect at the expense of my status, only I can see that if I'd stayed on and taken my diploma, by now I'd've got to the point where I'd've achieved enough to dictate my own terms, whereas here I am with a PhD and a pittance, watching my old colleagues getting £120 grand a year while I can barely afford a new pair of tights.

Nick isn't listening. He's watching Siddy riffling through his CDs.

– Av yer got Scratch or Shaka or owt like that? Meditation music for t'modern urban buddha inna laidback mellow stylee?

The best Nick can come up with is a Bob Marley compilation but Siddy seems delighted.

– Tuff Gong's da bomb! He grins and wriggles himself further back into his parka, as if making a nest for himself.

Niamh isn't paying attention. Engrossed in the back of a Marks & Spencer's carton she's plucked from the floor, she's closely scrutinizing the small print. Bored, she's thinking. This coke's pants. Cut to fuck. Trust Nick to pay over the odds for rubbish drugs. Should've left it to Siddy. Without looking up from her carton, she swipes her pale, manicured finger in the trail of white powder left on the mirror, and rubs it reflectively into her gums.

Siddy tries to catch her eye. He's twitching his head towards her and then at the floor, as if to say, *Look, look over there, what I've found, look at that.* He's spotted a lesbian-sex manual among weeks' worth of Sunday papers.

Niamh knows Siddy is trying to attract her attention but she ignores him, so as to wind him up.

– Have you seen Luella Bartley's new skirts? she asks in Eleanor's direction. – She's doing eighties retro as well this year.

– Is she? replies Eleanor uncertainly. She hasn't heard of anyone Niamh's referred to. Niamh has made her feel tongue-tied all night. She looks at her fingernails and plucks nervously at one that's snagged.

Hasn't she heard of nail bars? thinks Niamh. I expect she's got parrot earrings somewhere.

Nick is sitting on the floor intently scanning the morning's broadsheet.

Eleanor stretches voluptuously along the length of the sofa. She feels sexy in this little black dress. She hopes the effect isn't lost on Nick.

– What are you reading? she asks, peering over Nick's shoulder so that her breasts in their Lycra casing un-accidentally brush against the back of his shoulder.

– Did you know we've got domestic boar in this country? Nick says, sounding nervous. He was anxious in the restaurant, when they decided to come back here. Siddy didn't like the place he'd chosen, or the food. If Niamh were any more bored, she'd be horizontal. And Eleanor has tried to chat him up before, by talking about his paintings at great length. She's usually too inhibited to be predatory but the single line of coke seems to have unleashed something he'd rather she put back in its box.

– They escaped during Hurricane Fish in 1986 when falling trees crashed through estate boundaries, he adds. – And there are urban deer as well.

– I know that, says Niamh, without looking up. If she'd said *shut up* her message couldn't have been clearer. – Have you got a decent DVD we could watch? *Gladiator*? I love films with men fighting.

– They're not containable, says Nick, making himself sound as if he can neither see the elegant stretch of Niamh's long beige limbs, nor feel Eleanor's 34As brushing his Duffer-of-St-George-clad back. – They can get foot and mouth as well. One farm, just one farm, destroyed three hundred pigs this weekend.

– I could av done with a bit of pork pie before we left, says Siddy to no one in particular. – Or a bacon and egg bap. Were that what you'd call a meal? Big white plate and not much on it. Food with ideas above its station.

– If anyone's got foot and mouth, mutters Niamh in an undertone, we all know who it is.

Eleanor concentrates on winding herself slightly further round Nick's shoulder. He can feel the nub of her right nipple pressing under his shoulder blade. He shifts slightly.

– Nick? Do you think I did the right thing? she insists. – In giving up my career to fulfil my creativity? I can't decide if it was wilful idealism and the need for self-determination on my own terms, or just the necessity of rejecting the conformism of adhering to a career path. But there are long nights when I worry about having acted so impetuously. What do you think, Nick?

She half closes her eyes and inhales deeply so that 1989's Bodymap can get closer to 2001's Duffer.

– Time for another? he says, reaching for the mirror and creating a three-inch gap between their bodies.

– Too right, nods Siddy. – Bout bloody time. Had you down as a right southern jessie. Where I come from, we tek our drugs when we've got em. Not put em in fookin bank for rainy day. Got any draw? Oh well, askin costs nuthin, does it? Av to roll me own.

He rummages in the folds of his parka for his stash tin, then spots Nick's well-stocked drinks shelf and a glint comes into his eye. – Is that old Joe Cuervo? Few shots ud go down nicely.

Nick jumps up to do as Siddy wants. He doesn't want Siddy to write him off as a lightweight. It was what he'd fretted about the night he went out with Siddy, after the band had approved his cover designs in a terrifying half-hour during which Nick had been reminded of all the cliques at school that hadn't let him join in, and then whisked him off to a party under railway arches in Vauxhall, a part of town Nick had never been before. The club was dark, lit with occasional glimmers of black light, music pulsing like a giant heartbeat. Just being there felt dangerous, reckless, sexy. Being there with Siddy raised everything to another level. Scrawny Siddy, in his element, throwing shapes, taking the piss, controlling the vibe.

Siddy, the cocky urchin, at the heart of it all: eyes lit up, strutting from one pose to another with his feet at ten to two, grinning like a demon. Siddy who was so full of it that he made Nick's life seem grey and unlived. Siddy who had swaggered up to him and pressed a tablet into his mouth.

– What was that? Nick had squawked.

– E. Only cut with ketamine. Av addum before, they're nice. It were like time-lapse photography, where summat'd appen and then you'd av a bit uvva mem'ry lapse and summat else altogether'd be goin on. You'll luvvit. Avver good'un.

Nick had finally re-entered his usual headspace to find himself slumped next to a smoking Siddy in a stairwell halfway up a towerblock. His shoes were covered in black filth and his watch told him it was two-thirty in the afternoon.

– Think I'd best mek tracks, Siddy said chirpily. – Now yer back int land of living. There'll be hell to pay with wife if am not back before teatime. Are you all right doing stairs on yer own?

Nick had nodded blearily and, an hour later, unable to stand up without feeling as if the top of his head was about to fly off, he descended six flights of concrete steps by bumping down them on his bottom. It was only the thought of Siddy, his new mate, that sustained him. I've had an adventure with Siddy, he thought. I'm in with him. For the next week, every time his mobile had rung, he'd prayed it would be Siddy on the other end.

It never was. Eventually, Nick plucked up the courage to call.

– I wondered if you were doing anything this weekend? he'd stuttered shyly. – I wondered, if you're not doing anything else, if you'd fancy a bite to eat.

– Oh aye, Siddy had said immediately. – Am up for that. Ah luv a good scran. Ah'll bring wife. You bring your bird, an all.

This was where Eleanor came in. Nick hadn't got a bird. Wasn't all that lucky, in that department. The ones he fancied weren't interested and he didn't want to settle for second best.

But, as he somehow had it in mind that Siddy's wife would be a doughy northern dollop who spent most of her life in the kitchen, making cups of tea, he thought he'd ask Eleanor along. He knew Eleanor through friends. She was single, around his own age, reasonably attractive and had interestingly abandoned a high-powered commercial career to return to her studies, and she was always quietly thrilled to see him. That gave him a warm feeling. Nick needed to show Siddy that, in his own space, he too could command attention.

Blonde, beautiful, bored Niamh, Siddy's wife, is the most unattainable creature Nick has ever seen. From the moment he first sets eyes on her, Nick is instantly hard. He wants to wipe that disdainful look off her face. With his dick. But women like her didn't give men like him a second look. Next to Niamh's creamy smoothness, Eleanor's interesting monkey face resembles a crumpled paper bag and her clothes mark her out as someone who's forgotten how to have a clue. Eleanor's shocked, well-meaning innocence about drugs makes her come across like an overgrown schoolgirl. Nick feels as if he's been awarded the booby prize. And she makes it so obvious that she fancies him.

– Shall I chop em out while you sort t'tequila? Siddy shuffles his body further into his parka. He's warming up.

– I don't believe it. Niamh deliberately raises her voice, and she looks up from the carton. – They put potato starch in these.

Siddy looks at her sideways. Nick daren't look at her at all. Eleanor looks at Nick.

– Oo rattled your cage? snaps Siddy. – You've done nowt but read that fookin packet since we gorrit.

Niamh raises her eyes, and says nothing.

– Ey, Elly, says Siddy, in a friendly, jolly voice different from the one he used for Niamh. – You a'right?

– I'm having a lovely evening, she replies. She isn't sure why Nick seems so keen on this loud, shaven-headed, skinny Siddy with his big baggy clothes and his drugs and his snooty wife, but if he was the excuse for inviting her, then she's not going to look a gift horse in the mouth. – I've been so looking forward to seeing Nick's new flat. Isn't it beautiful? The end wall is such a wonderful setting for the new painting.

She looks up, and around, at the high white spaces of the new loft apartment which bear witness to Nick's commercial success and aesthetic judgement.

– It must get so cold, though, in winter, she says. – You'll need to make sure you keep nice and warm, Nick.

Niamh rolls her eyes upwards.

Siddy makes a fist with his right hand and places it at the top of his upturned left palm.

– Elly, he commands, beckoning with the fingers of his left hand. – Come ere an see what I've got.

She obeys, coming in for a closer look until her eyes are inches away from Siddy's middle left-hand finger.

– Smell the cheese, Elly, he says, and as she strains forward to sniff what's behind his fingers, he swiftly, none-too-gently biffs her nose with his balled up right fist.

Nick's face creases, his lips purse as he tries to contain his amusement, and then a tremendous bellow of laughter escapes. Siddy joins in. The pair clink shot glasses and down goes the tequila.

– That's right! crows Siddy. – Skull it, man!

Nick looks up and beams in the direction of Siddy's approval. Flustered with confusion, Eleanor escapes back to the sofa and rubs her nose.

– Take your coat off, Siddy, drawls Niamh without looking at him. – Nobody's going to steal it. You're not in Salford now.

The tequila has all gone, and so has the cocaine.

Niamh is flicking through a glossy magazine in a bored, desultory way, looking at spreads of clothes similar to the ones she's wearing. Eleanor is half on, half off the sofa. The mini-dress has ridden up to reveal ladders in her black opaque tights, her head is slumped forward, her arms are outstretched towards where Nick was sitting, except that he's moved out of her reach. Her eyes are half shut and her mouth is half open. Siddy, hunched forward and rocking slightly, is still in the best chair, still in his parka.

– So worrappened was, we were E'd up t'lot of us, really avvin it, I'd got a gram of whizz int mix an all, we'd robbed t'superglue from hole int back of warehouse, right, industrial container of it, and we give it loads, so when manager came back t'hotel, all t'furniture in suite were stuck t'ceiling. It were a right laugh. Stuff you gerrup to when you're a lad all designer-labelled up and off yer face and you think the world owes you. Right after our first single it were, job were a good'un.

– You do talk a load of bollocks, Siddy, says Niamh clearly.

– Shut up an read yer carton, snaps Siddy back. – And leave the bollocks talkin ter me. I am t'ninja king bollocks talker. Number one mirror licker of all time. I can talk bollocks until every other fooker has curled up an died.

Nick cranes forward so as not to miss any of Siddy's story. Eleanor shifts in his wake, as if pulled by invisible strings.

– We were gods among men. We loomed larger than life in our own mythology. But, you av to bear in t'mind that psychedelics an leisure wear and becomin yer own hero are t'lifestyle options of choice for average unemployed young males from the north-west, continues Siddy. – Drop a load of acid an mushies an go up moors in yer Helly Hansen, two hundred quid's worth of outdoor threads feelin ten foot tall on a KLF survivalist vibe.

Nick is lost for words, and opens his mouth like a fish.

– Ah berrit weren't like that when you were growin up, says Siddy, vicious all of a sudden. – Ah berrit were all school uniform an homework an fancyin art mistress but never doin owt about it. Wanking in yer bedroom t'Smiths. Lads like you never know what ter do wi real women. All mucky-minded thoughts an no trousers.

Niamh's eyes widen hungrily.

– Yer a nice bloke but yer just a posh boy wor ain't gorrer clue, says Siddy, relentless now he's turned nasty. – Like that poor nice little bitch oo'd be waggin er tail all over you if yer gave her half a chance, only yer've ignored er all evenin. Yer'd rather listen ter boy's own adventures than even pat er on t'head. Yer disrespectin her, man. Yer are. Yer never gonna be a real man because yer too busy mekkin up fer never avvin been a great big kid.

– Don't get all romantic, Siddy, drawls Niamh. – She was gagging for it, all over him like a rash, it's enough to put anyone off for life. One line and it went straight to her fanny.

Niamh stands up and gives Siddy a look that means business.

– Time for a waz. She yawns and strolls out of the room.

Siddy stands up too.

– Don't go without me, he says, and follows her.

Siddy slams Niamh up against the bathroom wall, presses himself up against her and kisses her as if he wants to suck the life out of her. She twines herself around him like a vine as he wriggles his hand under the satin skin of her knickers into the wetter silk of her skin beneath.

– Am goin ter give you one right ere, he pants as she comes up for air and fumbles expertly with the zip on his jeans. – A proper portion of cocaine sex, yer dirty beautiful bitch. I'll wipe that look right off yer face.

– I thought you'd never ask, gasps Niamh. She wraps her legs around his thighs and her mouth forms an exquisite O as Siddy's cock slides violently into her. – I've been waiting for you to do that to me all evening.

Nick sits on his flokati rug and surveys the debris of his evening. The Bob Marley CD, missing its case. Massive Attack's first. St Germain's second. J. J. Cale, which seems to have been on repeat play for ever. Friday's *Guardian*, open at a story about foot and mouth. The sleeve from Siddy's band's latest CD. A crumpled square of paper marked with origami folds. An empty bottle of tequila gold. Four shot glasses. An ashtray, next to where Siddy was sitting, filled with fag ends and roaches. A mirror flecked with white powder and smeared with fingerprints.

Eleanor, slumped on the sofa, in laddered black tights and a dress made out of sagging black Lycra.

Nick feels a pang of something – pity or fondness or exasperation, he isn't sure which – and tries to haul her body so she's lying prone on the sofa. Her dead weight is too much for him, and he has to let her flop back into her awkward position.

– I'll get you a blanket, he says, wearily, although he thinks she probably won't hear him.

– S'all right, she mumbles. – Just stay here f'you don't mind.

Siddy and Niamh appear at the door, clutching each other and grinning. They've been gone such a long time that Nick's almost forgotten they were still in his flat.

– We're offski, chirps Siddy. – Wiv adder laugh. Ah'll see yuh round.

Siddy bounces as he walks to the front door. Niamh glides. Nick reels to his feet to let them out.

– Nick, says Siddy, as Nick reaches for the latch. – Come over here a sec an see what I've got.

Siddy makes a fist with his right hand, and places it at the top of his upturned left palm.

– Smell the cheese, Nick, says Siddy, poker-faced.

Nick tries to laugh, but it comes out like a choke. – You can't catch me, he says. – You did that earlier. I'm not that stupid.

But Siddy doesn't budge, and Nick feels compelled to move in slowly until his nose is centimetres away from Siddy's balled up fist.

– Nick, says Siddy, fixing him with his eyes. – This is different cheese.

Nick brings his nose closer. When Siddy biffs it, really quite hard, he sees stars.

Hospitality

Gaynor Arnold

I sense it from the minute I wake up: I'm reaching the perfect pressure.

I lie on the bed unclothed, feeling the warmth of my body evaporate into the air, and the warmth of the air seep back through the pores of my skin. There's a complete osmosis, an exact equilibrium of heat. Days like this are rare, even in high summer, and the year has been disappointing until now. Grey, rainy, heavy. Lows on the chart and in the heart. I've stayed indoors.

But now I will get up. I will wash and breakfast. I will go to the park and walk among the flowerbeds, inhale the moistness of the glasshouses, and lie on the grass by the lake. Someone will come past. And stop. Things will repeat themselves.

I prepare eggs, toast, marmalade. In the morning room, on the mahogany table, I set a cup and saucer, two kinds of plates, a toast-rack, butter in a dish. I like the ritual of breakfast, the habit since childhood of starting the day properly. In this I am different from Rob. And from the others; the friends he brought to stay. They would get up at midday and stand at my windows half-dressed, squinting at the light, gulping at coffee and cigarettes. A little later they might bite at a biscuit, or crunch at an apple they would leave to brown on the sill.

Don't fuss, Rob would say if I cleaned up the crumbs or rinsed out a cup. *Just relax, princess. Relax and be beautiful.*

I tried so hard. It seemed such a good thing not to care about the material things in life, to be free from the slavery of habit. I watched the others, trying to copy what they did. But I don't smoke. And coffee makes me ill. And I am used to a tablecloth and cutlery. I am used to sitting down at eight o'clock sharp, clean and brushed and smelling of soap.

I sit down now. I pour myself tea from the big silver pot, milk from the silver jug. It is satisfying and civilized. I enjoy watching the clear liquid arc into my cup, the milk mingling it to opaque. *It's really no more trouble*, I would tell Rob, *than a tea bag in a mug. And a lot less wasteful.* But more ostentatious, he thought. And infinitely more bourgeois. 'Bourgeois' was his favourite word of condemnation as he lay on the Persian carpet, propped up with tasselled cushions, watching my colour TV.

He's gone now, of course. They've all gone. The whole thing was an aberration, a kind of hiatus in the pattern. They moved in, and then moved on. It's quite a while since they were here. But I dare say they remember me fondly enough, look back with a smile at my old-fashioned and solitary life. *Quaint Octavia*, that's how they saw me. A girl with a big house and a lot of money. A girl who was good to look at. A girl who always said yes.

You're like a little kitten, Rob would say, stroking my long blond hair while he read a book or talked to the others. They all did it, stroking, patting, as if they couldn't keep their hands off me. But they didn't seem to hear me when I spoke. They'd smile in my face, saying, *You don't mind, do you? If we have the meeting here? If we have the party here? If we move in for a while? If we invite our friends?* It was understood without question that they could all come to Octavia's house. That they could all eat Octavia's food. Drink Octavia's drink. Sleep in Octavia's bed. They thought I didn't mind; that I took sex like I took tea – calmly and with good manners. They didn't notice how stiff I was, how quietly I cried.

It was not what I'd been brought up to. It was not what Mummy and Daddy would have expected, not at all. But they were gone years ago and the big house had become so very lonely. The neighbours had carefully minded their business and I had carefully minded mine. But one blazing midsummer day by the lake, Rob had smiled and said I was beautiful. And I had taken him home.

He'd been kind at first. He said he respected my quaint way of life. *Don't ever change, princess.* But then he brought the others, with their easy laughter and their easy ways – and I felt out of step.

I watched them carefully – how they moved, how they talked, what they said. I believed that if I tried hard enough it would happen; that I would mirror them unthinkingly until eventually there would be no difference between us. I was twenty-one – just like they were; it couldn't be too hard.

I rode with them on buses and on the backs of motorbikes. I ate with them in greasy cafeterias. I sat with them on draughty walls outside corner pubs and drank beer in thick glass mugs. But it didn't work.

Just keep quiet, Rob would whisper whenever I tried to give an opinion. *I think your lot have had enough to say for the last few hundred years. Give the proletariat a chance.*

Jeni would put her heavy arms around me and tell him not to be so cruel: *It's not her fault. Octavia's not like the rest of them, are you? Anyway, it's her house, isn't it? And I think it's fantastic. Millions of times better than the last place we were in.*

Jeni liked my kitchen especially. She'd sit there, devouring handfuls of cornflakes straight from the packet, and concocting tumblers of thick, pink, slimming drinks: *Oh God, Octavia, something's got to work!*

The rest of them scattered through the house, the bedrooms, the library, Daddy's study – but mainly they occupied the drawing-room floor. They liked the Indian rugs, the cushions and embroideries, and the long curtains they could draw against the light. It had *atmosphere*, they said. Karen would sit cross-legged for hours, singing quietly to the Bob Dylan records Carl had told me I must buy, while Rob and Steve lay with their tangled hair against the sofa, smoking something strong and scenty and writing angry things on pieces of crumpled paper. They'd brood and chuckle together for hours. Often, Beverley would pull my head onto her flower-patterned lap and plait my hair the way she did hers – lots of little strands woven with coloured beads. Then we'd go into my room to look at ourselves in the tall cheval glass, my pale arm linked in her olive-skinned one.

You have such lovely things, she'd whisper, plunging her whole body into my wardrobe, caressing silk caftans, cashmere jumpers, chiffon cocktail frocks I'd never worn. She'd look at the labels and say, *Zandra Rhodes! Oh, fabulous!* And I'd let her have things, although she was a size bigger than me and split the zips in places where she couldn't see. She'd kiss me and say, *Don't let Rob know*. And she'd wear them when he wasn't around, twirling on the polished floors, catching her reflection in the window glass. *You're really kind, Octavia.*

Rob, of course, said kindness was meaningless, that it clouded the issues, the real class struggle, that there were no exemptions. *Property is theft*, he'd say with a grin, taking a five-pound note from my purse. I used to think about it a lot. And one day I told him that he was right. I'd give it all up. I'd sell the house, the furniture, the clothes, give all my money to charity, get a job in a shop, be ordinary. They were all silent. Then they shrieked with laughter. *Oh, Octavia, you are funny!*

Rob laughed too. But later on he came to my room, kissed my forehead and looked in my eyes. *Now listen, Octavia – about what you said. I think, my angel, I need to protect you from yourself. You don't seem to realize what a sheltered life you've led – nannies and governesses and all that crap. And money whenever you want it. I don't think you realize what the real world's like. It's dog eat dog out there, you know. Basically, princess, you wouldn't survive.* He put his finger under my chin and lifted my face, smiling in that way he had. *Now, I'm not getting at you. It's not your fault. You can't help your weirdo parents and their weirdo ideas. But promise me like a good girl you won't do anything rash.*

I kissed him and promised, and he smiled and lit a cigarette.

Rob was always rude about my parents. About anyone's parents. About families in general. They were bourgeois, of course. And a drag, to be cast off as soon as possible. He said I was well rid of mine. *You're a free spirit, you see. God, I wish I had your luck!* He always assumed I felt the same way. Only once did he mention his two sisters: older, married, and living in 'ticky-tacky houses' in suburbs too bourgeois for words. He'd been lying propped on the bed with an arm round me, drawing on a joint and rambling a little. But when I wanted to know more, he turned away on the pillow. *They're not important.* His mother telephoned once, late at night: someone was ill, he needed to come back. He refused to speak to her, wouldn't take the phone from my hand. *I don't know where she got this number, but if she rings again, hang up.*

But he was forever staring at the silver-framed photos on the piano and the mounted snapshots in the stiff, brown pages of the old albums. He loved the pictures of my grandparents – formal on studio furniture with potted palms; my bachelor uncles – overcoats and dogs in the Highlands, light suits and gins in front of Raffles Hotel. And, most recently, the end of our life in Delhi – my father against the white façade of government offices, our bungalow with its garden, the servants lined up, me a blond child in Manjit's arms just months before we came back to England. Rob would pore over them for hours, jeering at my father's moustache and droopy linen jacket, my mother's Dior afternoon dresses, wide-brimmed hats and long white gloves. *Look at them! The remnants of our glorious colonial history. Thank God you were too young to remember it all!*

But I did remember it. The pressure of the air. And the brilliance of the flowers, the huge red dahlias blazing just in front of the house. And the distant clatter of china cups in the afternoon shade as I lay on my mattress inside the veranda. We'd been happy, all three of us. Perfectly happy. But I didn't tell Rob all this. Rob always misunderstood about Mummy and Daddy. He'd turn the pages and snigger. *What parasites!*

I'd tried to tell him that it wasn't like that. Daddy had worked himself to death, staying up late into the night with his boxes of papers. Everyone in the Service had respected him. And they'd loved my mother; she was so hospitable – always tea parties and guests for supper. Rob would look at photograph after photograph, faded smiles in bright light. *She certainly knew a lot of handsome young men.*

So I stopped telling him anything, let him go on drawing his conclusions. It pleased him to make fun. *Righting the balance*, he said as he tried on Daddy's silk scarves and Panama hats, striding up and down, snapping his fingers. *I say, you there, boy! A cup of char for myself and the memsahib!*

Rob made them all laugh, and I tried not to mind. I tried not to mind when he started wearing my father's suits every day, staining them with food and cigarette ash; when Jeni went out to a dance in my mother's pearls and came back without them. And when Karen and Steve broke the Royal Worcester plates by sitting on them. And when Mandy burnt a hole in the pale blue Wilton when she fell asleep, stoned. They are my friends, I said to myself. And they must share what I have.

They stayed a long time, sharing. I can't remember how long. But gradually they drifted away, got jobs, sent me postcards: *Can you believe we've got our own mortgage and Bev is having a baby? And Steve's been offered this fantastic job in Hong Kong? And Carl and Jeni have a bookshop in Bath?*

Wankers, said Rob. He'd been the last to go. In the final months he lay about the floor, unshaven, gnawing at leftover food, slinking along the landings, turning knobs, opening boxes, pulling and picking at my life.

I couldn't stand it in the end.

And now, today, this warm summer's day, I will have to go the long way round to the park. When we first came to this house, Mummy and I could run straight there, out of our back garden gate, down to the lake. We'd lie in the sunshine under the dahlias, pretending we were back at the bungalow and someone would soon bring us tea. But the back gate is padlocked now, jammed tight with damp and I will have to go along the Crescent, past the mansion flats, through the railinged gate. But it won't matter. No one will be watching. Everything will be quiet.

It's almost noon as I leave the house, and the light is falling in solid blocks, cutting shapes on the masonry, dividing the road with hard edges of shadow, the geometry of pointed gables in triangles along the middle of the tarmac. A few parked cars reflect the sun along the bright side of the road, but there is no one on the pavements. The residents of the Crescent are very private. They sometimes smile at me as I walk along, but they never speak. Most of them are old, and stay indoors.

I have put on my big straw hat and my dark glasses. I have to protect myself from the sun. My skin is just as ivory-pale as it's always been. My eyes are just as large and blue. On a day like this I have to hide them from view. I wear gloves. A lady always wears gloves. I have many pairs. Today they are pale lilac, to match my frock. It's my favourite, a Jean Muir original. It makes all the difference.

I visit the glasshouses first. As a child, walking with Mummy into the sudden wall of heat, I was reminded of India. As I am now. I see splashes of shimmering red, a jungle of deep green. Everything moist, warm, scented. I drift along the rows of terracotta pots. My high heels skid a little on the red tiled floor. Hoses snake across my path. Sprinklers start up suddenly, tingling on my skin. My dress is damp. It clings a little to my back, my thighs. The heat is building up. I remove my hat, my glasses. It is time.

I choose the spot. I am superstitious; I keep to the same routine. Here in view of the lake, on a quiet piece of lawn, near the bed of dahlias. Spiky red dahlias. They are very tall; they reach my shoulder as I stand beside them. They have no smell; they attract by show. I hold out my hand, touch their tubular petals, their splayed open centres. I lie down. The heat of the day will soon start to wane.

I know him at once. I smell him, the acid of his aftershave, the faint odour of tobacco and sweat. The sun is behind his head as he stands over me. He is a dark shadow. Thinner than Rob. Taller. He pauses, deciding. I know what he will decide. The dahlias vibrate in the background.

'You make a beautiful picture.'

The usual words. I smile my usual smile.

He eases himself down beside me. He has long legs, grey trousers – grey flannel trousers. His face, as he turns, is pale and avid. He will be no trouble.

We talk a little. Very little. Then we walk, slowly, in the heat.

'We can go indoors,' I say. 'My house is very near.' I point out the back wall, the glistening windows of the Crescent rising above the trees.

As a lover, he is indifferent. I expect no more. He is too eager, too flattered to consider much beyond himself. He is a man who wears grey flannel trousers on a summer's day and is at the mercy of strangers.

He exerts himself, sweats a little, groans. Afterwards he strokes my hair. He looks around – the cornices, the mirrors, the mahogany furniture.

'It's a massive place. Do you live here all alone?' he asks.

'Not quite.' I like to tease on these occasions. He looks nervous, eyes the door. 'You needn't worry. We won't be disturbed.'

He senses something. He wants to be away, but my body is across his chest, my fan of still-blond hair scarfing his pitted complexion. He subsides. Strokes my hair again. 'I can't make you out. You're very – different – do you know that?'

Of course I know that. I accept that now. I smile. 'You're not the first to say that.' *No, not the first.*

He asks to get his cigarettes. They are in his shirt pocket, on the rosewood chair. I say I don't allow smoking. He laughs and says that isn't fair. I tell him this is my house and I make the rules.

But I bring him some tea. Indian tea. Strong and pungent. I bring it to him on a tray. White cloth, china cup. And a red dahlia head floating in a shallow glass vase.

He lifts the cup, reluctant. 'I don't drink tea, normally.'

But today isn't normal. Surely he can see that? Today is very particular.

'It's a special blend,' I tell him.

The temperature has dropped now. The pressure is falling. The windows rattle a little with the evening breeze.

I make myself supper. A slice of melon, cold consommé, anchovies on toast, a water ice. I cover the little folding table in my father's study with an embroidered cloth. I put out a silver knife, fork and spoon. I pin the dahlia in my hair. I pour myself a glass of wine.

No one will disturb me tonight.

Saturday Soup
Donna Daley-Clarke

Our mother liked the horses, so we were always a few furlongs short of our own house and the other things that people pass down when they pass on. When Mother died she bequeathed me a debt of £25 a week to a loan shark until November, rent arrears and her Saturday soup recipe.

Before dying, she asked me, as the eldest, *to care the family*. What she meant was: find Darius a job, buy a TV licence and make sure Nancy changes her underwear. But on days when I feel as if I am carrying everyone else's suitcases up the down escalator, I misunderstand Mother deliberately, and I make Saturday soup for the family, even if it is a weekday. I watch Darius with an empty bowl, sucking the marrow from a lamb bone and eyeing Nancy's dumplings and I think, *This is an easier way of caring.*

Peel and wash pumpkin with the green and yellow skin or a butternut squash. If you have neither you shouldn't be making this soup. Remove all seeds and chop into cubes. Peel the chow-chow, dash the heart away. Put aside.

'Don't start stuffing your face. I'm cooking proper food. I'm making soup,' I say to Darius who is folding digestive biscuits into his mouth as he opens and closes food cupboard doors.

He takes out a lidless, near-full pint of milk from the fridge and puts the bottle to his mouth. 'Why, what's the matter?' he asks as if he doesn't want to know the answer.

45

'Just making soup is all,' I say, respecting his wishes.

'Put in extra dumplings for me, sis,' he says, wiping his milk moustache away on the back of his hand.

I watch him take the last two spotty bananas from the fruit bowl. He has one leg of his jeans turned up to his knee and his T-shirt is knotted under his chest. His bellybutton still sticks out a bit because the midwife was slapdash when she tied the cord. The waistband on his briefs reads *Calvin Klein*. There's always something to read on Darius. I don't mind the words but I hate the numbers. £89.99 *Nike*, it says on the tag at his feet and I feel sad that he doesn't know he is worth more.

Take two fat cloves of garlic (or four thin), mash them flat with a spoon. (If it's good garlic you should be able to use the flat of your hand.) Chop the garlic small. Slice scallions (mind your fingers), then crush pimento and then wash thyme.

'Where you going?' I ask.

'Up the road,' he says and resumes glugging the milk.

I rub my hands with half a lemon to prevent the smell of garlic clinging. I can feel his eyes on me as I crush a juicy garlic segment with the palm of my hand. A few months after Mother died he would have said, *Don't ask my fucking business*, so even though I want to know the name of the road and the names of the people sharing the pavement, I say, 'Come back early for soup.'

Darius raises his forehead, which means yes on this occasion but can also mean *hello* if he's on the street with his friends and I'm wearing sad clothes.

'Nancy is in hospital,' I say.

Darius holds the bottle to his mouth as if he's still drinking, but the milk has stopped decreasing. He puts the dribble-mouth-dregs back in the fridge, banging the door so hard it opens again.

'I told you. I'm not interested. I don't give a flying fuck! You won't let me deal with it my way, so why not leave me be? You're doing it again . . .' he says in a way that might have been menacing if he didn't have a sticking out bellybutton and milk on his top lip, '. . . mistaking me for someone who gives a damn!'

'We can take soup for her and all eat it there. Like Mother used to say, the family that eats together stays together,' I say, finishing my sentence as if Darius's outburst never happened. I imagine us sitting on Nancy's bed, eating soup with the curtain drawn around us.

Darius sighs and presses cold milky lips on the side of my neck.

Strip the skin from carrots, yams (and leeks if it is the season). If you let Nancy wash the vegetables, rinse them over when she is finished.

Patrick, my nearly-brother-in-law, is coming for dinner. I'm making him a separate pot of soup with extra-special ingredients. Patrick and my sister Nancy eat with us most Saturdays.

Saturdays with my sister are my favourite day of the week. Nancy arrives early so we can shop for soup ingredients before the traffic wardens start ticketing. By seven-thirty a.m. we are already in Ridley Road market, standing up in the crowded bagel shop with the stall holders. We eat cream cheese and smoked salmon bagels and drink thick tea. We buy West Indian vegetables from the stall Mother started using in 1957. The stall owners are an elderly white couple, withered and lined like old spinach leaves. They gave us ribbons and sherbert fountains when we were young, and have always treated us with kindness, but since Mother died I want to be mean to them, just because they are still alive.

At the stall, Nancy often taps the ends of yams and holds eddoes up to the light like Mother used to, except we forgot to ask her why, so have no idea what she was checking for. Sometimes, after examination, Nancy says, *I'm sorry that just won't do*, and hands back a vegetable as if it has failed Mother's test.

On the other Saturdays Nancy pretends she has too much work to do. Really, she is hiding from Darius and me because she is as bruised as a three-for-a-pound mango.

Patrick joins us when the soup is ready, after he has finished lifting weights and sweating out impurities at the gym. He calls these sessions 'training' as if in the end he will become something important like a doctor or a priest.

At first I was surprised when Patrick (who is clean) and Nancy (who isn't) became a couple.

Nasty Nancy, Darius calls her but she lets it pass, partly out of sisterly love, but mostly because she knows it is true. Late in the day, when Nancy's eau de toilette has worn thin, she smells like old sugar dumplings, the cupboard under the stairs, and if you sniff hard on a hot day she has a faint tang of Dunn's River mackerel fillets. She thinks nothing of re-wearing dirty knickers – inside out the following day – and she uses baby wipes to wash her armpits before she sprays them. (This is her routine often enough for Tesco Club Card to think she has a baby and send her Mother and Baby vouchers.)

Patrick, on the other hand, keeps an oral hygiene kit (floss, fold-up toothbrush, toothpaste) in the sports bag that is with him even on Christmas Day.

They stayed over once, and when they were screwing I heard him call her a filthy whore, but then they were all lovey-dovey over the farm-assured eggs and carrot juice Patrick did for breakfast; so maybe it's true, opposites attract.

You can't tell Nancy anything. She's always had her own ideas and it's best to leave her be, because *those who can't hear must feel*, according to Mother.

Don't forget, Nancy, a plate has two sides, Mother used to tell her when she was washing up and when that didn't work she'd say, *Cleanliness is next to Godliness*, and slide Nancy's washed dishes back into the suds. But Nancy thought Mother had misinterpreted the Bible. *God was talking about living a good life; being clean on the inside*, she'd say.

Nancy sparkles inside. She always chooses the smallest slice of a cake she knows I like, so I can have the biggest piece. She buys two poached salmon and watercress sandwiches at lunchtime and gives one to the *Big Issue* seller at Farringdon station. She paid off the loan shark for Mother's gambling debt (again), financed Darius's training in computers (even though he didn't stick at the car mechanics course), and took me for driving practice in the BMW behind Patrick's back. Nancy is interested in my 'he said, she said' conversations. She thinks I'm beautiful and funny and clever like she did when she was five and I was nine, and when I'm with her I think so too.

If Nancy is right and God was talking about scrubbed intentions and pure hearts, then Darius and I agree: Nancy is squeaky clean and Patrick is rather grubby.

Fry all together until the onions turn clear and you smell the seasonings above the garlic. Slice carrots and take yesterday's seasoned neck of lamb. Swish out the fried things and then heat oil. When it smokes, add the meat and brown.

I am using a free-range baby lamb from a farm able to trace this animal's family tree back three generations. I don't want Patrick to stop eating until I can see the pattern at the bottom of his bowl. The lamb's young flesh is already broken down and softened with last night's seasonings. A toothless person could digest the meat from my soup. It is a shame Patrick's teeth will not be required, though, as Nancy's shopping lists reflect how hard she works for those teeth; soft bristle toothbrushes, waxed dental tape with fluoride, organic soya milk with added calcium. After all this investment his teeth get little chewing opportunity because, as Patrick is fond of saying, *Most food is processed and devoid of nutrients.*

Our sister Nancy, despite earning a six-figure salary, does not have a microwave or a freezer. She shops twice a week using a butcher and a greengrocer, like a 1950s domestic goddess. She does this for the love of Patrick, who places fresh food without technological interference and with a high enzyme count above Nancy's well-being. Every evening at eight o'clock, Nancy, in her pinstriped city suit, can be found braising organic meat and finding new ways of retaining the vitamin content of mange tout and purple sprouting broccoli.

Put Irish potatoes, chow-chow and carrots in the pot. If you have eddoes use them, if you have yam use that too; if you have neither, no worries. Add the pumpkin. Put red beans in, careful to boil them for a good time. (St Lucians will argue, but I think red beans add bite.) Have the dumplings ready. (If you can't make dumplings by now, I shame for you.)

Nancy is something in the City. She reads the *Financial Times*. She started out reading the *Sporting Times* sitting outside the paper shop with ten Silk Cut and a pint of milk for our breakfast cereal. If Mother, in her curlers and headscarf, hadn't charged round to the shop with the crumpled racing pages and threatened Mr Singh for selling a used newspaper, Nancy wouldn't have confessed to picking out horses and watching them race after school on BBC2 instead of watching children's TV on BBC1.

I remember Nancy in her brushed-cotton pyjamas pushing herself into the gaps of Mother's body spread out on the sofa. On the floor were two mugs of Milo and *Charlie and the Chocolate Factory*. ACCUM . . . AL . . . ATER. Nancy couldn't spell it but Mother kissed her behind the pages of the *Sporting Times* for knowing how an accumulator differed from a spread bet. Mother put the paper down and straightened up. Nancy moved with her, like a partner on the television show Mother watched where they danced the foxtrot and the waltz. Mother picked the book up from the floor but, before any words were read, Nancy bent the top part of her body away from Mother like at the end of a tango, and snatched up the newspaper.

'It's obvious that Charlie gets the golden ticket, but will Running Water win the two-fifty at Haymarket?'

Nancy thinks her nerve trouble and irritable bowel syndrome are due to the insecurity of our childhood. When I say, *If it wasn't for what Mother taught you, you wouldn't be where you are today*, she says *exactly*, forcing my words to support her own unexplained argument. But even though Nancy reads the *Financial Times*, carries a briefcase and has

Hollywood lips, she is still studying form – picking winners, assessing the odds of a new owner turning a failing horse around.

Add stock from a boiling chicken carcass. Drop the scotch bonnet and thyme in the liquid. When bubbling begins the dumplings go in with the chow-chow. You can put in chicken noodle or not.

I didn't use enough flour in the dumplings today, but I realized early and added cornmeal. Most things can be put right if you act early enough. With Nancy I left it too late. 'You know how clumsy Nancy can be,' Patrick said when he phoned from the accident and emergency ward after Nancy dislocated her jaw last year. And I chose to remember Nancy tripping over her feet and hitting her chin on the school steps.

From time to time, ugly thoughts bobbed up and down like scotch bonnet peppers but I could always remove them before things got too hot, until yesterday when Patrick phoned.

'Nancy's in the Princess Royal ward. She slipped on the kitchen tiles and broke her arm. Vintage Nancy!' He gave a little exasperated laugh. I remember thinking, *At least it's Friday. I can invite him over to eat tomorrow and he won't be suspicious*. The idea blew up like noodles in hot soup.

I swallowed my fury and said, 'Thanks for letting me know. I hope she'll be OK. I'll be making soup tomorrow, so why don't you come over after training and have a bowl?'

'Only if you don't use any stock cubes,' he answered, trashing Mother's memory and the only good thing she ever gave me. Sometimes there's a point of no return. A few grains too much and your soup can be too salty and even a potato in the stock won't cure it. It doesn't take much to tip the balance.

Throw in salt, black pepper and three mashed pimento seeds.

The counselling Darius had after Mother died has helped us all. After all the threats about what he would do to Patrick, Darius agreed not to smash the smile Nancy had invested so much time and money to keep.

The family soup pot sits alongside Patrick's little saucepan. I lift the lid on the little pan as the doorbell rings. I have created a work of art; water-lily yam slices, islands of dumplings and yellow-green pumpkin pieces float like speckled frogs. Perhaps too many red beans, but it's not easy following a recipe. No matter how often I cook soup there is always something I misunderstand.

Mother would be proud of me. I am proud of me, caring for the family.

Simmer and stir, simmer and stir.

Patrick stands at the door.

'Come in,' I say, taking his sports bag. 'Sit down. I've been waiting for you, the soup is ready.'

Patrick is washing his hands at the kitchen sink. He flicks wet hands in the air. I pass him a piece of kitchen roll knowing he won't want the tea towels because they breed germs.

'Aren't you eating?' he asks.

'Not till later,' I say.

He takes a seat at the table, laid with Mother's yellow and green checked tablecloth. I place a turquoise Pyrex dish filled with soup to its fluted edges. Steam rises. Patrick is sitting at my table with his big, nasty-clean self. He eats happily, clapping wet lips over chow-chow. His face is inches from the bowl that he hugs with one arm as if the food is homework someone might copy. But he needn't worry. I have made the soup for him alone.

Girlfriend

Gemma Blackshaw

He don't like the heat. Goes fucking AWOL. Can't keep still for longer than a second, moving from the fridge to the telly, saying, I've gotta get out of this house, it's doing my head in. And I think about telling him to just sit down and relax. Put a T-shirt on. Have a cold beer. I light a fag instead cos I don't want to wind him up. First chance to split, he'll take it. And I haven't seen him in days. So I just sit at the table and watch him cut across my eyes. Watch the sweat glisten through his crew cut and drip down the back of his neck. He's shining. Looks like he's just burst out of the sea. Like a Davidoff advert or something. And I was gonna tell him. Three years and he still fucking blows my mind. But I decide against it. You've gotta catch him right with shit like that.

The lounge sliding doors are open but there's no breeze. Not a breath. You give yourself a headache if you get wound up. Banging right behind the eyes. So I've just been sitting still, breathing in through my nose and then out slow through my mouth. Taking him all in. Feels like a waiting game, this heat that drops over your head like a wet towel. Feels like the sky's gonna rip and crack any minute. But it's been like this for ages. Not a stir. And he's uptight. His shirt collar's plastered to the back of his neck. He keeps on moving to the front window and back. Every time a car rolls down the estate he's up and off, like a fucking yo-yo, pausing between drags on his Benson & Hedges to point at me, the fag held in towards his palm between his thumb and first finger. Like a right fucking wide boy.

– I'd've killed him if Dean weren't there, he says. – I'd've ripped his fucking head off.

He stops and stands in front of me, blocking out the light from the window so all I can see is his massive shape. He's got great shoulders. Sometimes, when he's with me at night, I put the flats of my hands against them and though he's out for the count I swear the muscles quiver under my palms, like they're just itching to get out.

He points his finger at me, digging it backwards and forwards in the air.

– Little shit knocked over my pint. In the Clock House. Straight down my new shirt. You fucking believe it?

I shake my head slowly as he stops and stares at my reaction. And then he's off again, moving, wiping the sweat off his top lip and then running his hands over his head and then leaning across the table and shoving it back against the wall so one of his mum's china poodles falls to the floor and smashes.

– FUCK IT.

I sit very still. I breathe in again when he turns round to face me.

– I told him, I'LL FUCKING HAVE YOU.

My stomach clenches down so there's just a thin strip of muscle running from my tits to my belly. My stomach's always the first to tense up. Nerves. It gives me indigestion and everything. And then he whips round again, over to the mantelpiece and back.

– Bloke didn't know what hit him. I went for him. Just like that.

He jabs the air. I see the muscles through his shirt flex and release. He's so quick. He says he's got fine-tuned reflexes. Animal fucking instinct, he says. He's always going on about it, punching and ducking like Rocky. He knows whole bits of it off by heart.

He says, I'd've killed him if Dean weren't there.

I look away at the toaster and kettle on the breakfast bar. Focusing, really focusing on them. Concentrating like that calms me down.

– I'd've smashed his fucking face in.

He stands in front of me again, leaning low across the table with his hands gripping the edge. His face is very close to mine. He curls his top lip and pushes his jaw out. He speaks quietly, slowly, as if he's saying something he's had to go over time and time again, because I just can't get it.

– Little shit doesn't go down, does he? So I get him by the collar with one hand, don't I? And I start smacking him in the face. So fucking hard. Dean had to pull me off him. I'd've killed him if Dean weren't there. Ask Dean.

– Did you come straight here? I say.

– Nah. Went back to Dean's. He fixed my hand up with some TCP and shit. Washed out my shirt in the sink. Blood and beer all over it. My new fucking shirt.

I think about Dean bending over his face, then washing the blood and beer from his shirt with his bare hands in his mum's peach bathroom.

He opens the fridge for the fifth time and slams it shut again.

– Watcha get all that fucking yoghurt stuff for?

I say, There's a beer in there. Why don't you have a beer? Cool you down.

He brings his face down to mine so quick I jerk my head back.

– If I wanted a beer I'd ave one, wouldn't I? All right?

I look away from him at the china dog in pieces on the floor. I don't say nothing. He gets aggravated in this heat. Thirty-eight degrees for two, three days now. It said on the TV, no signs of letting up. The weather girl stuck an ice-cream cut-out over the south east and issued Essex with a sun-protection warning. It's always hot on my birthday.

He takes one of my fags out and screws his face up as he lights it.

– I'm off out, babe, all right?

– You're coming back, though? You're gonna drive me tonight, aren't you?

– Yeah course, he says. Be round at eight. I've got your pressie over at Dean's. Forgot to pick it up.

I smile at him and flex my bare toes.

– You didn't have to do that. You're skint, I say.

I hadn't reminded him or anything. I hadn't even mentioned it. He surprises me like that.

– You got me car keys, darlin?

I point to the breakfast bar and then look up at him. He's a big bloke. You wouldn't shit with him. His lips are cracked and there's a graze down the side of his cheek. I was about to run my tongue along it but he bends over me for just a second and then I'm watching him move through the lounge towards the front door.

– See ya later, I say.

The sun smacks me straight between the eyes as I step through the sliding doors to the patio. Heat like you wouldn't believe. Everything is dead still. I run across the concrete slabs to stop the soles of my feet from burning and reach the garden furniture his mum bought in Argos last week. We were there for an hour deciding between black plastic or white plastic. She thought the black was stylish until she got it home and burnt her arse on the seat. I told her, white reflects the sun *away*. She still won't have it.

I look out across the estate back gardens. It's mid-afternoon so everyone's slowed down, sitting on the scuffed grass with ice pops, in shorts that are too tight. Me, I've got my new high-cut bikini on. His mum bought it for us. She didn't wrap it up or nothing but I didn't care cos it was the one I wanted. – Book yourself a holiday, she said. – Leave the cunt for a fortnight, she said. But it's like abroad anyway. The black plastic sunlounger. The Tia Maria and Coke. The adverts for Bounty bars and cans of Diet Lilt. Like a mirage in my head.

Joanne's coming with us to Clacton tonight. She said, You

can get tanked if you drink in the sea air; cocktails and things with umbrellas and pineapple chunks. Something a bit different, she said.

I look at the ice cubes melting in my Coke. I hear the sliding doors go and I shield my eyes with the back of my arm. The skin's warm on my face and smells of coconut Hawaiian Tropic. Joanne's just had her hair highlighted. The blond hurts my eyes.

– Hey, babe, she says, look what I got you.

She holds out a card. The envelope's still wet with her saliva and the gum smells sweet. I open it. There's a badge on the front, which Joanne pins to my bikini top. *Twenty-one*, it says, *and ready for anything*.

I fix Joanne a drink. I like fixing drinks so I take my time running water over the ice cubes to get them out of the tray, going over to the bottles of Duty Free Vodka and Malibu and Tia Maria, and thinking up a cocktail to make her. She turns the slatted blinds down on the sliding doors and stands in the dim blue light from the TV his mum never turns off, only down.

– He's gonna pick us up then, is he?

– Yeah, he's got the car tonight. He'll be here about eight.

– Give us a chance to get some drinks in. Cheers, babe.

I put a Black Russian down in front of her on a cork coaster. There's a whole set of them, Flamenco dancers and bull-fighters. I rest my drink on my stomach and lean back against her. Her skin's covered in freckles. Hundreds and thousands of them. I used to trace patterns over her legs like I was joining the dots. I rest the side of my face against the top of her arm, feel her skin squish under my ear so there's a rushing sound.

– What did he get you then?

– Dunno. He says he's giving it to me later. When he picks us up. He'll bring it over then.

– Cheeky cunt. What was wrong with this morning, for fuck's sake?

– He forgot it. Left it over at Dean's.

– So he's definitely coming over then? What time?

– About eight, eight-thirty, something like that. You know what he's like. I didn't want to get on his back.

– It's your birthday.

– Yeah, I know.

– Cunt. Watcha gonna wear then?

We can say stuff like that to each other, me and Joanne. We go back a long way.

Saturday nights are good nights to see him. He'll be here to pick us up. He said so. He just had a few things to sort out first. With the boys, you know. You know how it is. Babe. So I wanna look hot tonight. Like a million dollars. Me and Joanne get in the shower and she shaves my legs so I don't get no nicks. We wash each other's hair, standing facing each other and shrieking when next door's washing machine goes on and the water turns ice cold. She holds on to my bicep as she gets out the shower. The muscle tenses as she lifts one and then the other leg out. I've been working out. Joanne's got a weekday job at Riverside Leisure and she's given us a free gym pass. Thirty, forty minutes on the cycling machine until the sweat pours off me and I've got stains under my armpits and tits. Pounding away the afternoons. I could put my Walkman on but I like to hear my breathing and the spin of the wheel going faster and faster. The burning down the front of my legs and then nothing at all, just that feeling that I could go on and on. I've biked from Chelmsford to Romford and back in a fortnight. Joanne says I'm overdoing it.

I hear his mum come in the front. I know she's done a shop at Asda cos she heads straight for the kettle and switches it on and we'd run out of tea bags this morning. – That boy of mine, she'd said, drinking me out of house and home, he'll bleed me dry he will, just you watch, no fucking consideration.

I get bored of hearing it. Drinking my black coffee and smoking her fags, nodding as she leans against the kitchen units with an empty packet of bacon in her hand.

– Why does he bother to put it back in the fridge? she'd said.

– I mean, tell me that, will ya? Little bastard. Thinks I won't notice. Thinks I was born yesterday he does.

I've got used to it now. It's like listening to the breakfast show on the radio. Day in, day out. Same fucking story.

It was meant to be a stop off, his mum's, till we got some cash together. I saved up and everything, working in Star Burger all hours. Eating chips dipped in barbeque sauce when the Greek was out the back. Five hundred quid I've got saved. I got it out of the post office account one day. Just for five minutes. Just to feel what it's like to hold that much money in my hands. We were gonna move out and everything. Get a place of our own in the developments round Chelmer Village. We were gonna do it proper. Give it a paint job. Get a king-size double bed. I used to lie awake at night and think about it. The side of my face against his hard pec, moving as he breathed in and out. And I couldn't believe my fucking luck.

– YOU UP THERE? she shouts up the stairs. – Cor, it's like a bleedin oven! You been out yet? Bringing me out in blotches. It's that heat rash, in'it?

She trails off and I hear the drag of her flip-flops on the kitchen lino. She turns the TV up and as she lifts the shopping carriers up on to the breakfast bar tins drop out on to the floor. She's making fruit cocktail and Angel Delight tonight. She said, We never have treats, it'll make a nice change.

She comes to the bottom of the stairs again and shouts up.

– That Joanne up there, an all? JOANNE? You two gettin ready? Come down and ave a cuppa tea. Cool you down.

Joanne switches her hair diffuser off and says she'll go on down without me. She cups my jaw in her hand as she squeezes past.

This is just a box room. It hasn't been done up since he was a kid. There's a framed poster of a red Ferrari on the wall with an Arsenal rosette pinned underneath. I'm sitting with my back to the door on the edge of the bed. The sun's just started to dip and it fills the room with orange. And I think about calling after Joanne, Look out the window, look at that colour, isn't that great? But I decide against it. My legs have gone pale from shaving and I reach for the Instant Leg Make-Up for that Summer Time Shimmer. I think about doing my toenails in Rimmel Pearl to set them off but then decide against it. I fasten the straps on my heels and run some wet-look gel through my hair. It's three inches all over my head and a dark, dirty blond from where the roots are growing out. He went fucking mad when I cut it. Down my back it was and white with Sun In. He said he'd smash the hairdresser's face in. He said it made me look hard. Said I looked like a bloke when his mates started staring like they'd never clapped eyes on me before. One of them walked me home that night. – You look fucking great, he said. Walking up Chelmsford High Street with him, away from the Rendez Vous, taking really big steps cos it was suddenly easy. Cos it was suddenly like I was invincible.

Downstairs, his mum sits opposite Joanne at the breakfast bar, tipping Super Kings into the ashtray.

– You look nice, darlin, she says. – I used to have a figure like that, before the kids. Ruined it they did.

She starts to laugh and it turns into a cough, phlegm cracking in the back of her throat. I look at her fat arms the colour of corn beef underneath the T-shirts she buys from Tesco's cos they're easy to iron and they come in pastel mix and match packs of three. And I grip on to the kitchen worktop.

I bring the bottle of Tia Maria and two cans of Diet Coke over from the drinks cabinet and pour out two full pint glasses for me and Joanne. We don't bother with ice.

– He gonna meet you there then, is he?

His mum throws a packet of Mr Kipling Chocolate Swirls down on the table. Takes one out, unwraps it.

– No, he's gonna come and pick us up.

– Ah, in't that nice? He's a good boy. What time's he coming then?

– Fuck knows, says Joanne. – Bet ya he's down the Clock House.

– He's at Dean's, I say. – He's gone to get my present from Dean's and then he's coming to pick us up.

– Ah, in't he good? his mum says. – He'll be here in a minute, bet ya.

She eats the Chocolate Swirl in two bites.

It was my twentieth birthday and he'd just got out. Didn't go to his mum's and change, nothing. Twenty-four hours they kept him in. Said he must've smashed the windows at Comet. Said they had it on CCTV. Him and all his mates. Videos, cameras, Walkmans, tellies, the whole fucking lot. Friday night and me and Joanne were down the Rendez Vous. Necking bottles of peach and passion fruit Thunderbird and I was thinking, Cunt, not showing up on my birthday. Smoking Joanne's fags like there was no tomorrow. And then I saw him heading over with this split nose and I thought, Fuck, what's he done? And the bar just divided in two like the fucking Red Sea and his mates were saying cheers into their pints, knocking back their shots and turning to the bar with stiff tenners between their fingers to buy him a drink. Cos they knew all about it. And I watched him come over in slow motion, like in a film, like I was the only girl in the whole wide world. Cos everyone was looking and he was heading straight past them, straight to me. And he went, All right, gorgeous, and put his hand on my arse. He smiled so I could see the gap where his two back teeth are knocked out. He leant against the bar and all he had to do was raise his eyebrows and he was served just like that. And he bought me a drink without even asking if I wanted one. And he was right up against me so I could feel his jeans pressing down the length of my bare legs. And I felt smoothed out flat by the strength of him. Like he'd taken all my creases out. And he said to some blokes he was kicking around with at the time, Look at my girl, isn't she great? Isn't she fucking great? Like he couldn't believe I was real. And he put a cocktail with a sparkler in it down by my elbow and said he wouldn't miss my birthday. Not in a million years.

Joanne and me eat some of the fruit cocktail his mum's done for us instead of birthday cake.

– Where the fuck is he?

– I dunno.

She stands by the mirror and pulls the shoulder strap on her top so it don't cover her tattoo. It's a butterfly. She screamed blue fucking murder when she got it done.

– D'ya really like it? she says, straining back to look.

– Yeah, it's great. D'ya want another drink?

– Yeah, go on then. Fucking hell. It's nine o'clock. You sure he's coming?

– I said so, didn't I?

– All right.

She sighs and lights us two of his mum's fags out the packet on the breakfast bar.

– Only we could have been there by now if we'd got the bus.

– He said he'd be here. He's got my present and everything.

– OK.

I stick Essex FM on. Joanne goes to look out of the window.

– We could walk and get the bus. Wouldn't take long, she says, then comes over and strokes my bare arm. – You go really brown, she says.

I keep looking out the front-room window at the estate.

– Come on, babe, she says, he can meet us there. We'll walk to the bus station. It'll be a laugh. I'll get us some bottles of Hooch for the way. Come on, babe, it's your birthday.

We cruise on up through the estate to the main road. It's nine in the evening and the sky's blood red. Like someone's run across the clouds with a kicked in face. It's about a twenty-minute walk into town to the bus station but it saves getting a cab. And we don't drive. No girls round here drive. We've finished off the Tia Maria so I don't feel the straps on my sandals cutting into my skin like they usually do, and we walk fast. Up the Broomfield Road with cars honking and minicab drivers slowing down, their windows open, and groups of lads outside Kentucky Fried Chicken wolf-whistling and asking if we want it. The air's thick with exhaust fumes and the smell of K9's burger van from the shop parade car park. No wind and it's difficult to breathe. Joanne stops at the off licence and buys us a four-pack of Hooch for the bus trip to Clacton. I stand underneath the air-conditioning vent in the offy and raise my face up. Outside, she opens a bottle, kicking the top between her shoe and the brick wall.

– You're not gonna be sick, are ya? I say.

– Nah.

– Only I don't want puke on me.

– Nah. Honest.

She goes as if to throw up over my shoes and I start to laugh and feel a bit pissed, walking even faster to the bus across the road. She sticks the Hooch down her top and holds her denim jacket over her tits and winks at the driver. He drinks with her dad down the Broomfield Angel.

– All right, Des, she says, you're not gonna make us pay, are ya? It's her BIRTHDAY.

He slaps her on the arse as we get on the coach and tells her she better watch herself. And then we're coasting along the motorway, the light getting dimmer and more blue as we reach Clacton sea front and see the neon signs of the arcades on the pier and the fish and chip shops. I run my fingers through my hair that's so short it still surprises me every time, and I finish the Hooch and smoke a fag looking out at the enormous sea.

It was when the slow dances came on. Joanne calls it the erection section but I like to think of it as when the slow dances came on. It was dark and there was just this disco ball spilling light over bits of the dance floor like rain. He was drinking JD and Coke cos his eyes were flashing and JD and Coke always makes his eyes flash. And I was smiling at him as he came over cos he really had it going on that night. He had all the gear. And then I saw that his jaw had gone tight and his eyes were just like slits and Joanne was above me on the balcony snogging Dean but then she looked down and started to push through the crowds. And I stepped back. And there was this bloke I'd been talking to cos I'd gone to school with his sister, and he starts to back off away from me, holding out his hands and saying, Look, mate, I don't want no trouble. And I swear he nearly fucking went for him, cos he can be vicious, my bloke. But then he wasn't looking at the bloke, and he was just staring at me. And he had his hands out by his side and he was saying, Look, I'm not gonna fucking touch ya all right, and he was leaning his neck into me and his shoulders were thrown back like he was about to take off or something and he kept jabbing the side of his head with his fingers really hard like he was knocking it against a wall and he was saying, Do you think I'm fucking stupid or what, do you think I ain't seen ya, what the fucking hell do you take me for? And I couldn't understand how he didn't know that he rocks my world, that I'd do anything for him. Sitting on the floor in the Ladies down Dukes and all I was thinking was how pink they'd done it up. Pink loo roll, pink frames on the mirrors, pink bloody carpet. Like we was all still little girls. And Joanne was sitting next to me and she was saying, Why d'ya do it, girl? Why d'ya put up with it? And a thousand reasons flicked on like light bulbs in my head but the only thing I could get out straight was, I dunno. I dunno.

There's a massive queue running right down the length of the concrete sea breakers but Joanne's walking past all these people up to the door. And I want to tell her to slow down cos I'm clocking everybody to see if he's here with his mates but I know it'll just get her back up. Joanne's not into hanging around. And blokes are shouting out, Oi! Where the fuck d'ya think you two are going? And she's turning round and swinging her hips and blowing kisses with her hands that are fucked from her weekend job on the deli at Gateway. And I'm following her thinking if he's here then he must've seen me. Thinking, any minute now he's gonna call out, All right, gorgeous, or he's gonna run up behind me and grab my arse and say, Babe, where were ya, d'ya want your pressie or not? But Joanne's saying, Watcha! to this bloke she's never met before cos we're at the top of the queue and it's the best way to barge. Tried and tested. And I slide in behind her and smile at him and his mates who can't believe it's their lucky night. And Joanne goes, Cheers, babe, I hate to queue. Chatting them up so they give us some swigs of their bottles of Bud. And they're saying, Who's your mate, then? And Joanne goes, Oh it's her BIRTHDAY. Giving me a wink and a giggle as one of them pays my five quid entrance. And as he turns to give me my ticket he holds my fingers longer than he should've and he says, Cheer up, darlin, it might never happen. And if Joanne hadn't dragged me off I'd've punched him in the face. On my life.

I don't know how many times I've walked round the club. Past the aquariums with the tropical fish and the wall to wall sofas lining the dance floors and the scaffolding holding massive projection screens and the bars on the balcony and the bars in the chill-out room and each time I think the next person I touch is gonna be him. Sure as anything. I go into the Ladies with Joanne's handbag and comb my hair through with cold tap water. The mirrors all steamed up from the heat. Holiday heat that falls wet and soaks through your clothes. So my hand slides over my skin like I've just come out the shower and my legs are shining, feet slipping inside my sandals. And I think about Joanne bringing those brochures over with deals to Ibiza, pointing at photos with her chewed up fingernails, saying, Just you and me, babe, that could be you and me.

– You got any bog roll? she calls out from another cubicle.

– Nah. Jo, I'm gonna do another circuit.

She comes out the cubicle, door banging behind her, standing with her hip against a sink blocked up with tissue and fag butts.

– HE'S NOT HERE. We've been walking round for an hour. For fuck's sake, girl.

– I'll just check, won't take me a minute, come on, Jo.

– He's not gonna find you if you're charging round all night. Let's go get a Bacardi Breezer. I'll treat ya.

– I've gotta find him.

She looks away. Sweat's running through her hair and down behind her ears. She wipes her face and looks at me hard.

– You need your fucking head read, she says. – I'll be at the bar.

I start at the laser room again, round the left to the DJ box and then down the right to complete the loop. Halfway up the left side I decide to cut quickly across the dance floor and back, just in case. Just to make sure cos I'm going near frantic, my stomach squeezing down, heart battering behind my tits and then higher. And I'm saying to myself, Steady, don't fucking panic. This doesn't mean a thing. But I wanna puke or something. Thinking, Where is he, where the fuck is he? And I reach the chill-out room and he's not there and I feel this wave of something, I don't really know what, rise up from my stomach to my nose. And it makes me want to gag.

I must've been gone for ten, twenty minutes cos when I get to the bar Joanne's on her third bottle. – These are really nice, she says, really refreshing. She pushes a bottle of Bacardi Breezer into my hand.

– He's over there, she says.

Everything starts to pound at once. Enough to make me go deaf. I look over. I don't notice at first and I start to make my way down from the balcony, feeling this kick in my chest so hard and fast it could knock you for six. I'm thinking about what he's bought me and how he's gonna feel under my hands, under my fingertips, cos he always feels different. It's like I'm always touching him for the first time. And I'm almost falling over to reach him with this fucking smile on my face that splits it in two. And then I look up cos Joanne's grabbed me tight at the top of my arm and she's saying, What the fuck are you doing? You stupid cow. And then I see he's got some bloke by the neck of his shirt, keeping him at arm's length, with his other hand raised up by his head. And I see him smash his fist down and down into this bloke's face and he's shouting stuff I can't hear. And it's like watching him on TV with the sound turned down. It's like I'm watching him at his mum's place.

I'm standing with my legs pressed against the concrete of the sea wall and my arms wrapped around my shoulders, taking huge gulps of air. No fags. Joanne's calling from the doorway but I can't hear what she's saying above the crash of the sea. I'm looking out ahead of me at the lights down the end of the pier and further still but I can't make out the horizon line. I wonder when it's gonna decide to rain. Fuck knows, the place needs it. And I think about that five hundred quid in the post office account and how I could go to Inta Travel tomorrow and book myself on a package deal or something. And just for a second I see myself by a swimming pool in my new bikini, drinking a Harvey Wall Banger or something exotic like that. Cos shit like that can seem possible when you let yourself think about it. Just for a second.

Joanne's waiting with a bottle of 20-20. She's sitting on one of the bouncer's laps and smoking his fags. She holds out the bottle and sticks a bendy straw in it.

– Come ere, she says, you've smudged your eyeliner.

Playing the Joker
Penny Simpson

'You should have "I do" printed up on your bastard T-shirt, Clance. Said it that many times and with that many different men. Why don't you just saves your breath to smoke those ciggies you got stashed?'

Dermot delivered his verdict with a flourish: he flicked a beer mat into the air and watched it perform a near-perfect arc before slipping down Clancy's logo-free chest. She didn't like the idea – had learnt young to avoid attention from unwanted men. Ironic, then, that she'd ended up in this line of work. She had the one suit for the registry office. Pastel pink with a matching plastic flower for her hair. The mobile went and she was told the day and time of the job and off she went, twisting her poppy in her ponytail and rehearsing her lines like an actress poised in the wings.

Clancy bit her fingernails and tried to damp down Dermot's scorn. She didn't get married, not properly. He knew that, so why did he cod on about her 'appetites'? Truth was, she was never curious about any of them. Some barely spoke English, so it was hard to strike up much in the way of a conversation. Others were anxious, fussing over non-existent paperwork. They were lined up for work in fruit fields, if they were lucky. And if they were unlucky? Clancy didn't ask. You lived on sites as long as she had, you knew all about random injustice. Picked on, picked up. Angry protesters emptying rubbish bins on the caravan steps – and worse. *You gonna fucking ruin this place anyways, so we's just saving you some time . . .*

The council produced documents which said the same but in fancy talk. Sean Choke up at the Wentloog site understood them, he'd made a study of the law in prison.

'Can't fucking argue with letters, lovely,' he told Clancy. 'Black and white, see? No muddle.'

She had always understood muddle better than she did the alphabet. And here she was on the eve of Wedding Number Eight and she was still trying to reason with Dermot.

'It's just a job, yeah? So what's the problem?'

'But have you never wanted to . . . you know?'

'That's not what the deal is. I just have to say "I do". They needs someone to stand there and go through the motions, that's what Mikhail says.'

'He's a smug smuggler. Don't like his cut.'

'He don't like yours, neither.'

Clancy had liked Mikhail straight away, though. Short and wiry with bright green eyes; his suit was too big for him, his Caterpillar boots were worn at the heels. He paid her with bank notes wrapped up in glossy magazines. 'Something to read on your wedding night,' he said.

He didn't know she couldn't read. He bought her *Tatler*, *Vogue* and *Harpers & Queen*. Clancy asked Sean to read the picture captions.

'Fuck me, five grand for a coat!'

Both were stunned into a new awareness of the cost of living. Clancy liked the party photographs the best of all. Smiling guests with pipe-cleaner bodies, wearing clothes that cost more than all of her weddings put together. Another illusion, but it didn't seem to hurt anyone, except their wallets maybe. Pretend didn't have to be a mockery. Clancy wished others could cotton on to this idea. As it was, her Wentloog neighbours always joked about her 'weddings'. She tried to keep her transactions quiet, but everyone knew what she was up to the minute she showed in her pink suit and pink slingbacks.

'Making an honest woman of you again, is it?'

Dermot stood back from their loud catcalling. Brow corrugated; hands tucked up under his armpits. His whole body a question mark that spelled resentment. Clancy was aware of his confusion but was powerless to change it. Since the wedding scam had started, her mind had turned into an alphabet soup that hardly matched with Dermot's view of the world. *That* took the form of a game he called 'The Perfect Do' – which as far as Clancy could tell was anything not blown together by a man in worn-down boots.

'Gretna Green is supposed to be *the* place,' Dermot sneered. 'Not for me, mind. I fancy something more upmarket, yeah? Like a country house with a koi carp pond. You like them, Clance? Sort of posh goldfish, they is.'

'Who you gonna marry then, Dermot?'

'Well, you're spoken for. Dozens of times. That would be illegal, that would.'

'It's just different names all juggled up. Me mam's, your mam's, whoever. I learns the words off by heart, but I don't really *feel* them. Not like when I say things in my own way.'

Dermot remained unconvinced, even after she'd bought him four pints of Brains in a row. Clancy tried another tack.

'We should give the poor buggers a chance of a party at least,' she reflected. 'Year ago today, right, I marries a man who lost all his family. They burnt him in prison. Battery acid. His lips melted together . . .'

But Clancy knew she was getting nowhere with her explanations. Dermot was always uneasy when she talked about her on-off job as a bride. They'd been going out for nearly three years and the pretend weddings had begun shortly after they first met, in a stifling registry office in Bethnal Green. A licence, a box of confetti and a *Vogue* full of bank notes, but no bridesmaids, or best man – unless you counted Mikhail – not even a flute of dry champagne. Bride and groom turned up ten minutes before the ceremony started and introduced themselves. The groom spoke enough English to recite the words Mikhail had written down for him on the back of a shop flyer, no more.

They'd stood smiling awkwardly at each other as Mikhail telephoned yet another fixer in the little drama that was unwinding around them. The groom had blue eyes and a suit lent him by Mikhail. The sleeves concertinaed up his biceps and the trousers barely touched the tops of his socks. Clancy had on her brand-new pink suit and a gold necklace that had been a present from Dermot.

'It means good luck,' she'd whispered to her groom. 'We've kept to the tradition. Something old, something new, something borrowed, something blue.'

He hadn't understood the words, but Clancy had no time to explain. They were back outside when Dermot sneaked up on them, shades glued to his face.

'Who is he, Clance? I'll kill the bastard.'

It wasn't till after a flurry of punches and Mikhail biting his flailing hand that Dermot had let the sight of his own blood subdue him. Explanations in the café over the road. The stranger in the borrowed suit thinking . . . God knew what; Clancy nursing Dermot's torn palm and pleading: 'The licences are just pretend ones, I get £100 and my travel.'

That had always been the way with them, Clancy thought. Dermot was hot and furious, like a forest fire; she was calm and took her time. Brushed her hair out with fifty strokes each morning and applied her eyeliner as straight as if her life depended on it. She didn't want to understand more than she already did. The odd revelation dropped by the unknown husbands had scared her. She didn't have an alternative script to the one she'd prepared with Mikhail's assistance. *My name is Clancy O'Riordan. I do. Love and cherish. Thank you. Good luck. May the wind always be at your back . . .*

Later, heading for the train back to Cardiff, she had nearly trodden on a baby mouse scuttling through the feet of the London Underground commuters. The thumb-sized mouse was lost, panicking amid the caravan of moving feet. That's how the strangers must feel, she thought. A confusion of airport lounge, wedding, a safe house, a derelict house. Fruit picking, sweat shop. The choices were few, but how many did a man need before exhaustion swept him down into chaos, like that baby mouse? She'd grown up on the sites, had little idea that other people's lives could be as miserable as her own. No right to settle anywhere, no running water, no jobs, no money, no respect. A verdict made and delivered – no appeal heeded. And then the chance encounter with Mikhail in a pub off the Broadway. A chance to put some money her way, to have an adventure; to say, *I don't love, honour or obey*.

'Always excuses with you, Clance. Nothing ever bastard doing.' Dermot thumped down his pint. 'Why stay in your da's caravan now he's passed on, an all? Move in with me. It's not the weddings I mind, see. A scam's a bastard scam, but stalling on me, that's unnatural that is, Clance. Bastard unnatural.'

She had her excuse ready and waiting: Wedding Number Eight.

'It's going to be a breeze,' Mikhail promised. 'Reading. Eleven-thirty a.m. You meet a guy wearing a leopardskin hat.'

'As you do,' Clancy replied.

It was a bright June morning. She treated herself to a punnet of peaches from a stall by the railway station. Mangy pigeons and a dreadlocked youth with a dayglo waistcoat emblazoned 'Friends of the Earth' dogged her footsteps. Clancy felt like everyone's friend that morning. She decided she would keep hold of her wedding money, no more 'loans' to Dermot. *What is mine is yours*, he always said. In truth it was a one-way traffic that kept her from moving on. There was nothing stopping her from leaving the Wentloog site, if that was her tickle. She wasn't like the pretend bridegrooms, trapped; relying on someone else to make their world as fresh as a spring crocus for them.

Clancy found Bridegroom Number Eight sitting on the pavement outside the registry office playing a trumpet. She stood on the opposite side of the road and listened to him playing something slow and jazzy. His face crumpled up around the mouthpiece like a flower not yet ready to bud. He was oblivious to everything else going on around him, intent only on looping the next coil of notes into his melody. Clancy's curiosity was aroused – the first of her bridegrooms to step out of the shadows and meet the challenge of the day head on. She crossed the road and planted herself in front of the trumpeter; he finished his music before acknowledging her.

'Hello. I'm Clancy O'Riordan. I'm marrying you at eleven-thirty.'

'Clancy?'

'Yes.'

'I'm Louis.'

His voice was as good to listen to as his trumpet. Like her da's, which had swooped and curved like a bird's wing. The minute she heard its echo in this stranger, Clancy found herself breaking the rules of her short lifetime as a much-married woman. She sat down next to Louis and asked him about himself.

'I'm from Zimbabwe.'

'Do you play there?'

'Sometimes. In a club, on a street. People always want to hear music even if they don't want to hear about you.'

Clancy wondered if he might be hungry and offered him one of the peaches.

'The wedding breakfast?'

He gave a smile, which revealed two front teeth that made a shape like a butterfly. Clancy had to resist the urge to tap them with her fingers.

Their wedding was delayed by the party in front of them – they watched a gaggle of sailors file in behind a teenage bride and groom. Louis shook his head.

'Everyone in such a rush, Clancy. People should put on the brake. Shake the dust out of their shoes.'

She took him at his word. Pulled off her slingbacks, loosened

73

her hair and prayed that Mikhail would get diverted – arrested even. Let it all come to light. She had a conversation to finish. Louis put down his trumpet and touched her hair.

'Look at me nice,' he asked.

She smiled at him.

'You really married, Clancy?'

'No.'

'You even with anyone?'

'I'm not sure. You do this for a living, how do you know what is your life any more? Everything's all shuffled up.'

'Good money?'

'Enough to get me through the gaps. I don't have any qualifications, see. Not many of us do where I live. We travel a lot. No putting down roots, like a tree does.'

'The man who set this up for me, he says I must take "pot luck". What is this, Clancy?'

'More of the shuffling.'

'Waiting for the aces?'

'Could be.'

'You can be my Queen of Diamonds and I shall be the Joker in the pack. What else can I be? I stop laughing, who knows?'

'Then stay laughing, Louis.'

Clancy dug her toes down on sun-hot paving stones, her fingers were wet with peach juice. Louis slipped his trumpet into its case and put it up on his back. 'Ready?'

'As I'll ever be. But, look, what if I helped you find places to play, maybe you could make it as a musician over here?'

'Not in the plan.'

'What plan?'

Clancy felt anxious. She remembered Mikhail muttering about people crushed under pallets of rotting fruit. Bones folded up and cutting into their bellies like knives.

'The plan they give you when you pay up the money. I owe a lot of money.'

'How come?'

'You think I fly over here with the birds? There's always a

price to pay, Clancy. Even this old corpse has a price. But look, I've met you.'

'I'm only pretend, Louis. And I'm paid to do this.'

'Sure. You are what I want you to be. It's a deal, yes?'

'I'm the Queen of Diamonds.'

'Marrying into royalty. It will impress them back home.'

'Will they ever know?'

'One day, perhaps.'

Clancy was grateful to Louis all of a sudden. Usually, she gave legitimacy to someone else by signing away one of her made-up names. Today, she knew it was different. She could add little more to this man's life – he had everything he most needed when he played his music; he wore the challenge of his new life like he would a mohair suit. He would make it fit into his way of being just like he did his trumpet's notes. And when he talked to her, he made her feel that she was his equal. No catch-out questions or drunken rows. Clancy walked into the registry office, electric with anticipation.

'Your shoes, Clancy. You going to wear your shoes?'

She turned round. Louis stood outside, his trumpet held up in one hand, her shoes in the other. Clancy strapped them back on her feet in the reception area where the registrar, a tiny woman in a ruby red suit, bounced up to welcome them.

'Don't you two look a picture?' she exclaimed, hurrying them into the adjoining room where Mikhail stood, a copy of *Vogue* rolled up in his coat pocket.

'I don't think I'll be needing a magazine tonight,' Clancy whispered in his ear.

Mikhail started, but she moved on. Louis sat on the table where the registrar hovered. Seeing her approach, he put his trumpet to his lips and broke into the wedding march.

When Should We Live?

Rachel Bentham

She watched him take his clothes off. He had always been unselfconscious about his body, about the breasts beginning to pout, the fat almost forming ripples down his sides, the little swag of belly poised above his knicker line. He didn't try to hold his stomach in, or straighten into a more flattering position as he spoke. Most women probably would, she thought. She supposed he thought his fascinating mind outweighed considerations of mere flesh. He gingered towards the lake and turned.

'Are you coming then?' He was grinning, and she couldn't help smiling back.

'Just working my way up to it.' She strolled towards the lip of the lake, aiming for casual, probably failing . . .

It was hard to work up any enthusiasm for a swim without the encouragement of sunshine. The weather had been the same since they'd arrived in Connemara; not really raining, but a fine misty drizzle that settled on your skin like a barely perceptible sweat, and encouraged wild Irish curling of the hair. If it had been raining hard they could have stayed beside the turf fire and given way to cosiness, or found a pub and settled with a Guinness, waiting for music to release them from the need to talk. But it was what the Irish call a 'soft' day, and on a soft day you had to go out and make the best of it, not be deterred by a little damp, though it might seep through your skin like ill humour. There was something about it, though, that encouraged her to just sit and think. He seemed to find that mildly irritating, as if she wasn't attending to him quite enough.

She could imagine he might find it somehow bovine; the inactivity, the just being. He was very directed, even when relaxing he consumed newspapers and serious magazines as if his mind needed constant feeding to satisfy its ravenous hunger. She grinned to herself as she suddenly had a mental picture of him as an overfed hamster in its cage, cheeks stuffed with food, frantically shredding *Marxism Today*. Maybe it was a kind of animal thing – he had to feel completely up-to-date and well-informed to compete with his fellow academics.

To be fair, it suited her that he usually occupied himself so thoroughly – it gave her a certain kind of space. He made few demands, beyond tacitly expecting her to do the bulk of the domestic work. That was a tricky one. He'd moved into her flat, and since she already cleaned, washed and cooked for herself it would seem churlish to demand he sort his dirty washing from hers, or clean the kitchen . . . She knew that if she mentioned it he would look surprised, would behave as if he was hurt and disappointed by such pettiness.

But, all in all, he was convenient for her, exempting her from the stresses of being single and available; he was reliable, and a boyishly energetic lover – if maybe a little over-focused on performance, rather than tenderness. But hey. They kept each other company.

She wondered what she was to him. Interestingly, he never asked what she thought. Never had. She was just a PA, a glorified secretary, but he was far too PC to say that. Occasionally she'd tried to formulate how she felt, tried to find a question that would stump him: 'But what if there was a colour that we couldn't see?' He generally laughed – such childish ideas couldn't possibly be serious. She knew she wasn't very good at it, but she kept trying. He had once said that if women didn't want to be oppressed they shouldn't live with men. He didn't twig that she was feeling her way towards something. Something important to her. Anyway, he never asked her opinion, though he was happy enough to hold forth for hours. He treated her rather like an empty vessel to be filled with reliable information from the inexhaustible fount of his own knowledge.

He cleared his throat. 'Well?'

She nodded and stood up. She looked across the lough towards the island as she quickly stripped off her clothes. Of course it was utterly beautiful; a ruin draped with ivy perched romantically among misty trees on the island, the lough spreading out like pitted glass, mountains huddling protectively around. It reminded her of a child's snowstorm toy; the perfect little scene contained within mountains, within curved glass walls. There was one of those toys in the cottage where they were staying, the only childish thing there. Perhaps that was how she seemed to him: a curiosity; pick her up and shake her from time to time. Pretty, but very limited.

She shivered. He waded in. She'd told him of her fear of water, but he'd dismissed it as illogical – he used the word 'irrational' – laughed it off as a rather feeble, girly thing. His head bobbed, sending calm ripples out across the water. He was a strong swimmer; she was not. She'd always been afraid of water, as long as she could remember. She walked as briskly as she could into the lough. She knew she could swim that far in a pool; of course she could do it, of course she should at least try.

One sentence kept flickering in her head: 'When should we live, if not now?' It had leapt at her like a sudden spark from the Sunday papers yesterday, and stayed with her, glowing . . . It was a quotation from Seneca. She knew the name, but couldn't place it. She felt she should know, and didn't like to reveal her ignorance by asking. The words alone were enough, though, particularly poignant in this bleak landscape. People had been sent to Connemara as if to prison in the past, to learn the meaning of meagre, to grow the caution of the bog dweller, walking on uneven, treacherous ground. To scratch sustenance from a wilderness. To starve. And she had choices, a wealth of resources in comparison.

Last night there'd been a huge sunset; grandiose, cinematic, staining the mountains all around the deepest pink, the lakes burning back the magenta of the sky. There was something almost terrible about it. She'd run out of the cottage and stood on the road, soaked in the drama. *When should we live?* She felt expansive, hungry for experience. *If not now?* So many people lived in spite of, managing, and she didn't have to.

She waded through the soft mud into the water, determined. When the water was halfway up her thighs she stopped, trying not to gasp with the shock of the cold. He had turned, was shouting, 'You'll warm up once you're swimming!' Her legs were purple-white marble. Try. Try. Inching this cold up over her belly and breasts would be too excruciating. Now or never – she fixed her eyes on the island and pushed forward, forcing her arms to slice two strong arcs through the water. It was unutterable. She could hardly believe the strength of her own will, not allowing her to run out of the water screaming: 'It's – absolutely – unbelievably – freezing – you – bloody – maniac.'

Breathe. Remember to breathe. Breaststroke; she didn't want to splash noisily across such stillness. Every nerve stung. She sliced her arms through the water, pulled them hard to her sides, sliced them out again. Swim hard, get warm. Be confident. It seemed much harder work than in a pool, or in the sea; less buoyancy. Slice breathe pull, slice breathe pull. Not warm yet. She looked round. The shore looked quite far away, maybe three lengths; forward, the island about as far. Hard to judge, down in the water. His arms rolled over and over in a steady crawl. He never looked round.

No birds on the lough – just the sound of water, fat dollops of water, rolling over her limbs. She tried to focus on the beauty, the calm; tried to keep her mind occupied, to keep the panic from edging closer. Think about something else. She searched for an image.

This morning, hands in the sink, warm water, bubbles, washing up the breakfast things while looking at Our Lady, a flat plaster image smiling calmly, placed strategically between the taps. Another plaster figure knelt before the Madonna, arms outstretched, supplicating. Probably St Bernadette, who seemed very popular around here, kneeling in desperate perpetuity before a radiant Madonna at every roadside shrine. In fact, she thought, there should be an image of Our Lady on the island; she'd look good there, cold and blue and smiling. Faraway. Their rented cottage had a Virgin Mary in every room, even one in the bedroom that glowed in the dark. In the main room there was one with a 'perpetual flame' red light bulb that couldn't be turned off.

Standing at the sink, she'd been angry, thinking of generations of women standing at sinks, thinking of Our Lady's suffering, and 'Sure, wasn't it greater than our own', and carrying on, stoic. Stuck. He was reading the paper in the other room. Of course he would have washed up if she'd asked him. He would have done it kindly, as if it was a favour to her.

The middle toes in her right foot began to cramp. *Damn. Crawl, bugger the silence, kicking might help.* She splashed out vigorously, dropped her face under the surface. *Pull, pull, pull, suck air, down again, pull pull pull.* When she put her head under, there was the deafening noise of water churning. Only water.

She could feel a taut line of muscle knotting tighter between toes and heel. *Damn. Help?* She looked forward and back. It looked further to shore than to the island. His arms rolled over and over, smooth as a paddleboat. How could he be so oblivious? He seemed close to the island. *Relax. Confidence . . .* She tried breaststroke again, to calm down, to get her breath back, to relax. The rope of muscle began to tighten painfully up her calf.

Two lengths to the island? She tried to tread water, tried to hold her foot and pull the toes up, stretch the muscle – she went under. The worst thing; water closing over her face. Fighting panic, she crawled again, one leg trailing. She forced herself to look around, take stock. Where was he?

Standing! He was there, on the island – there! Now he could see her.

She lifted an arm, shouted, waved frantically. 'Cramp! CRAMP!'

He waved back, then he raised both arms above his head, joined his hands together in the gesture of victory, and shouted something, triumphant. It sounded like, 'Yeah, champ!' The sound spread across the water as he turned away; her arm was still upraised, in mid-wave. She gasped with disbelief – he'd turned away! A few steps up the bank, then he disappeared among the trees.

The rage began in her belly and hissed quickly through cold-mottled limbs. Her cheeks felt as if they were burning, so hot the water would fizz on them, evaporate. She flipped over onto her back, leg still trailing. It didn't feel so bad now. Perhaps rage could override pain. She backcrawled, windmilling through the cold, rage sizzling to the ends of her fingers. Anger, leaking out into the water, overflowing. It felt like voltage, vitalizing all the water around her. As she flung her arms over and over, she pictured the flat, gloriously emptied it of his belongings. *When should we live, if not now?*

Her body began to feel warmer. His books, his dirty washing, his caffeine-free bloody teabags. Gone. Bliss.

Birds

Kwa'mboka

In summer 1977, my sister Sophia and I left our Equatorial African homeland to go to a school on the outskirts of a little green village in the Northamptonshire countryside. We had spent many school holidays travelling the world with our father. This, and the nostalgic England of well-mannered expatriates, gave us false confidence in our understanding of England and the English. Father was considered radical and rash for educating his girls in Europe.

The school, established in 1125 for the sons of the clergy, was chosen by our Oxbridge father for its reputation as a station on the road to Magdalene or Kings. We arrived on an August afternoon and drove through farmland draped in ripening wheat and aromatic rape, unaware that the picturesque village boasted National Front marches on scorching Saturday afternoons; that too soon nationalists comparing Sophia and I to primates would create fractures in our safe worlds with every volley of spit and rough shove. We couldn't understand how people who didn't know us could believe that they did, and that their beliefs could turn to conviction and their conviction become the right to abuse. Nothing in our short lives had prepared us for the hostility of the natives. I took this experience badly, felt exposed, as though my skin was being torn slowly off my body. Sophia simply disengaged from her emotions.

Stonebridge was a boys' school which accepted a few girls.

Of the six hundred pupils, only a handful of children came from Asia, Africa and the exotic Elsewhere. The masters and mistresses, matron and the reverend delivered egalitarian care for all their students; so our trials in the village were all the more distressing. Kai and Ling, the friendly, happy Hong Kong twins; Sophia's special friends, the Indian boys from Zambia; clever, shy Mona from Kuwait and the green-eyed Iranian boy, Reza, were all shunned, called Pakis. The Honourable Hope Howe – a child of Biafra, adopted into the family of the Earl of Stonebridge – Odebayo and his sister from Nigeria, like me and Sophia, were for the first time called Wogs. At first we kept our own counsel, then sought small comfort among ourselves by sharing hilarious intellectual deconstructions of the etymology of words hurled in our faces. Finally our English schoolmates, unable to watch or bear the humiliations, spoke to the headmaster. Foreign children were banned from going into the village in case the words turned into sticks and stones. Imprisoned for our own well-being and doubly deprived of a prized treat, we watched the other students turn right out of the school gates. Sophia, Mona, myself and the other girls quietly following the backs of the English, German and Italian girls rushing towards rough village-boy leers and knickerboker glories with lipsticks and eye shadow stuffed into their blazer pockets.

In 1978, during our first summer holiday home, Sophia went to her mother's people for a month. She returned as a woman. Our three mothers, our grandmothers, brothers and father spoke to her in adult tones, with a special kindness. She wore heels, straightened her hair and spent many hours alone in her bathroom. I missed Soppy, sat on her bed for hours watching the closed bathroom door. A week before we returned to Stonebridge, Soppy came out of the bathroom, checked the corridor and then locked us in her bedroom.

'They cut me. I am a woman now. Clean. My sons will respect me and be buried close by me.'

I hated the confirmation. 'They circumcised you? How could Daddy let that happen? It's illegal.' I was kneeling on the bed, leaning towards Soppy.

'I know, but every self-respecting woman still makes sure her daughter is cut. I'm sorry, I didn't mean anything about your mother. Mummy Lola is wonderful but, well, she is so different – look at the way she left you and Markie.'

My mother held a gun to my father's head, Babycham in hand, so they say; she was questioning Father about his affair with her best friend and when her suspicions were confirmed, she became too hysterical to shoot. She lives alone now. Daddy only allowed her to see us for an hour a month when we were in the country. But he respected her wishes, and when she told him she would not have me cut, she said it in front of me and Markie. Daddy had tensed, nodded curtly and asked us to wait in the car. If it wasn't for Lola I would have been cut at the same time as Soppy.

'The aunties spent loads of time talking to me in parables,' said Sophia. 'Mad-chat, but they were kind, they made me feel like a real woman. My mother was there when I woke up in the private clinic. A nurse showed me how to care for myself and I've almost healed. It's not that bad actually, I can't feel a difference.'

Staring at the ceiling, Soppy thrust her hands between her thighs. 'Actually, there is a difference. I shouldn't think like this, let alone talk like this, but Boo, have you ever stirred your birds to flight?'

'Felt them flutter, alight and explode into the horizon, taking you with them into the white light, shaking your womb? Yes,' I said, sitting back on my heels.

'I have lost my birds,' said Soppy. 'They slaughtered my birds.'

She sat very still; I did not know what to say so I pulled her back on to the bed and we lay side by side, holding hands and swinging our legs off the end of the bed, lolling and mulling the way we had since we were two.

*

So, at the age of seventeen, Sophia and I stopped listening to the songs of our spirits. The world was not a safe place and we agreed that the only way to survive was to use and abuse. We did not find it hard to give away hope, trust and faith and it was easy to construct hard transparent shells, so to everyone else we were still the same Boo and Soppy. This became our education in isolation. We distrusted affection and were sure only of the rejection of those who liked us least. Our shells grew welts and weals, which grew calloused as Little England lashed at our confused longing for singularity and acceptance.

Maybe it was because spring came early in 1979, maybe it was a rite of passage, it doesn't matter. Sophia decided to lose her virginity to a man-boy who had befriended her at school. She hoped he would awaken her pleasure on the chipped wooden slats of the school's cricket pavilion. That Sunday evening Soppy crawled into my bunk and held my hand in the dark.

'Boo, he couldn't penetrate me and gave up gentleness for the thrust and force of battle.'

'What? Who? Sopps, what are you talking about?'

She told me how she'd silently willed him to complete his task, clenching her teeth in pain. Finally, when he broke through, he asked her to turn her face aside because, he said, beautiful, gentle Sophia looked like an ape. She'd stared into his straining white face and felt nothing, absolutely nothing. I couldn't bear the detachment in her voice and turned my back on my precious, animated sister. I imagined her prone, impaled body looking up into his grimacing face. Soppy spooned into me, one arm holding me tight, the other gently tugging my plaits. She started laughing when she told me she had asked herself in that moment, 'Are we no longer in love?'

I wept.

Sophia and I got into Cambridge but, fearing the duplicity of beautiful old villages and towns, we risked our father's anger and attended university in London. Bava, our maternal grandmother, had calculated our bride prices and demanded he bring us back for marriage. She worried that the amount Father spent on us would never be recovered through our dowries.

The Honourable Hope went to Cambridge and, like Mona, Ling, Sophia and me, rushed into the fray, disclaiming our privileges, nascent values and gods. Suddenly we were hip, acceptable, exotic dates. During those three years we topped up each other's bank accounts, shared our wardrobes, nervously supported each other at Brook Street and Marie Stopes clinics, and all the while reassured one another's parents with our apparent wholesomeness.

Sophia and Mona accompanied me for my first hymen replacement surgery; if you mention the name Dr Hermione Stone to female graduates of the 1970s and 1980s from Africa, Asia and the exotic Elsewhere, many a president's wife, Minister for Women's Affairs, and a good proportion of Businesswomen of the Year will stand and in unison cheer, 'Honour Restored!' The first thing Dr Stone always said as she secured the final suture.

In July 1986, after grand graduation ceremonies at the Albert Hall, we had a sleepover to celebrate all our parents' departures from England. Over four tubs of ice cream, we shared our memories: school, university, sex, but not family, not yet. Mona said she'd known she was a lesbian since the age of thirteen, that her mother knew and had sent her abroad for her own safety.

'But you fucked Hugh Maxwell-Smith and Reza, and you're the one who knew about the hymen replacement,' I exclaimed.

'Honour Restored!' Sophia and Ling shouted, saluting and laughing.

'Yes, well, I wanted to be sure about my sexuality,' Mona told us. 'Hugh couldn't help me in that department and Reza wanted to understand what to do with a woman. I taught him how to make love and to fuck like a woman . . . if you know what I mean, but then, you're all straight so of course you don't.' We protested loudly. 'As for the clinic,' Mona continued, 'I know these things because I'm switching to medicine. I want to work in women's sexual health, actually *do* something.'

'Mona, Mona, Mona, my God, we're your best friends, like your sisters and you never let on, hey . . . wait a minute, does this mean you and I can finally get it on?' Ling's mouth was almost on Mona's.

'Fuck off, tease, we're here tonight to be ourselves, to honour the love we have for each other by being exactly who we are,' said Mona in a mock-American accent, then, turning to Sophia, asked, 'Was Hugh good for you?'

I knew about Soppy's lovers but I'd never guessed Hugh was one of them; we hadn't seen him for at least three years.

'You could say he proved to be emotionally challenged,' said Soppy. 'The saddest part is that we lost a good friendship. Did I ever tell you about the Easter weekend we spent at his parents' home? They'd lived in Ghana and did the whole "we understand your people" thing. On the Sunday afternoon I was helping his mother in the kitchen and in between nips of vodka – she had little bottles stashed away in the cupboards – she suddenly tears the tea towel out of my hand, grabs my wrist and says, "Darling, you are such a handsome Negress, truly, I would love to paint you, beautiful. I want you to know you are very dear to us, our little African princess, but Hugh will never be more than a friend, you do understand that, don't you?"'

'Not that tired old line,' Ling said, and I shoved her gently.

'Anyway, a few weeks after the Easter holiday, Hugh and I had missed tea at school,' Soppy continued, 'so we decided to go for a walk and I seduced him in the cricket pavilion. I wanted to do something to shake his bigoted little world. It made sense at the time . . . he avoided me for ages after that.'

She paused and smiled. 'Hey, Ling, do you remember how we chanted Larkin in the shower on Saturdays when we were banned from going into town?'

Soppy and Ling struck up in chorus: 'They fuck you up your mum and dad, they don't mean to but they do!' Mona and I smiled, yeah, we remembered.

Soppy sighed. 'They fucked him up. They fucked me up.'

Hugh was a kindred spirit, not only because he'd grown up in Africa: he was an outsider and outsiders recognize each other. He'd spent his industry placement year in London. Sophia and him had spent a lot of time together, clubbing and showing off new friends to each other.

'Do you remember his coming-out party, at your place, Mona?' Soppy asked. 'That peaked leather cap, chaps and pink organza tutu? What you *don't* know is that towards the end of his year in London, he decided to tell his parents. I warned him not to, but he went home and came out screaming.'

Soppy was in her own world again and we were getting restless. This was stuff we mostly knew, what was the point of going back over it?

'We had coffee together the night after he told them. His face was crimson, voice shaking with rage and disbelief. "My father says he's changing his will and my mother asked me if you and I were still close. She suggested that I 'try it' with you, after all you're a nice girl and brown grandchildren would be utterly charming."' A tired groan went round the room. 'I looked at Hugh and just couldn't help it, I pissed my pants, coffee shot out through my nose and tears sprang out of my eyes. Hugh started laughing too.'

Sophia rolled closer to Mona, peered into her ice-cream tub and scraped out the last of the chocolate. 'After we calmed down, I said to Hugh, "If they ever get over themselves I hope they can handle your preference for African men." Hugh smiled, he was thinking about Wole, the dentist from Benin he was dating. Hugh and I lost contact after that evening.'

Mona and Ling looked bemused. 'Sophia, that was deeply disappointing, profoundly forgettable and I know I missed something,' said Mona as she trailed off towards the fridge.

Ling went to change the music and I asked Sophia, 'And?'

'And I asked him if Wole always turned his face aside when they fucked,' she said quietly. My stomach knotted; the one who'd called her an ape was Hugh.

'It's time to get married, have babies, be a dutiful daughter,' said Ling. 'So that's what I plan to do: find nice Chinese boy from nice wealthy Chinese family, make good marriage and make first-born son.'

Mona muttered something in Arabic.

'Anyone special in mind?' asked Sophia.

'Nope, I reckon I'll set it up during my postgraduate studies.'

'Let's do it together,' said Sophia.

So, Mona became a doctor, Ling and Sophia married the right men from the right families and gave birth to boys within a year of the three of us gaining our doctorates. Sophia returned to our country of birth with her correct husband, lived in a magnificently suitable house and from all accounts distinguished herself as wife, mother, daughter, sister and aunt. She stayed with me during her frequent trips to Europe.

In 1994, Ling, Mona, Sophia and I shared my flat for a week at the end of July, just as we did every year. We decided to attend the Old Bridgarians reunion, arriving the night before to join a house party given by Hope's parents. At the end of the evening we congregated in Hope's old room and, not wanting to exclude Hope, we pretended we had more to catch up on than we really did.

'Cambridge was more or less as expected,' she told us. 'Lots of sex, which was amazing at first, but none of the boys ever wanted to be seen out with us.'

We hummed at Hope.

'I don't know where I got this weird puritanical idea about virginity from, certainly not from the old parents, but I thought nice girls had intact hymens so I "lost" my virginity five times in three years.'

'Oh my God! You too? I did it three times and then I stopped counting,' said Sophia.

'Dr Hermione Stone, Harley Street?' asked Hope.

'Honour Restored!' saluted five women in unison, then we collapsed in giggles, talked in stage whispers, smoked too many cigarettes and, swathed in duvets, huddled in Hope's huge bed, watched the sunrise.

Sophia stayed with me for two more weeks. She was chasing her climax, her birds.

Lying side by side, swinging our legs off the end of the bed, holding hands, she talked me through her world of unkempt beds and disorderly encounters with unsuitable men. From time to time when she loved, truly loved, the pain would be so great that melancholy would lay her low for days. She fucked like a man with men and women, always hoping that this time, this position, this mutual passion or unbridled lust would bring her to climax. The correct husband, the beautiful children, the perfect home were a sham; normality tortured rather than comforted her.

'Now I understand your mother, Mummy Lola,' she told me. 'After you are cut, one of two things happens to a woman: either you lose interest in sexual pleasure and the clitoral orgasm in particular, or you torment yourself with the memory of childhood orgasms which grow more fabulous because they're no longer yours to have. No one has released my birds, so I'm going to see if a specialist can help. Come with me, Boo, please.'

I would go anywhere, do anything for my sister.

Darling Soppy required the replacement of her clitoris and we both assumed that if honour could be sewn back under local anaesthetic, her pleasure, her treasure, would surely be a small matter. We talked long into the night, sipping for ever. In between giggling and congratulating ourselves on our inspired medical ingenuity, we would fall silent and sad. My sister was willing to forego the tip of her tongue, the lining of her womb, a nipple or small body part from any area the doctor considered appropriately sensitive.

And that night I lay awake, thinking about her desire and the carelessness with which I treated my treasure. My intact clitoris may as well have been incised. I never caressed or stroked. If another's fingers touched this place, alarm paralysed pleasure and guilt blotted out sensation. Memories of lying still under impassioned fingers feeling only pain, dull pain, sharp pain, prolonged pain. Was my companion trying to wriggle my clitoris out by the root? Other times I imagined the fingers were picking at me as though my clitoris was a particularly stubborn stain on a highly polished surface. To end the torture, I moaned, feigned excitement, faked orgasm and pretended gratitude.

At ten-thirty the following morning, my sister and I sat side by side; rigid, articulate, aubergine beauties. Dr Ash, erect and relaxed in his black leather swivel chair, gathered up our words with glass-grey eyes and a slit-lip smile.

'How novel,' he exclaimed. 'We do not have the technology yet, but in a few years we will. Why, we might be able to clone you a new clitoris.' He took out a business card, and his shaking hand scribbled across the back. My sister's fingers touched his as she took the card. 'This is my private number. Stay in touch. Perhaps we might meet again before you leave.' He looked up, this man with grey hair, grey suit, and clipped grey manner. 'Tell me, Sophia, do you not find pleasure in other parts of your body? People who lose their sight, for example, often develop a heightened sense of smell or touch. Your mouth perhaps, your breasts . . . anus?'

Time, hope, breath, all stopped for us. The doctor held on to my sister's hand. I retched as we flew out of his office. Sophia flew back home to her husband, sex addiction and search for climax.

A year later, I sensed a strange excitement among the women of our household. Coded conversations, a suppressed thrill and discreet preparations for something special. I soon found out. Sophia's eldest daughter, Nonie, just thirteen, and in sight of her first blood, had decided to be circumcised. The youngest of our mothers set herself apart from the excitement, but the other two and Sophia's maternal grandmother could barely contain themselves.

'Don't let this happen,' I said. They looked at me with pity – thirty-six, unmarried, living abroad and without a son to care for me in my old age.

'Don't worry, Boo, these days we always use a surgeon. No infections or dangerous haemorrhaging for our daughters.'

They smiled and walked on by.

The women said Nonie had made the decision. Had my sisters, her aunts, not spoken to her? Held her back in a private space to share their experience, their loss, their grief and their attempts to reverse the cut? I wondered. Sophia not only became the most active member of the initiation clique, she seemed more and more excited as the day for the cut drew closer.

Me? I asked Sophia whether we might invite Nonie to one of our regular lolls. They came, and Nonie watched in amazement as we lay on my bed, side by side, swinging our legs off the end.

'Come on, Nonie, join us. Here, get in between us. Your aunt Boo and I have done this since we were little, it's a woman thing . . . Come.'

Nonie joined us on the bed.

'How do you think things will change for you, Nonie?' I asked.

'I'll become a woman . . .' she replied.

'And your sons will bury you and be buried close to you, you'll be clean . . . respected . . . wholesome,' said Sophia. 'It might be coincidental, but look at Boo here: beautiful, successful, kind. But no husband. No son, just a doctorate to keep her company. Me, I have them all: doctorate, children, husband, all. No offence, Boo, but . . .'

I stopped listening. It wasn't unusual for her to publicly shame me for having a clitoris. I never did tell Nonie not to go through with it, never told her what she would face, couldn't tell her what risks her mother took in the dingy and dangerous sexual encounters she pursued.

The night before Nonie's transition, I asked Sophia quietly and clearly, 'Why? How?'

'It is Nonie's decision,' she said. She walked away, humming a sweet melody. This time I felt as if my skin was peeling itself off my body.

Our lolls were never the same after that.

Long after midnight I called Lola – she and I hardly saw each other – 'Mamma Lola, it's Boo,' I told her. 'I'm calling because tomorrow they're going to cut Nonie, Sophia's baby girl, and I want to stop it.'

I cut into her replies.

'I know I'm not her mother. It was a figure of speech, she's thirteen . . .

'Oh, for heaven's sake, it's illegal . . .

'Lola, you can't mean that, how can you wish you had agreed?

'It is not your fault I'm not married; I like it this way . . . this is about Nonie, not you or my choices . . .

'No, I won't have a child just so you can prove my fertility to your friends.'

Lola thought she'd made a mistake with me, that in saving me from the silence of a nerveless sex, she had lost a daughter, a son-in-law and her grandchildren.

I extended my holiday. Sophia and I watched Nonie recovering. She was quiet, spent most of the time in her room, hours locked in the bathroom. Sometimes Soppy and I would force her to lie between us on my bed, we would hold hands with her and include her in our rambling conversations. My sister knew this was the only way she could include me in the transition.

When she came out of her room, Nonie held her head high. My gift to her, lunch and a day's shopping, became her gift to me. The young woman looked at me with sly pity, her pretty lips curled into a condescending smile.

'Why are you looking at me like that?' I asked.

'Like what?' the teenager replied.

'Like I'm God's special simpleton.'

She picked up her iced tea, took a sip, gracefully rearranged herself at the table and held my eye. 'They were right. You are not a woman. Because you are unclean, uncut, no man wants you and you will not have sons to bury you. You're old, Aunty Boo, old and alone all because Mamma Lola was too selfish to care about your future. God, what a bitch your mother is.'

I saw Father, Sophia and myself in Nonie's face, heard our mothers', grandmothers' and sisters' confusion behind her words and the shaky fear of a child in her voice. The sun felt so good on my skin. For the first time since 1977 I was awake and breathing. The hibiscus and bougainvillea framing the veranda became luminescent and I pulled Nonie into a tight embrace.

'Maybe so, maybe no. There are many things I would change about my past but getting cut is not one of them,' I said.

Nonie pulled away but kept hold of the last three fingers of my left hand. We sipped tea in silence for a few moments.

'Nonie, you're going to Stonebridge next month, come and see your old unclean aunt when you want a night on the town.' I kissed her brow and we got up to leave.

A year later Sophia called, asking me to help find a new school for Nonie. It was whispered that she 'liked' the boys too much.

Likes of Him

Jackie Gay

Last night he told her she was as sweet as Tupelo honey. Pitching and rolling round the living-room floor he sang it in her ear, *You're* as sweet, *you're* as sweet as Tupelo honey. They got up, though – 'The hardest thing in life, getting out of bed,' he said, and she laughed – and went straight to the pub, still pretty spaced. Sat steadily sipping pints and watched the men draining a quick few before Sunday dinner; the air hot and meaty through the open windows.

'Under manners,' said Clint.

Clint as in Eastwood, he'd told her last night. Swaggered round the room like a cowboy, except he couldn't hardly walk and kept falling around her, which Ju hadn't minded in the least.

'Huh?'

'Got to get back to their wives.'

The blokes sloped off, one by one, leaving the bar nearly empty. Motes floated in planks of sunlight stretching down from the sky, twisting the angles of the room.

'The nutters'll be in soon. *Ding*. Round two.'

Last night seemed more real to Ju than now, here, and it bothered her, that only the past was tangible. He hadn't even put his arm round her today – couldn't keep his hands off yesterday – although he did say 'nice night' when they woke, sliding his eyes away from hers, talking to his ribs.

Someone pulled a curtain to see the telly better and the room went dark and treacly. No one was serving, two blokes were up at the bar, one slumped on a stool with his face in his hands, the other shifting his eyes and legs about.

'Reckon they've got no wives, then?' she said, trying to get into it, living in the moment, instead of wishing last night could have stretched out for ever and they were still in the middle of an hour-long snog or scrapping like tiger cubs; batting, scratching, feeling his weight on top of her as sleep crept up his body.

'Crackhead; alky,' said Clint, nodding in turn. 'They've got no nothing.'

She thought it was all going to fizzle out there and then, was about to grab her bag and leave – always better to be the first to give in, she thought, although when she was younger she'd hung onto them, saying, *Why? What's the matter?*, as if she had a right to a boyfriend and they were obliged to explain. Now she sometimes left before they even woke up and she never said any of those things: *What's going on then? Will I see you again?* That was up to them, if they wanted it, and mostly they didn't.

'Tone!' said Clint. 'Maxie! Nice one, mate. Good one.' And he was up: slapping backs, grasping hands, touching fists. The bar snapped back into life as if they'd been statues waiting for the music; the crackhead all over Maxie, already trying to steer him in the direction of the bogs. Clint's mates all touched Ju too, squeezed her shoulders and nudged her chin; *Hiya, girl, you all right?* She was in because she was with Clint – cos he felt OK bringing her here, she guessed – and all she had to do was laugh at their jokes and carry on drinking.

'Wicked night,' said Clint, touching her thigh. 'You going down next time?'

'Might do,' said Ju.

Have to get someone to come with me, though, she thought, perhaps Andie'll come, if she can get away from that psycho boyfriend of hers. Wouldn't want him turning up stomping and ranting and demanding attention off everyone. Imagine if a woman behaved like that – strutted into the pub sticking goggly eyes into people's faces, bellowed out stories to everyone and no one, like one of the blokes had just done in here: *Jimmy White, he was in the snooker hall, on my babby's life, I mean Jimmy WHITE!!*

There was no future in thinking like that. She had to stop it.

The table was filling up with pints, rings vibrating outwards, some had beer mats placed over the top – I hope some joker isn't dropping pills into people's drinks, thought Ju, my face is going to be enough of a mess come Monday morning as it is. Maxie had brought some tapes in with him, banging house, and the girlfriends were arriving: tight white trousers, intricate gold bracelets and earrings, wings of hair slicked over one eye and springs of curls frothing behind their ears. She wasn't in with them, not by a long stretch, and wished she had a hairband, there was probably still a mussed up patch at the back of her head from all that thrashing about. Clint was sucking hard on a fag and grinning as wide as last night.

'Drink up,' he urged, drumming on the tabletop with his hands and the music was catchy, *ding ding ding* in her head but then it suddenly stopped and everyone roared, snooker cues clashing like swords, blokes up on stools blaring at the barman like he was the ref who finished Blues' dreams of the play-off finals.

'All right, all right,' said the landlord, fumbling with the tape machine. A power thing, Ju realized, watching them watching him, this is *their* patch. A phone rang into the silence and all the blokes frisked their chests and hips, but the ring was coming from Ju's bag; her surprise broke the tension somehow, the music started up, people laughed. *Andie* was on the display.

'My mate,' she said to Clint. 'Hiya, And, you all right?'

'Ju . . .' Hiss and crackle and *ding ding ding*.

'Hang on, love, can't hear a bleeding thing in here.'

By the time she got outside Ju already knew what had happened. She vomited, right there outside the pub door, *whoosh*, projectile splat into the wall, then *heave*, her guts in a puddle and her sick-looking face reflected back at her from the slosh of water.

Sunday was nutters' day but having to work all next week was taking the edge off it for Clint. A rake of Maxie's charlie and he wouldn't make it at all – no point in kidding himself – the poor cow without a bathroom for another week and he'd have to lubricate the gaffer with a good drink to get back on the job. He was a surly bastard, though, that Murray, puffing and grunting all day while he dug out footings, mixed concrete and lugged breezeblocks around, fag in mouth. The radio tuned to Capitol FM playing Marvin Gaye and Percy Sledge, all those bloody songs about soul. Stevie Wonder – 'You Are the Sunshine of My Life' – Clint couldn't get it out of his head, one reason he'd gone down Atomic Jam, some mad techno to proper blast the thoughts away. Granted, working with Murray was better than the factory, he'd hated that place. Making boxes not even fucking cars and all those little Hitlers just around the next stack – any excuse to have a pop and they didn't need much of one what with his record. Worse than fucking school and he used to jump out of the windows to get away from there. They'd sacked him for gluing the arms of the supervisors' overalls together, all joined up like those paper people kids cut out, he'd laughed his tits off watching the tangle they'd got into. Maxie got the elbow too – just for laughing – and they'd strolled out of the gates singing 'We Are Not Going Back'. He wasn't either, that much he knew for certain. Ju had thought it was a great story, 'I love the Housemartins,' she'd said. 'And Fatboy.'

Where the hell had she got to? He hadn't taken her for the sort who'd just piss off. Fucking knew those songs would get him into bother.

Emergency supplies: tea, milk, sugar, baccy and Rizlas, spliff, leccy on the card – she can have a bath then. Arnica cream, painkillers – Ju had tried to get sleeping pills but no one was about, they never bleeding are when you need them. It had taken her ages, lynching a taxi, home first for lotions and pills and then the bank, prayers at the cash machine, then the shop and then to Andie's, running up the steps and bracing herself. The *ding ding ding* still there in her head and it seemed obscene that her brain could be occupied with that, although she supposed it had to, had to keep your lungs puffing and your blood pumping around carrying all the good things to everywhere and taking all the bad shit away, messages jumping over your synapses so you could run and pick up things and remember some plasters and a bag of peas to use as ice and she was sure she'd forgotten something as she rapped on the door –

'Hello, girl,' said Andie.

Ju thought her synapses had finally laid down dead when she saw Andie's face. She stared at her feet, willing them to move but they didn't seem to belong to her, the reflective strips on her trainers throbbed.

'That bad?' said Andie.

'Fucking worse,' said Ju, and she could move again, an arm on Andie's shoulder and in through the hall and then a massive, massive hug until Andie started shaking so much she had to sit down. Ju wiped the tears, snot and grit from Andie's face, smoothed on Savlon, made tea and held the cup near to Andie's lips, switched on the water and felt her bones for breaks – she had a huge bruise on her shin and her foot looked like he'd fucking stamped on it. She fed Andie some Co-Prox and rolled them a spliff each. 'I mean, what the fuck, Andie? What happened? Where is he?'

'Dunno.'

'Has he got a key? We should get the locks changed.'

'We were pissed . . .'

'Oh for God's sake, don't start making excuses.'

'But we were. He got it into his head that I'd been eyeing up some bloke in the pub, just said it, "go over and talk to him if you want", and I'm like "you what?" and he goes "that fella over there, you've been staring at him for ten minutes" and I'm like "don't be ridiculous". And I think it was that *ridiculous* that got to him . . . But I didn't *do* nothing, Ju. I was just staring into space –'

'Course you didn't do anything. You don't have to *do* anything.'

They'd both smoked their spliffs right down to the cardboard but Andie was still sucking on hers. Ju started rolling. Better do a few, she thought. Look at the way her hands are shaking.

'I've *told* him. I say it all the time – I love YOU. Yeah, I talk to other blokes – I *have* to talk to other blokes at work. Yeah, I went for lunch with my boss last week but what am I supposed to do? "Sorry Mr Roberts but I can't come for a sweaty fucking ploughman's in the shiteiest pub in town because my boyfriend thinks I might have a weak moment and shag you for the hell of it." Why won't he believe me when I tell him, "I love YOU. No one else matters because they're not YOU."'

It was as clear as the hard blue sky outside to Ju. He doesn't trust you out of his sight and that's because you fell for HIM. Not a good time to pass on this painful piece of logic, though, so Ju made some more tea. 'Where did he do it, then? Did he batter you out in the street or have the decency to wait till you got home?' she said.

'Don't . . .' said Andie, but she managed the weary half-smile Ju had been waiting for, hoping for.

'That's you and him finished, then?'

'That's me and *men* finished. Looks like it's sex toys for Christmas for us, girl.'

Ju left when Andie finally crashed, put a duvet over her and tucked her in, grazing her brow with a kiss. Outside the sky was turning pink. She walked across town, whole streets wrapped up like those weird public artworks, tying up the town hall in a giant cherry-red bow, that stuff, except here the buildings were bundled into clear plastic. No frills for us, she thought, stepping on to the temporary pontoon over the crater where the Bull Ring used to be. The sides of the canyon had been clawed out, cranes swung great planks of wood over the holes opened up in the skyline – there was already a body or two down there, so she'd heard, casualties of the new Brum. She tried to imagine what it would look like, how the place would come together when everything was finished, but right now the site just made the towerblocks look lopsided. It seemed to Ju that the city was at long last coming out of black and white into colour, like telly when she was a kid, but the hole in her gut was as big as the one underneath her. 'When are they going to think of something else to do but batter us?' Andie had said and Ju knew that her own answer was to stay in the shadows, feigning nonchalance – come out in full colour and the scrapping would soon start. At home in bed she couldn't sleep, bits of music from the pub still trapped in her brain – *tearing up tights with my teeth teeth teeth* – and Clint, grabbing her from behind and swaying, together for a moment in the middle of the baying, restless crowd.

'What happened to your bird, then?' said Maxie.

'Dunno. Her mate phoned. You know what women are like.'

It was another lull. The death, really. Clint put his feet up to avoid the landlord's broom and the table collapsed. 'Fucking hell,' he said. 'You want to get some new furniture in here.'

'Nah,' said Maxie. 'All this broken-up stuff reminds me of our house.'

Clint thought the bar looked like a Van Gogh painting he'd seen somewhere: shattered faces, blind corners, patches of vivid texture picked out by the last long fingers of sun. He wished he could paint it, make it as real as the worlds he saw in films: *Taxi Driver*, *On the Waterfront*, maybe. But this was a dog-rough pub on a forgotten estate and no one, anywhere, gave a toss about the likes of them. Him and Maxie had been using it since they were boys, used to hang around outside like the kids out there now, fetching fags from the offy and scrawling their names anywhere they could reach.

'She seemed all right, though,' said Maxie.

Clint wished everyone would stop saying that. All fucking afternoon in his ear. 'Cool bird, her.' 'Wouldn't say no myself.' Billy Mac had even said, 'Get a ring on her finger, son. Stop arsing about for once in your life.' But Billy was a soft old fool.

As if I'm ever going to get married, thought Clint. I'd rather die than see a bird like Ju turn into my mum, never a word that's not sniping, the house a battlefield and me the target from the day I started looking like *him*. In Billy's day they might have got married and just got on with it but now no one knows what the fuck to do . . . So all he could do was wait for love, which was about as likely as a spaceship landing on the car park out there, if it did it'd drop right down on Murray's bust-up works van – the only vehicle on the acres of concrete – and the kids would have it tagged before the doors even opened.

He was in a bad mood, no doubt about it. Knew it would be best just to go home and get his head down – he hadn't slept since Thursday, not properly, last night just a couple of hours of floating, waking up wide-eyed and twitchy and getting up quick before the day was lost for ever. He remembered looking at Ju, splayed and sweaty, and getting this urge to say something to her, but the words never made it to his lips, just joined the trillion other unsaid things swirling around his blood; some days he thought he'd black out from all the things he kept inside.

Maxie nudged him and nodded at his pocket but Clint slid a beer mat over the top of his pint. 'I've had it,' he said. 'Off to get some kip.' They clapped each other's shoulders: *Later then, safe*.

He walked to Pershore Tower but knew if he went up to his flat the mess would just piss him off even more, and anyway, he was starving and there wasn't a scrap of food in the whole place. Fucking Weetabix and Pot Noodles, what kind of diet was that? The diet you provide for yourself, you tit, said a voice from the sky, and that was the last fucking thing he needed so he legged it, as the crow flies, over garden fences and through the lock-ups and a foot on every other stepping stone over the stream and quietly round the back – there was a light still on in her bedroom – to let himself in to the kitchen. The radio and the oven were on low and inside was a Sunday dinner, drying under brittle tinfoil, and on the stove a pan of custard with skin gone to rubber. He ate the custard cold first, then his dinner while reading the *Sunday Mercury*, his mum's TV choices carefully ringed in blue biro.

He stared at Ju's number on his phone and wondered if he'd ever ring it – tried to remember if he'd said he would. One minute he was there with his hand on her knee, rushing like Ian fucking Rush, and then she was gone, some dark thing happened to her eyes in two seconds flat. Something to do with men – he just knew it; some weight he'd have to carry if he ever wanted a woman of his own. He hoped he hadn't promised to bell her, didn't want to be a liar when he hardly ever even fucking opened his mouth.

Ju and Andie lolled on the sofa eyeing *EastEnders*, swinging their feet from crossed legs and spitting cherry stones into the bin. Andie had worn sunglasses to work for the last two days – the biggest pair they could find – and made up some rubbishy story about eye correction.

'They seem to believe me,' said Andie. 'Even the women make out they do.'

'Easier for them that way,' said Ju.

'In the short term, maybe.'

On telly Jamie was talking earnestly to Sonia, a hand on her shoulder: 'But I'm your boyfriend, I'm supposed to look after you.' Ju and Andie spluttered red skin. 'Have you ever had a boyfriend who could look after you?' said Ju.

'I've never had one who could look after *himself*.'

'Fuckers.'

'Tossers.'

'What about that one you met Saturday? Has he phoned?'

'Has he bollocks.'

Ju tried to ignore the dive of disappointment inside her. Didn't want to put Clint up in the bastards gallery just yet, although he *could* have phoned her; she'd grabbed his mobile and plugged her number in just before chasing off to Andie's – only got the balls to do it because of the surge of fury, the fucking tsunami which was forever slopping round her blood now, one tremor and it was off, rolling dangerously inshore. *So phone me, you fucker.*

Andie had seen the psycho off magnificently – 'Understand this, shit-for-brains,' she'd said, dismissing his apologies with an imperious wave, 'you've blown it.' Ju could see the notes she'd written to herself afterwards on envelopes and scraps of paper: *Treat everyone like a cunt until they prove themselves different. You don't get what you deserve, you GET WHAT YOU FUCKING GET.* Hard-boiled phrases, hard-bitten words from women who've been bitten hard, totems to ward off victimhood. Ju had been trying to dodge that way of thinking for months, body-swerve it; up, under, over or around it, because how do you talk to people when your mouth is full of that? It was all she wanted, really, to talk to a bloke. The physical stuff – whatever sort – she knew about instinctively, ferally, her body was there before her, if someone raised a hand to her now she'd be had up for GBH herself, wouldn't need no earthquake to set her off. Part of her would quite like to see it, the look on his face when she punched him in the gut.

'Don't suppose you'll call *him*?' said Andie.

'No way.'

'You like him though, don't you?'

'No way, Andie. I can't take the knock-backs.'

'Show me someone who can.'

'You gonna bell her, then?' said Maxie, whipping away the triangle and smashing the balls to all corners of the table. It was quiet in the snooker hall for a Saturday morning, old men shaking over their first beer and some reedy old Beatles tunes playing on the tape machine.

Clint tried to imagine the phone call. *Hi, it's me* . . . What if she went *Who?* She might not remember – they'd been pretty spannered. He was sure he'd said some things he shouldn't have – *I haven't felt like this for ages* – that sort of thing, he might even have *sang* to her. The words did tend to spill out sooner or later, usually when he was too wasted to remember exactly what.

'Nah.'

'Why not?'

'Give it a rest, will you.'

'Text her, then. Walk past her fucking house if it comes to that.'

Clint laughed. When he was a kid he'd dragged Maxie round Tinkers Farm Grove every night for weeks because that was where Wendy Foxkirk got off the bus.

'Pint?' said Clint, holding up his glass.

Maxie sliced the snooker cue within an inch of his head. 'Go on,' he said. 'Get a drink down you and you might not be such a fucking wuss.'

The tape had stopped but Clint could still hear the words. All about love, telling her, having to get a belly full first. 'Her Majesty' – someone out there talking to him again. Fuck *off* out of my head, he thought – but it was getting harder and harder to ignore the glimmering which he sensed, somewhere, behind all the gloom. He knew it, had always known it – how could you not when every song coming out of the radio is about love, yearning, souls? How to wade through all that darkness without it swamping you? Five blokes from his and Maxie's year at school had topped themselves, one way or another, fucking *five* – what chance did he have? Better stay misjudged and alone than end up a fucking statistic.

Say nothing and you get nothing.

Fuck off.

A sign was jammed into the mirror behind the bar: Cheap

Doubles. He sank two brandies while the beers poured then sat with his fingers hovering over the buttons on his phone. *See you later?* – erased – *Fancy a drink?* – course she did, but with him? In the end Maxie grabbed the phone and typed in *Pick you up at eight?* and pressed *send* before Clint could stop him.

'Pick her up in what?' Clint asked.

'Oh for Christ's sake – borrow your mum's car, get a taxi, do what you fucking like but don't bottle out.'

Clint had said something now – kind of. He was still trying to think how he'd front out a brush-off when his phone chirped. *Twist my arm then. See you later, Ju.*

They went out to the country – his mum's mud-coloured Metro rattling through the tunnel of trees over Icknield Street – and sat on a wall outside the Coach and Horses chucking sticks for a black and tan mongrel whose tail wavered above the long grasses.

'I'm getting a dog,' said Ju, fingering its ears and stealing glances at Clint. She was going to have to do something this time, still winced at the gap it opened up beneath her. But she was already out on the wire and the realization buoyed her.

'What sort?' said Clint.

'Dunno. Like him, maybe.'

'That's a she.'

'Is it?'

Clint shrugged. Clouds were sinking into the busy landscape – hedgerows and odd-shaped fields, farm buildings clustered under trees, a maze of paths and tracks and ancient roads – but there was still a shine behind them, the sun wasn't gone yet.

'Want another?' he said.

'Might do . . .' She was flirting – no doubt about it. Her legs were dangling, there was a swing to her shoulders and she sat up straight, like a queen; if it hadn't been for the grin on her face and the rays of sunshine fanning out across the fields he'd have felt utterly helpless. She was humming a tune – he kind of recognized it – and swaying recklessly, an awful moment when it all might have crashed down in a heap.

'Watch you don't fall,' he said.

'Think I'd fall for the likes of YOU?'

Five pints later and he was driving like a granny, weaving along close to the hedgerows. The radio played handbag house. Ju tapped her fingers and flashed him smiles although once he thought he saw her mouth, *you fucker*.

'Best leave the car at the pub,' said Clint, when they could see the towerblocks by the Man on the Moon. 'Come back for it tomorrow.'

'Yeah,' said Ju. 'Stay out a bit longer, hey.'

A mix of 'The Passenger' came on the radio, tinny beat and loads of high hat. They glanced at each other, drew in a breath and sang together the *la la la la la-la la la*, bouncing around the car like they were in a B52s' video. Perhaps moments like this *could* flush all the bad shit away, Ju thought, feeling a grin grow fat on her face. Clint pulled up underneath the pub sign of a smirking moon, *Apollo Five* hurtling towards it, and thought that for once in his life he might just have got away with something.

Aqua Blue

Naylah Ahmed

She peels onions as if she were unwrapping jewels, jewels that belong to someone else. She is careful and gentle. But the onions are not. Her eyes leak and swell at the clear juices tainting her fingers and blurring her vision.

She likes that. When her vision is obscured she feels that were the knife to slip and slit her translucent wrist instead of the onion, it would not be her fault. It would be an accident.

One nick would free a torrent of scarlet words in capital letters, followed by exclamation marks, explained and re-explained in brackets and inverted commas. Inside she bleeds two languages in constant italics.

Outside she is responsible, responsible for her actions and the actions of those around her. Because she is she, and not he.

He is free to – anything.

Somewhere exist the *they* that make it so. *They* that taunt and jibe. *They* whose tongues would slice her wrists in a moment were they given to licking the wounds they inflict. *They* are everywhere. People she knows as everyday 'you-and-me's are *they* when they want to be.

So who would dream of escape?

For now, escape is from the chopping board to the sink. A he-shaped pile of dishes, pots and colanders blink at her, reflecting the sun. Outside.

In here, rays bounce off clinical surfaces and cut through her face with blades of light. But out there it is intimate and warm –

out there it is unprejudiced, interrupted only by clouds and tall buildings.

Outside there is sun.

The kitchen is clean. All elements are under her control here – until, that is, *they* will begin to arrive from outside and consume and disrupt before taking their rest.

And she will start all over again.

There comes a point when a stainless-steel kitchen sink is so clean and free of water that she can see her face in it, but just one trickle of liquid, one drop from a silent tap, causes her reflection to bubble and inflate unnaturally. The frightening thing is not the deformity of her reflection, but how clearly it sketches what she feels.

When he barks at her, she wonders how she could be an elder sibling and still the recipient of such violent tones. But she knows that in this household age is a weak second to gender. Her shoulders tense and then sag, but she resolves to hum a tune in her head – a happy tune. She finds a song, fixes it in her mind and sings. A smile fights to free her lips – only slightly more elegant than a tremble. He is barking again.

'Why are you laughing? What's so funny?' he wants to know.

She loves that tiny bit of mystery too much to give him the satisfaction. The thin slice of 'I-know-something-you-don't-know' that she can wedge between their bodies before his rhetoric forces out the tune and replaces it with tears.

There is no room for tears.

Yet there are many rooms in which, were tears available, they would drown everything in sight. Rooms that still hold bitter interchanges on their walls like *they*-shaped trophies. Rooms where it was decided that he could do and she could not; that she *must* do, and he needn't bother. Cubic spaces with doors running on silent hinges; doors he slams at three a.m. after OD-ing on freedom – her freedom. Walls she's had her back to, floors she's pressed cold soles on while being asked the why-where-who-and-how of her daily routine. A routine as constant as a straight line, unlike the violent zig-zagging of his.

These spaces are constantly refurbished. He moves things and she replaces them; he fills ashtrays and bins and she empties them; he throws mean words like icy snowballs and she catches them in her raw, bare hands, holding them like babies until they melt, and then cleaning up their liquid aftermath.

There is always an aftermath. Then all eyes focus on the television – lives that are too real to be real, but so easy to watch – anything to fill the gaps between awkward bodies.

Washed three times, the colander is gleaming. But her wrists have become entranced by the circular movement: swirling water which, mid-swirl, is forced to evacuate through the small holes. It escapes. She doesn't want to let go.

Finally, giving in to the call of duty, she places the clean colander amid a pile of glasses on the draining board. After all, a kitchen is only one room in a house.

She moves to the bathroom soundlessly.

The bathroom: if ever there was a place that reeked of anger, separations and – at the very least – the promise of an argument, it is this space. This no-man's-land is a necessity, used by all several times each day. Around her lie the provocations of war: a deformed tube of toothpaste (half full yet twisted as if the culprit had fought to squeeze the last drop). It lies helpless, refusing to recognize its cap sitting bewildered beside it. The sink sprouts tiny hairs from a razor hastily removed and replaced. The toilet is yawning. A pubic hair coils, almost proud, on the edge of the porcelain, next to a content-looking drop of urine refusing to slide either way.

Armed with yellow Marigolds, she is careful not to let her skin make contact with her surroundings. Her busy elbows nudge the air as she scrubs. Of all her tasks this is the most trying, as the smells of strong chemical cocktails – insufficiently laced with lemon – strip her of her self-respect. What excuse is there for this?

Boys will be boys after all. The words sit motionless in her head – as stubborn as the spiralling body hair.

They are back.

Yes. Boys will be boys – and girls will be anything you want them to be.

In schoolrooms throughout her youth, she sat among boys that smelled of soap and sweat at the same time. Boys whose ink-stained fingers never used a pen to scribe what bald-headed teachers demanded. Teachers with clear eyes that stared out, searching for the brown in the Union Jack, momentarily becoming peers with their pupils in a universal search for one colour among many.

She didn't mind that. She didn't once mind being colourful.

What she did mind was being typecast, being as non-present as the life-size cardboard cut-out of an air hostess in a travel agent's window: a smile that flexes painfully wide, but clothes and hair and face stripped of colour by the everyday sun.

Boys were genderless in the academic race. Too enthused with moseying in the general direction of independence to concern themselves with pluses or minuses. Yet, in the outside world, they seemed to sprint in turbo-boosted Nike, while she attempted to catch up with a bucket on each foot and an entire household strapped to her bare back.

These boys were now men. Men in suits forming grey queues outside sandwich shops come one o'clock; men in taxis pulling into the drive-through. While women clip, wax, pluck and snip at their beings, their men sit (ever discontent) raising eyebrows as unkempt as roadkill – stroking bellies pregnant with six-packs of beer, and twisting nose hair which meets ear hair which finally travels down the neck and into the great unknown.

Boys will be boys . . .

*

Water slides over her head, racing to reach her ankles. Her skin inhales, drawing in the warmth. However, at this moment, the white tiles and shiny basin under her feet have lost their appeal. Having scrubbed away their filmy shadow on reluctant knees, she takes no pleasure from the cleanliness of her environment. The grimy remnants of daily chores remain tattooed in her skin's every line. Washing is futile.

An image of diluted colour looks back at her from the misty mirror as she steps out of the shower. Disinterested in her reflection, she dresses hastily, pins her scarf in place, and heads downstairs.

The pale blue carpet remains soft and dirt-free un-tampered by the intentions of others. She finds comfort in rooms that don't permit shoes. The feeling of her vulnerable bare soles on any surface gives her a sense of belonging. She lays out the Ja Namaaz with the enthusiasm of a shopkeeper spreading out fancy fabric for an eager customer. The carpet and prayer mat are an identical blue – if they were going to have a prayer room, everything must match. So, while *they* laid carpets in a particular shade, she was left to search for God in aqua blue.

There are two scars on the mat where her feet have worn down the nap. A place where two perfect size fives have stood and recited verses from the Qur'an so often that soft, still feet have worn away fabric as if they had been jogging on the spot. His size twelves do not come here – his size twelves are only present on Eid and during the Holy Month.

She stands reciting Arabic as familiar as her name – repeated more often. There is a beat to words born from practice. The rhythm carries her from verse to verse without thought. Sometimes this is a good thing – her tongue acts like a foot tapping to music: no thoughts, just a beat, and time seems to move at a reasonable pace. Today, however, she is weary and the beat hides below a meandering whine. Tears sit under her lashes like glass beads and, though her head is bowed, they refuse to fall. Closing her eyes, she ensures their capture and stoops to submit for the second time that day. Her forehead rests on the hand-woven image of Ka'ba – she doesn't want to move. Fully clothed, with only hands, feet and face exposed, she chooses to stay in a foetal ball at the foot of faith.

This rectangular mat is the only space she inhabits where *they* are not present and cannot interrupt. Her desire is to expand this safety zone until it spreads out around her and leaves them on a periphery just out of sight.

When the phone and doorbell ring out in unison, she knows it is time to resume – everything. Time to fold the mat, leave the room and wear shoes again. Her brief moment of atonement is over.

He is back.

A coat sits below its hook, like a frightened child crouching. She knows to avoid the large rubber-soled shoes he's stepped out of and left in the middle of the floor. A pair of discarded socks lie inside out, seconds from the shoes, spread across the carpet like two streaks of butter. She knows what to expect and so plans ahead – picks a song – and begins humming quietly before she reaches the kitchen. The television is on in the lounge; she doesn't have to look to see the stale feet resting on a newly polished table, or the cigarette smoke curling around a bowl of pot-pourri.

As her feet slip back into shoes, her body finds itself in the kitchen again. Everything is where it shouldn't be; she is the only object in place. The worktops are crowded with crumbs. A layer of sugar dissolves in speckles of water, a moon-like marking etched in it from the base of a mug. The floor is sticky. Once again, she will begin at the sink.

My song isn't working. Gloria won't play – she's not singing 'I Will Survive'. The tune's the same, but the words are telling me I won't – I can't – survive. She's screaming at me 'cause she knows what I know, knows that when the others get back they'll do the same. They'll mess it all up, and I'll have to start again! Just the music by itself makes me feel stronger – usually.

But where are the words? All I can find are two: afraid and petrified. I know they belong somewhere in sentences – powerful, Gloria-kick-ass-Gaynor sentences – but they're the only two I can hear. And they're the wrong ones. That's not what the song's about – being afraid and petrified. It's about not being those things! But I can't seem to find the link, I can't find her words. The music isn't enough.

She jumps at an unfamiliar sound – her hands clinging only to the memory of an object. The walls hold their breath. She looks down at the population of tiny glass fragments at her feet.

Did I drop the glass, or did it fall?

In the lounge, he turns the volume down. He heard it too. She can see his questioning brow – inquisitive, but an easy loser to his lazy arse that is never curious enough to move. She is the sound-maker, the creator of unfamiliar. She likes that.

A muscle twitches in her leg as she raises her foot, clad in a delicate hand-embroidered slipper. Nerves drunk with anticipation fail to register the tiny cuts on her feet. The glass fragments splinter into ever-smaller grains under her size fives, unwilling companions soon to be strewn about the house.

Blood trickles down her skin with the fine artistry of henna – as if there were anklets of barbed wire stitched inside the cuffs of her shalwar. She walks on. The house expands in front of her as she strides through rooms, disrupting. Breath comes easier at this moment – her only restriction is that of the shoes choking her feet, interrupting the dialogue between sole and ground. The doorbell is ringing again, and more coats crouch below hooks. But the walls are making space, throwing back the inquisitive bodies, inconvenienced by her change of routine. Questions are launched into the air around her:

'What's for dinner?'

'What the hell are you doing?'

She wafts them away with a carefree hand. Someone asks about the blood – but she doesn't even look to see who expressed the belated concern.

She steps out of the shoes and into the room. As exposed skin meets soft carpet, her body tingles. The only thing she shares with *they* is a love for the calming blue. Her tongue wets the corners of her mouth preparing for the foreign beat before the Ja Namaaz is even unfolded. Her smooth forehead aches to rest on cool velvet. Curiosity pushes against the door, but is unable to enter. *They* know better than to interrupt in here.

Gloria's empty rhythms are now filled by an ancient beat. One that needs no music, no sound other than her mouth, tongue and throat working together to pronounce the elegant curl of the Arabic letters.

Blood pumps ferociously around her unmoving limbs. She stands on the mat watching the blue turn to purple at her feet.

Obeah Catastrophe

Ifemu Omari

*R*eports are coming in of a road accident in the Midlands.
An oil tanker has exploded on the M6. We'll bring you
further details as soon as they come in . . .

Beverley ran back and forth from bathroom to kitchen
transforming her tatty morning self into that of a sophisticated
professional. Uncle Manny's portable television, propped on
the kitchen counter, blinked fractured images every few
seconds for the attention of no one in particular. Beverley
inspected herself in the mirror and giggled. I bet Robert hasn't
finished that bloody report. I'm sure it was his PA who did the
last one for him anyway, she thought, as she dusted her
shoulders and looked at herself approvingly.

The telephone in the hall was flashing red again. But each
time Aretha's number showed on the display, Beverley
convinced herself that she'd face it all later: *I can't allow
anyone to mess with my head just now. Aretha'll understand.
I'll phone her straight after the meeting.* She grabbed her coat
and briefcase – early for once.

As she turned the key in the ignition, the car radio crackled
out the eight o'clock pips and another news flash:

*Details have now been confirmed of a fatal pile-up near the
Spaghetti Junction. A leaking oil tanker swerved across the
motorway and exploded, setting fire to at least ten cars. No
survivors have yet been found. Concerned friends and relatives
should telephone this number . . .*

Beverley rushed back into the house, switched the TV back on: the screen showed a burnt hill of twisted iron. Black smoke clouded the morning sky. She stared, open-mouthed, at the scene, held in limbo by the magnitude of the horror for a few splitting seconds. She didn't go to work that day.

In the last few years Beverley had borne witness to the deaths of both her parents. They'd died within ten months of each other. Twice over Beverley sang 'Meet Me by the River' and 'Abide with Me'. Twice over she was greeted by the same mourners with their twin condolences. Her emotions had been seared raw, to numbness. No healing time. Too soon, especially for an only child. So she was glad of Uncle Manny.

Uncle Manny was Beverley's mother's only brother. He'd been a steel polisher at Patent Shaft's for thirty-five years, beating hot iron for cold white people. He'd started work the same day Beverley was born – 22 August 1961 – and believed the new baby had brought him luck.

'It's a sign,' he'd said to Beverley's mother, and from then on he'd treated Beverley just like the daughter he'd never had.

Uncle Manny prided himself on living frugally. In the 1970s he bought a terraced house, but lived in just one room and rented the rest of the property out to students. He didn't like spending money. When Beverley was small, his greatest joy was giving her his blue savings book to inspect.

'Tell me, girlchile. If I put in ten shillings a week extra, how long it will take to double my money?'

Beverley would sharpen her pencil and work out the sums in long multiplication, as Uncle Manny quietly watched. When she finally came to an answer, he'd pat her gently on the head and say, 'You have a good head, dawta. Here's two shillings for that good head.' She often fretted for days over whether she'd put the decimal point in the right place. But Uncle Manny had no worries about his niece's abilities.

During the summer holidays of 1972, Uncle Manny stopped sharing his savings book secrets. To him, Beverley was no longer a child. 'You can't trust big pickney,' she heard him say.

'I wish I could stay little for ever,' she complained to her mother. 'Uncle Manny only likes little people.'

Her mother only stopped laughing when she saw the tears in Beverley's eyes. 'Your uncle has a way of seeing the world, but him got a real big love for you, dawta,' she said, hugging her tight.

Those 1970s summer weekends saw the domino men – as Beverley secretly called them – flocking to the big creaky house on Waterloo Road. Beverley and her parents lived upstairs and the other rooms were rented out to an Irish couple and their four children. The domino men were Uncle Manny, her dad Samuel and his workmates: Longman, Blu, Lieutenant and Mr Pol. They played in the attic from Saturday afternoon through till late Sunday night. Beverley was fascinated; those domino games were the only times she ever saw men skylark like children. She would bring them the crate of Davenport beer, tuck herself neatly on the second flight of stairs and listen.

'So, Manny, you still hoarding your money to build that dream house in Jamaica?' teased Mr Pol.

Uncle Manny slammed down his domino. 'Deuce. Yep!'

'Seems to me you can build ten hotels, never mind houses, the way you hate to part with money,' Mr Pol continued.

'Tell me, Samuel,' said Blu to Beverley's father. 'You ever see your brother-in-law with so much as a ten shillin note in his hand?'

Beverley's father's domino hit the table. 'Nope.'

'Pure coppers,' they choroused.

For a while the only sound'd be that of wooden dominoes slapping the table. The men mumbled under their breath, all focused on the last domino cupped like precious water in their hands. With perfect timing, Uncle Manny tickled their concentration.

'But you all forget something,' he teased.

'Huh huh,' they all whispered.

'You know, I'll be looking for a woman keep me company . . .'

'And that's where your problem begin, Manny,' said Mr Pol. 'We know how Jamaican woman got expensive taste. Not one will put up with a mean English like you.'

'Well, that's the kind of problem I'd love to manage – last card!' Uncle Manny replied, triumphantly flinging down his last domino. Much laughter and crashing of dominoes as that game broke up, and Uncle Manny was declared the winner.

By the time Uncle Manny retired, he'd got the house built in Constant Springs, St Andrews. He'd begged Beverley to go out there with him.

'Your parents dead a while now, you might even decide to stay in Jamaica. Wha you say, dawta?' But Beverley was about to start a new job the week Uncle Manny was booked to fly home.

'When I get settled into this new company, Uncle, I'll come for a long break,' she promised. 'Say, a fortnight this Christmas.'

Uncle Manny left England with his head held high. He'd given his sister and brother-in-law a decent send-off and left his only niece a sum of money along with his terraced house. When he stepped onto Jamaica's hot red tarmac, breathed in the scents of hibiscus blossoms and morning glory for the first time in thirty years, his heart gasped for more. Like a goatfish out of water, his eyes and mouth stayed stark and open.

That was 6 June 1995. The porters at Norman Manley International Airport moved quickly to the shocked group of passengers from flight JA602. Mr Emmanuel Saunders was unceremoniously pronounced dead, and his lifeless body bundled up and zipped into a body bag. The new supervisor, Mr George Montcrieffe, would tolerate no delays, even if an old Englishman *had* dropped dead on the tarmac. Not after those reports criticizing standards in international arrivals. So the bag marked MORGUE in stiff bold letters shuffled limply along the conveyor belt with all the other baggage, suitcases stuffed fat with gifts from the UK.

George Montcrieffe prayed that God would forgive him for the perfunctory way he'd speeded up Uncle Manny's departure. From that day onwards, international baggage was always spot on schedule whenever he was on shift – an achievement not missed by the Directorate. A man with Montcrieffe's standards could tighten up the workforce, pay dividends for the airport. By Christmas 1995, Montcrieffe was promoted to senior supervisor; a year later, he became manager for international carriage and baggage handling. But despite his neighbours' suspicious whispers about obeah practices and rumours that he communed with the dead, George Montcrieffe never worked on 6 June again. Instead, he would drive up to Constant Springs Community Cemetery taking his best wishes, flowers and a little labrish to the graveside of Mister Emmanuel Saunders.

Five such anniversaries had passed without incident. Then, on an ordinary working day in May 2001, Montcrieffe picked up his office telephone, promptly after its third ring.

'Mr Montcrieffe, Mr Jones from Customs on the line for you.' Esmina Jacob's shrill voice ended on its usual high note.

'Put him through, Esmina. Hello, Jones, what's your query? . . . What are you talking about, man? . . . Run it by me again . . . A woman? . . . An empty coffin? Be they black or white, these English people have some foo-fool ways. What happen to the body? . . . Oh yes, that big road accident. OK, Jones, I'm on my way. Put her in the first-class suite, I'll be there in half an hour . . . Delay? Who cares about delay, man? Haven't you heard of respect for the dead?'

Montcrieffe grabbed his car keys and dashed out, his mind racing, so much so that he didn't notice Esmina filing her nails. He'd moved too quickly for her to start strumming those glossy red fingernails on the old Canon typewriter.

That date, 6 June, and the old man's death, had come back to haunt him. The body bag, the disrespect he'd shown. Five years of visiting a stranger's grave and now a woman arrives from the UK on flight JA602, this time with an empty coffin. What kind of coincidence was this? he asked himself.

Deep in thought, Montcrieffe didn't notice the stares from passers-by. '*Why is he driving himself?*' '*Where is Errol his chauffeur?*' Onlookers tut-tutted and kimboed, amazed at the speed of the steel-grey Cadillac as it flew towards the airport. If Errol'd been driving, he'd have tooted the car horn at Viola Chin in her dumpling shop. And she'd have waved flirtatiously at Montcrieffe, while thinking, *It's easier catching fish with your bare hands*. But today, as the car cut along the dusty road, Viola was busy labrishing on the phone with Esmina.

Since his career took off, his employees and neighbours didn't say much to George Montcrieffe, but they watched him. They noticed who he dated, where he shopped, what mail came for him, what visitors came to the 'big house'. They were waiting for the monkey to climb up the tree. *Bound to get a fall*, they whispered, willing the monkey on. They watched him visit the graveside of the stranger from England. Miss Ira had said that time would reveal the truth about George Montcrieffe. So they passed the story on, adding their own texture and colouring. *Monkey must fall*, they agreed.

The story was moving fast now, quickly changing shape.

Lester Jones from Customs phoned his ladyfriend Esmina Jacobs. 'Wha happen, Esme? Montcrieffe fretting like when puss mooma dead.'

'Is the woman, as you mention har, him fly out the office like mongoose tail catch fire.'

'How you know about har?'

'In the urgency I forgot to turn off the telephone conference switch,' she said, trying to sound official before continuing excitedly, 'You see har? Wha she like, Lester?'

'She very small, almost like a child, dressed in red from head to foot. And she don't talk. Har eyes just look right through you.'

'Jesus Christ!' shouted Esmina, banging the phone down. She just had to call Edwina Francis, Montcrieffe's neighbour, who lived a quarter of a mile from the big house in Stony Hills. She kept an eye on Mr Montcrieffe and the house. She never got invited to his private parties, but bore him no grudge. He was too uppity for her liking. And now, even more peculiar was the description of the staring woman, dressed in scarlet. Edwina had to phone Miss Ira, out of duty of course . . .

Miss Ira was agog with excitement. Not since the disappearance of Precious Townsend had she felt so thrilled and intrigued. Then the whole community had looked to Miss Ira for answers and she'd given them what they craved: Precious had been spirited away because of her bad-mindedness. No relatives claimed Precious's house, and as Miss Ira had the definitive story, she was declared the rightful inheritor of the property. Even when a journalist tracked down Precious in Barbados with her toy-boy lover and brought back photos as proof, Miss Ira's credibility remained in tact.

'These young, educated people think they can prove everything. Well, I have faith and I need no proof. That's not Precious.' Faith-healer, body-healer, fortune-teller; bring any evidence and Miss Ira would have an answer. Photographs, strands of hair, clothing, she could read them all, drawers and briefs excluded.

Business had been a touch slow since then, so this news of the woman in red, the empty coffin and George Montcrieffe's odd behaviour could only mean an upturn in Miss Ira's fortunes. To nudge events on a little, she phoned three employees of the Constant Springs Pentecostal Church: the preacherman, the gravedigger and Kitty, the church cleaner.

George Montcrieffe's car squealed into the airport's executive car park and half a dozen boys swarmed over it with cloths and buckets of soapy water. As he strode tall in his linen suit, Lester and Elbert stopped chatting loudly about the hot news item and greeted their boss in deferential tones.

He opened the door of the first-class visitors' suite and felt the quiet intensity of its lone occupant. A diminutive, copper-coloured woman, dressed in a matching towering red head-wrap and a long kimono-style gown. She was gazing at a gloriously shiny white casket, edged with gold rope and with a gold cross over two-thirds of its lid.

This is all for someone very special, he thought.

'Good afternoon, I'm Mr George Montcrieffe, manager responsible for international carriage.'

'My name is Beverley Clarke,' the woman responded.

'Mrs Clarke . . . I gather –'

'Ms,' she interrupted.

'Ms Clarke . . . In delicate situations such as these, we at Air Jamaica Incorporated try our best to accommodate the needs of our international customers.' George faltered, knowing he sounded like a marketing executive.

'This is my partner's coffin. There are no remains . . . no body, my partner was killed in a motorway accident.'

'Yes, we heard about the disaster. On behalf of Air Jamaica International Incor . . . Mrs . . . Ms Clarke . . . Please accept my personal condolences.'

'It was my partner's wish to be buried in Jamaica. I'm obliged to honour that wish. It's important to me to hold a fitting burial ceremony.'

'I understand, Ms Clarke,' replied George, struggling to find words appropriate to this conversation. 'So how can I best help you?'

'Simply to treat the coffin as if it did have a body and to help me transport it to my family's plot in Constant Springs.'

Montcrieffe gulped. Then, regaining his composure: 'Are the authorities aware of your arrival?'

'It's been very difficult organizing the burial from England, but the ceremony takes place tomorrow.'

'Do you have anyone here with you? Perhaps some family in Jamaica who can help?'

'My close relatives are all dead,' she said sharply. 'I do have an uncle buried here in Constant Springs.'

'He lived here?' George couldn't help probing further.

'No, he had a heart attack when he came back to retire.'

Montcrieffe held his body rock-still. His mind chipped away, frantically trying to shape this information. The woman in front of him, dressed like a priestess from a Pocomania church, was the niece of the man whose dead body he'd treated so badly five years ago.

'I'd be pleased to take you to the cemetery for the burial service tomorrow,' he said. 'I can arrange to have the coffin transported, and for a priest to be present. I'd advise that we begin early. And you are most welcome to stay at my home tonight, as my guest.'

Jamaica was a different kind of Jamaica as night fell. Rich with the smells and sounds of Kingston. On the roadside: roasted corn, children's voices singing, '*Kisko pop, kisko pop.*' The oily succulence of jerk chicken, the sharp aroma of white rum, a heavy tide of reggae. Then the quietness of the countryside, patterned with the flashing lights of peeny wally, the whisperings of fierce crickets and mosquitoes claiming the night as their own.

'Home at last,' hummed Montcrieffe.

Beverley followed him towards a huge sand-washed house with elaborate iron gates. Greek-style columns, lavishly curtained french windows, half a dozen Alsatians on guard. A man and young woman ignored the dogs and rushed towards Beverley and Montcrieffe.

'Good evening, Mr Montcrieffe. Good evening, miss.'

'Good evening, Iris. Good evening, Junior,' Montcrieffe replied, trying to control the unruly dogs.

Once inside, they entered a spacious room with floor-to-ceiling columns, cream leather sofas, white floor tiles, low coffee tables and a few austere tree-like plants.

Uncle Manny would've loved a place like this, Beverley thought, smiling to herself.

'Iris will show you to your room, and I shall I meet you on the veranda at seven for dinner?'

'Junior will bring your luggage up in a few minutes, miss,' said Iris. 'A bell will ring when the meal is ready.'

In the privacy of the vast white guest bedroom, Beverley took out a silver frame from her case. She stared at the photo of the woman's round, coffee-coloured features. Black bubbles of hair encircled the face, filling the picture. Deep set eyes. Plucked eyebrows. No smile, but smile lines around the mouth.

Stifled laughter outside the bedroom drew Beverley towards the window. She peeled her ears to listen.

'I hear say she's a obeah woman come to bury her man,' said Iris.

'Woman, stop talking foolishness,' Junior retorted.

'Foolishness? Is that what you call it? Well, hear this, there's no body in the coffin. She come all the way from England to bury an empty box.'

'Who tell you so?'

'Your own brother Lester tell me.'

'Half-brother.'

'Now you being foolish. Same belly, you're still brothers.'

'Well, how come he don't get me a job at the airport?'

'Hell, man, you have the same boss. You ever tell Mr Montcrieffe you want a job at the airport?'

'Mr Montcrieffe don't take me seriously,' Junior said grumpily.

'You'd better start take yourself seriously. You too damn lazy.'

'It's not easy on this island for a black-skinned Jamaican like me. Lester have the high colour to suit them American tourists and that speaky-spokey way they like.'

As she shamelessly eavesdropped, Beverley smelled the heavy aroma of marijuana.

'Talkin bout foolishness, what does Lester have to say bout this woman?' Junior asked.

'When he see how quick Montcrieffe come to the airport, he was so worried he phone his girl Esmina, an she phone Miss Ira . . .'

'That mouthamassy woman who can't tell sunshine from cheese?'

'Miss Ira says the red-dress woman is a obeah woman an we must watch har because she dangerous. She say that empty coffin is for Mr Montcrieffe. She come to repay him for something bad . . . hang on . . . he's callin for you, Junior. You best hurry.'

'Lawd have mercy. If he find out I smokin weed on his premises again . . . I comin, Mr Montcrieffe. I comin.'

The dinner was as vast as the house. Beverley sampled all the delights of her first Jamaican meal. Escobvitch fish served with all manner of peppers. Sweet potatoes, plantain, green bananas, yams, rice and peas. She gave the dessert of pineapples and mangoes a miss, and settled for a cool glass of sorrel.

Montcrieffe was utterly polite to Beverley, but his tone towards Iris and Junior at the dinner table seemed mocking.

'Iris, Junior, dinner was delicious, congratulations.' He dabbed his mouth with a serviette. 'Such attention to detail, the food, the house . . .' He stopped and sniffed the air. 'The furniture has been washed in what, Iris?'

'Camphor, Mr Montcrieffe,' Iris whispered meekly.

'And I see we've been invaded by bush. Have you noticed, Ms Clarke, every nook and cranny of the house has bush in it? What kind of bush, Junior?'

'Cerasee and fever grass, sir,' mumbled Junior.

'Has this got anything to do with our guest?' Montcrieffe's voice was booming. The word 'guest' crashed like a heavy mallet. 'I'm warning you two, if you so much as breathe the same air as that Miss Ira woman I'll take it you no longer desire to be employed by me. Am I understood?'

'Yes, sir,' they both muttered.

'Clear this bush out of my house. Junior, get the car ready for tomorrow. I'll drive Ms Clarke to Constant Springs myself.'

Back in her room, Beverley went to pick up the photograph

from the bedside table but it was gone. She didn't even begin to look for it – she knew this had something to do with the dinner-table scene.

Beverley slept restlessly, disturbed by flashing peeny wally, trying to swat whining mosquitoes. And the laughter and melancholy music? Real or a dream? She was grateful when the cocks crowed, the dogs barked playfully and sunlight filled her room to the brim.

The silver car gleamed as if fresh from the showroom. As Beverley got into the front passenger seat, her eyes fixed on a green shrub, tied with red ribbons on to one of the gates. Montcrieffe followed Beverley's gaze. He turned on his heel, ripped out the bush and sent it flying into the veranda.

'I'll deal with those two when I get back,' he muttered under his breath.

After this tense start, George tried to maintain a pleasant and buoyant manner throughout the journey.

'. . . However, I must warn you that quite a gathering may attend the ceremony. As we discussed, I've arranged for a priest to be there. I'm not sure if your husband was religious, Ms Clarke, but Father Kohl is excellent. The tourists use him; Muslim, Christian, Hindu, he can cater for any religion.'

Beverley knitted her brows and said a terse 'thank you'.

This woman was odd indeed, Montcrieffe thought. Iris must've sensed it, no wonder she got to thinking about obeah. He really couldn't wait for the ceremony and burial to be finished. Over the years, he'd tried to distance himself from gossip and suspicion, and now here he was at the centre of rumours about witchcraft. As the car approached the cemetery he wondered if helping Beverley Clarke had been wise, but it was too late now.

A throng enveloped the car, forcing it to slow down. Montcrieffe glimpsed Miss Ira's brightly coloured headdress. Edwina Francis was standing just behind her. He was sure that all the others would be there somewhere.

A rubbled pathway led to an open grave over which the white casket was resting. A plump-faced, ashen-white man dressed in a long purple gown stood by, clasping a Bible in his left hand. The babbling crowd lulled to a hush as Beverley and Montcrieffe approached Father Kohl.

'Father, may I introduce the deceased's wife?' said Montcrieffe.

'No, I'm not a . . . I wasn't a . . . a wife.'

'No matter, my dear, we're very liberal, even in these parts. I've buried many a co-habittee. It's love that counts,' Father Kohl assured her.

Montcrieffe sensed Beverley's unease. 'Father, this is a little awkward. Everything's happened so quickly. I can't even be sure that she wants a priest.'

'I want a priest, my partner was a Christian,' Beverley said quickly.

Montcrieffe's face relaxed; Father Kohl seemed glad. 'Shall we start now?'

Beverley felt tearful as the ceremony began. She hung her head low. The hypocrisy, the mess. Honouring the wish of a lover she hadn't loved for years, among strangers whose presence she resented, with an escort whose attempts at kindness made her suspicious. And then being expected to recite prayers to a God she didn't believe in.

Father Kohl intoned, 'We are gathered here to bury Mr . . .'

'What's his name?' Montcrieffe asked Beverley urgently. 'Your partner, what's his name?'

'He is not a he,' said Beverley. 'Her name is Aretha.' She forced herself to meet Montcrieffe's gaze. 'Her name is Aretha Lee.'

His stare was horribly expressive. *Why didn't you say? Have you come to make a fool of me? I have to live among these people.*

And in the silence that followed, Beverley thought: She loved me. I lived a lie. Nobody knew about us. Nobody. All those years and then she died.

Montcrieffe's look was adamant. *A lesbian lover? Whatever next? An empty coffin is bad enough! I'll be a laughing stock.*

He went over to the priest and whispered in his ear. The priest smiled thankfully and resumed his intonation. 'We're gathered here to bury Miss Beverley's sister, Aretha Lee.'

The crowd welled with approving whispers.

As Beverley looked towards them, a flashing light blinded her. She saw a smiling woman in a tall, colourful headdress holding a silver frame. As she walked towards Miss Ira, the crowd parted.

'That's my partner's picture you have there.' She stretched out her hand and took Aretha's picture from Miss Ira.

'God have mercy on your soul, child.'

But Beverley was now walking purposefully back to the white and gold coffin, her poise in defiance of the suddenly hostile mood. In spite of herself, she began to sing a slow dulcet ballad:

> *Sometimes truth hurts and love is painful*
> *Pain is when growing begins*
> *Truth is a weird place to be*
> *Today, in love I'm beginning to be free*
> *To be free, to be free, to be free.*

Many of the bystanders fell quiet as they recognized the melody – an old Kumina dirge. The song lulled the stirrings in the air. The priest gathered his sense of solemnity, and Aretha's casket was buried, in a rapt atmosphere of wonder and respect.

All those present at that graveside told their own stories. Iris and Junior said they'd seen an arrow of light shoot through Beverley, keeping her in a trance. How else would an English woman know that old Kumina song? Miss Ira claimed that she'd exorcised the evil spirit from the photograph and assured her followers that Beverley could no longer do Montcrieffe any harm. Esmina was certain that Junior had stolen the picture simply for its silver frame and had sold it to Miss Ira. The whole experience moved Father Kohl to revisit his faltering faith, leaving him convinced of a living God. But he wouldn't tell his story, not for money or love.

Like He Was Just Anyone Else
Amy Prior

I was wondering about Jarvis. How, for a while that night, we thought he was just the look-alike who had been spotted a few times on the bus in Kentish Town. How, when we didn't know he really was a popstar, we just saw someone trying too hard to look cool in velvet during high humidity; a shy man who bobbed jerkily when I handed him the flyer about the boutique; a poser who wore dark glasses in the gloomiest corner of the pub. Then, when it was confirmed that the look-alike was, in fact, the real thing, we suddenly realized the aesthetic qualities of his stoop; the character in his unsymmetrical profile.

I was thinking this as I wheeled my trolley past the vegetable section, when I was half-wondering about the kind of mushrooms to buy: the plastic container of washed and regular-sized ones branded with a clean-cut name like Charlotte or the loose grey ones, which were of course cheaper but less convenient, being both softer (so harder to chop) and dirtier (so more likely to need rinsing). The decisions of the supermarket were, I found, a microcosm of those in life. Of course, the consequences only affected your stomach and your change, but you encountered the same dilemmas.

What I did like about the supermarket was that it made me feel normal for a little while. Well, more normal than being in our house, with just the two of us. I mean, you could go in there and look like a space alien and there would always be

131

someone stranger than you. Because the whole world has to eat, even maybe someone with studs everywhere and a cork through their earlobe. They all have to buy food, and here the supermarket is really all there is, unless you want to go to the shop round the corner that never closes, but where everything is so much dustier and you are watched down every aisle by men growing old before their time.

I was shopping for a meal. I say meal, Joel says dinner, but it amounts to the same thing. Some food cooked for some people he knows to impress them. The people were from his work. I had met them once at a party and thought they were dull. They had just come back from somewhere exotic and talked a lot about snowboarding. Joel's plan was to make some sort of stir-fry with the vegetables and then crème brûlées for dessert. He always made such an effort for these meals and had spent three evenings deliberating over the right recipes.

I went round the supermarket in a kind of stupor. I think it was something about the lights and the colour and the fact that I was listening to Jarvis on my Walkman and remembering how exactly one year ago he had been a firework-lit demi-god singing to a crowd of thousands. And then I think back to the man I saw in the pub yesterday and can't comprehend that this was really the same person.

When I got home Joel was there with the Chinese vegetables he bought from a supermarket in Soho, chopping away at them fast like those chefs you see on TV. And, as I was unpacking, he said, 'Did you get the mushrooms?'

And I hesitated for a moment and said, 'Yeah, they're here somewhere,' when I knew they weren't. By the time we'd emptied the last bag and put everything away I hoped he would have forgotten, but this was not the case.

'You didn't buy the mushrooms,' he said very slowly, looking at me without smiling as if he were building up to something. I tried to explain about the choice and how difficult it was, about the different mushrooms and what they were like and about how I couldn't make up my mind between them. I didn't know which ones he wanted. And he said, 'You get every single vegetable: carrots, onions, potatoes, broccoli, but you forget the mushrooms I need for my stir-fry. You remember all those things that you like – all those chocolate mousses – and you forget the essentials. When you go to the vegetable section you should always get potatoes, carrots, onions . . .' He counts out the different kinds of vegetables on his fingers and the total comes to ten.

And I know, as I watch the fingers, that this is a test. If I care about the meal and his work people enough I will make a trip to the local shop to buy some mushrooms, which of course I do, and on the way I'm reminded of all the other tests we had put ourselves through. Like the one when we first met and asked each other: 'Would you go out with me if I had a harelip?' 'Would you go out with me if I was in a wheelchair?' 'Would you go out with me if I was paralysed down one side?' And the answer was yes, yes, yes to everything and the skies were always blue and the sun shone.

The trouble between us started, I think, when I gave up my job. I was working on reception in a publishing company but after six months I began answering my phone at home with, 'Hello, Redbox Publishing, nice to do business with,' and my friends would say, 'Oh, sorry I've got the wrong number,' and then put the phone down, and then I'd have to ring straight back and say, 'No, it was me, Daisy – I just forgot where I was.'

You could say that work worked me up.

Other things preoccupied me more. Jewellery had always been the most important thing to me and at the time I had just got a boutique interested in a new design: little heart-shaped earrings in pastel colours with messages on them like 'make eyes at me' and 'meet me at midnight'. I got the idea from my favourite sweets. Anyway, since then Joel had been edgy about a lot of things and he was always asking what I was going to do for a pension.

*

The first boxes arrived just as Joel was about to start frying. He was concentrating hard on heating the oil up to the right temperature, and I went to the door. I knew he was stressed about dealing with his inheritance: a bizarre assortment of possessions from the household of his uncle. His mother lifted the boxes out of the back of her Volvo, one by one, handing each one to me in a flurry of perfume and excuses. There were six altogether, and they contained dusty hardbacks that had probably remained unopened for quite a while and would remain so for a while more. I dumped them on the landing next to the place where the cat sleeps.

I went back to the kitchen and when I told Joel what had arrived he said, 'Jesus. Where the hell are we going to put all this stuff? Uncle Harry never threw anything away and we can barely fit in everything we've got now.' It was true: this man had hoarded many things over his lifetime, mostly money, though now he resides in an older persons' home on the Isle of Man with no clue of his name or his fortune. And slowly his house was being emptied for sale, the possessions of a life half-lived now cast off to the younger generation.

I was silent for a while. Joel had made the oil too hot and it was sizzling the vegetables so they'd started to smoke a little, but I didn't say anything. Then I said, 'Maybe we could give the things away.'

Ben and Emma enjoyed the stir-fry.

'There's something about its nuttiness that blends so well with the carrot,' Ben said, and I had to agree. Joel had excelled himself this time.

The table on which we were eating had arrived half an hour previously, having been whisked over sixty miles by a transit van and hauled up three flights of stairs by a man of five foot five and his companion. And now that I was sitting at it I noticed how out of place it looked in our landlord's kitchen. Its unblemished oak clashed with the more familiar, tea-stained pale Formica surfaces. The ends of the legs, shaped like eagle's claws, rested precariously on the worn lino. Of course, if you looked carefully at it for any length of time you would realize that it was, in fact, a seventeenth-century antique, and so for this reason, Joel had covered it with a thick linen tablecloth in case it got stained by the red wine.

Ben and Emma had just bought a garden flat in Bow and they liked to talk about it, about its windows and doors and walls and green spaces (front, back and side) and about how much they were going to do with it.

'God. I can't believe what the previous owners did. They panelled up the old fireplaces and the banisters and underneath there's just this beautiful wood,' said Ben, taking large gulps of his wine. His face had the rosy glow of someone who likes his drink and I imagined him every night in Bow, cracking open a bottle of wine with their dinner, talking about the deadline that had long since passed or new corporate web design concepts.

'And the bathroom – green paint on the ceiling and yellow walls! I can't wait to get rid of that,' added Emma, wiping a speck of marinade from the hairs on her top lip which, I noticed, had been lightened artificially. Maybe it was the wine or maybe the company, but my attention was focused elsewhere.

It was the first time we had drunk from these glasses. We thought they were more books, because the box they came in was marked 'Bonfire?' in heavy felt pen. But once we saw the careful way with which the objects inside were wrapped, we realized otherwise. I think the one I was drinking from that night was really a Champagne glass, or a special kind anyway, because it was cut so that light refracted through at acute angles and it was so thin the slightest pressure would shatter it to pieces.

They were talking about the weather, about how there had been a hosepipe ban for three weeks in Bow, about how their lawn was brown at the edges and getting browner by the day. People they knew had been spotted using a sprinkler by council officials, and were waiting for court summons.

I remember becoming distracted by the glass, not by the actual object itself, but by a small white thing, half an inch long, wending its way up the fluted sides. It was only the width of one cut, but its power came from the muscles inside that allowed the body to contort itself into the curved shapes needed for propulsion. The thing was edging towards my thumb, so I moved it out of the way fast and, in doing so, caused the glass to fall on to my plate. I shouted then, just one word – *maggot* – very loudly and at high pitch. They could do no more than me to rescue it before the smash, which left shards like transparent, fatal, vegetables. And after that there was a good deal of flurry, cloths wiped over and newspapers torn and scrunched up and talk about the insects this summer and how the heat had really brought them out.

And then later after they'd gone, Joel said, 'In Uncle Harry's house there always used to be insects. Little flies everywhere. When I was a kid I remember having to eat an ice-cream cone that had maggots on it and when I showed it to Uncle Harry he just told me to wipe them off. I didn't want to hurt him, but for days afterwards I imagined these little things in my stomach getting bigger and bigger. That house was his life but it was infested and he just ignored it.'

I remember we were talking in the living room and in that room there were big windows that we kept open a little way to let the air circulate. It had been humid all summer, and left to its own devices the room would ferment obnoxious smells. Stray apple cores left under the sofa would grow brown and turn to a vaporous mush; the leftover yoghurt in the yoghurt pot on the table would coagulate and grow a green covering.

As we were talking, we became aware of music from the street, something fast with big beats. When we looked out we realized it was coming from a car, open-topped, with Ken and Barbie look-alikes in the front seats chatting loudly about futures and investments.

'Look at that,' said Joel. 'Who are they?' He was leaning out of the window to get another, closer view.

It all looked so perfect, like a still from a Hollywood film. The man had his arm draped possessively around the back of the woman's seat; she, meanwhile, tapped her long, painted fingernails on the pristine black paintwork; the chocolate brown interior blended perfectly with the colour of their clothes.

We decided on a weapon without fuss: tomatoes, baby ones, the kind that degenerated on impact. In that weather, though, the refrigerator was straining to keep things cool. Even on the highest setting, the milk was on the turn. The vegetable compartment was so full I could barely pull it out.

I looked for the tomatoes, but couldn't see them, and then I remembered I'd finished them the night before: in the absence of biscuits and sweet things to pick at I would sometimes turn to raw vegetables. Then my fingers fell on something liquidy and rotten. I moved the leeks and cauliflower out of the way to get a better look at the cause of this, and my eyes fell on them then: small, grey things, in a plastic container; no longer regular-sized but squashed by the vegetables on top and tempered by the warm so they were turning to an unpleasant-smelling mush. I thought, He didn't use them after all.

The first landed on the road, just inches from the left back tyre. The second hit the boot and broke instantly into several grey fragments, leaving an outline – white on black – like a crown of thorns. Then Joel whispered, 'Get down,' and we ducked below the frame so we couldn't be spotted.

And at that moment we knew everything. We knew that Jarvis really had been the shy man in velvet with strange, nervous mannerisms. We knew that when he went shopping he wouldn't have any trouble deciding what to buy. We knew that the real superstars are actually geeks who choose the kind of mushrooms that are loose and dirty and come in all different shapes.

The Uniform
Helen Cross

It is hanging at home, over the door of the wardrobe, the yellow and black tie coiled into the pocket of the blazer like a viper. It smells of crumbed biscuits and chewed grass; of long, gone schooldays.

The doctor says you've drunk so much Hooch in the last two years it's altered the shape of your blood cells. That's why you've put on weight recently and have spotty skin. You've to cut down to just one glass a night, which you could do, but just one in the right environment is enough to make you forget you ever had altered blood cells and so you'll go right ahead and have another five bottles and a couple of shorts.

She says the reason is not enough oestrogen and, because of this, crusty ovaries. You picture dinosaurs. Like it's *Jurassic Park* down there.

Then you want to pick up your mobile and shout *TESTS*, and tell Mr Part-Time Maths Teacher how they're doing *TESTS* for Argonauts, whole armies of things, *TESTS* for bird life, for fish and fowl, for the poisons he's slipped into you on purpose.

'Therefore,' she says, not looking you in the eye, 'you should go back on the pill.'

There's a pause.

You imagine how the shirt won't fit. You won't be able to do up the middle two buttons and the cuffs will end way above your wrists. The tie'll be a big loose knot. Outside, a nipple-gnawing dog'll be growling like thunder and the sound will make surf in the fish bowl.

Meanwhile, doctor suggests a pill called Celeste – some goddess anyway. *Woman's Own* recommends losing weight with an organic vegetable soup diet and now she's insisting on pumping an ocean of chemicals into your body *every morning*. She says you must stop drinking and take the pill if you want to be thin, with clear skin, and start having periods again. You say you've been on *the pill* for quite a while before and you can't stay on the pill *all your life*.

'Melody,' she exclaims, suddenly looking up over the top of her rectangular, rimless glasses, 'you are seventeen!'

She gives you a hard stare, which suggests your sequined hipster jeans and green chiffon butterfly-bra top is an inappropriate look for this appointment. Actually it's already occurred to you, in recent anxious moments, that the outfit makes you more tramp than lady, more hag barmaid than killer cleavage queen.

Then doctor looks at the computer again and asks why you came off the pill in the first place, and you say because you got headaches, and then she asks why you went back on it after that, and you say because they made you after the abortion and she sighs, 'Ah yes, the abortion.'

It's six months since the day fifteen girls waited one hour in the silent hallway of the clinic. A nurse came round with square brown envelopes and quietly everyone, the entire flock of too-fertile girls, were de-jewelled: gently dropping their skinny rings in the envelopes, silently getting unwed.

Doctor looks concerned and smiles and says, 'Don't worry, this is the latest pill, you won't get headaches. You're young enough to be on the pill for another twenty years. You'll be fine as long as you cut down your smoking and *stop drinking*.'

'But I'm so shy that if I *stop drinking* I'll never get laid again,' you want to say, and it's like she hears you because she whispers, 'Which might be a good idea, Melody,' and looks round sympathetically from the computer, 'because of the infection.'

There is another awkward moment, which is enough time to worry that the skirt will be too tight around your waist now (it's been one whole fattening year since you left school). On the bedroom dressing table will be a tumbler with a faint purplish stain of lipstick frowning round the rim, and you'll sniff the inch of whisky, and then, though the surface is furred with fine dust, you'll drink it, knock it back in one, and the bed will have to catch you while the room rocks like a cradle, and you'll be alone with the fun-fair fish, both swaying on the waves of dog bark, maddened with fear.

For the first time, it occurs to you: what if Jason Almond isn't a part-time maths teacher? His text-sex spelling is worse than your own.

'The infection, Melody?'

The infection. You look out into the car park at a bird table. You think of the Owl and the Pussycat and how did it happen that you've got an aviary in your pussy. She says they'll need to do tests for other things, but she's 99 per cent sure. You look out up into the sky.

'It most likely is,' she says, 'but it's hard to tell because this happens immediately before your period,' and blah blah because of the fibroids and the dinosaurs you don't have periods, so vampires'll suck out your bad blood and archaeologists'll examine it for ancient life-forms.

'Did you hear me, Melody? I asked if there's any history of breast cancer in your family.'

Later she shows you a long plastic stick with a tiny bucket at the top: Europe's very latest cocktail stirrer. 'This,' she says solemnly, 'is the applicator. And this,' she says, waving a chalky tablet the size of a brick, 'will, if used correctly, hopefully clear everything up.'

Hopefully, it occurs to you that if, when you meet Jason Almond this afternoon, you need a party trick, something to break the ice, you can get trigger happy with this applicator

and catapult the bastard tablet right up and out your mouth –
da da!

An hour later the tie lolls out of the carrier bag like a dry
tongue. It licks against your leg as you walk. The uniform is
unclean. Those first dirty thoughts have turned the white shirt
grey and the blue wool's clouded pale by old sunlight.

It's 1.39 p.m. and you've been tramping the streets,
conspicuous in the butterfly-bra top, for what seems like
hours, sipping Hooch and watching women. Eyeing pretty
young mothers with babies, and some with big, kind, cuddling
husbands, helping them push padded prams. And you wonder
if dark diseases are turning tricks deep inside these perfect
ladies too, if it's what being female *is*; if enough infections and
invasions to open a hospital are always mushrooming up
within.

Or, if you're the only one.

He's waiting at the high window, a grey cloud behind the net
curtain, sucking on a cigarette. Your legs (bare, as requested)
have great pythons curling through them. You turn the
package from the chemist's over and over in your pocket and
look up at the trees but you still can't tell a thrush from a
sparrow or a penguin.

'My sister has a dressing gown like that,' you say when he
opens the door and the pink silk flutters above his pale, hairy
knees. He doesn't smile; your jokes never work on him. He's
the humour equivalent of an amoeba; can only laugh with
himself.

'Nice,' he says, scrolling his stare down over your
inappropriate outfit.

'It's called a butterfly-bra,' you explain, because this is
where his eye-popping gaze has settled. 'It's the latest thing
from America.'

'Manufactured in heaven,' he smiles creepily. 'Sold only to
angels.'

'Oasis. £12.99,' you reply.

That first night you met Jason was at a disco, two days after the abortion and you were out celebrating. No one understands why, like a bootilicious grim reaper, you always go after these sad-looking, unhealthy, tired, old men. Even when you explain that every good Christian must do something for charity. No one ever questions why these crinkly grey-hairs – husbands, fathers, eminent professionals – always, always, always, go for you.

He didn't mess about – said it was good he'd met you because his wife, Natalie, the chiropodist who works afternoons, was looking for a girl to do babysitting. After that Jason moved quickly through text sex, night drives, sofa afternoons, twice upstairs – and now this.

He keeps you waiting on the doorstep while he pulls a finger through the silky belt and the dressing gown falls open and his stomach's an udder the way it hangs fat and low, his swollen bellybutton a nipple, his cock a short gnarled thing that could star on *Pet Hospital*, and when he leans down for the wet kiss – teeth, tongue, tonsils – you feel like a rag doll in the jaws of a lion.

'Hey, good girl,' he snarls, nodding at the yellow and black tongue. 'Come in.'

Indoors, Baby Leo's in a highchair at the table. He smiles, kicks his legs and you think about it but not with any regret, though you sometimes get this feeling that out in the dark of cyberspace might be floating a little ghost baby that belongs just to you.

'Hey, d'you want a drink?' Baby Leo's dad shouts from the kitchen.

'Apparently I've drunk so much in the last two years of my life it's altered the shape of my blood cells, so I guess I'd better not,' you want to say but instead agree, though now you mustn't operate heavy machinery or drive.

'Hey, why don't you go upstairs and get ready, yeah?' he calls. 'I've bought you a magazine. Go up and relax, yeah?' This is the good thing about real men, the way they get on with things; if they had a deadly disease they'd be too busy to notice.

Breezily you grab the bag, in which the tie, blouse, skirt and blazer now wiggle and squirm, and head off upstairs, feeling, as you carry your old impish self, like a glum ventriloquist with his grinning dummy.

The bag floats, weightless.

In contrast, the wife's room is heavy. It smells of baby sick and spicy deodorant. It's messy, piled with clothes, toys, nappies. Natalie's stab at girly lightness is a pile of teddies on a pine chest. The biggest has arms stuck out in rigid welcome. One says: *Mmmm-mummy*. Another has toes that go: *This little piggy went to market, this little piggy stayed home . . .* On the window ledge is that single orange fish in a bowl. Natalie won it at a fair. It moves, drugged, in a slow figure of eight. The sun against the bowl makes it swim through silver gold.

Downstairs, Leo's howling.

Her skin creams are the expensive type in squat pots. For dry skin. Natalie has cream for getting hair off legs and bikini line. She has perfume in clear bottles: Juniper, Azor, Venus, not ones you've heard of. She has the pill, not the goddess Celeste but another daintier one, though Jason says they've not had sex for a hundred years. She has a pot called Moisturizing Nipple Lotion and again you imagine her marshmallow nipples savaged by hounds. She has Super Plus tampons and a packet of Maternity Panty Pads and a flaky, creased old tube which, when you unroll it, says: For Vaginal Itching.

'Coming, ready or not,' Jason shouts from downstairs. His voice sounds trembly.

Off you peel the tight sparkly jeans and black lace thong, and on comes the faded skirt, then those blue nylon gym knickers. Even when you really were at school you did everything to avoid wearing this skirt, and of course you didn't really have these knickers but he likes to think you did. Though he should know, Mr Part-Time Maths Teacher.

Draping the butterfly-bra carefully over the back of a chair you struggle into the white shirt, then knot the yellow and black tie.

You reach for the magazine and turn to a page that says, *How To Know If He's Crazy About You*, and wait.

From this angle you see Natalie has books on aromatherapy, stress-management, teddy-bear collecting, astrology, beauty, and novels fat and soft as pillows. You consider, with some excitement, clearing out your tattered pop posters and adopting a similar bookish look for your own bedroom. Also on the bookshelf she has a box called Single Arm Breast Pump Kit. You find, to your surprise, that if you clench your fist a muscle bubbles up in your arm and your breast goes hard as iron.

'OK,' he says when he comes in, 'close your eyes, yeah?' and he tears his dressing gown off like it's on fire and leaps onto the mattress so heavily it makes a tidal jerk. He hasn't given you the drink, he's forgotten. 'Hey, OK, you're at school and you've had a really bad morning, everyone's been telling you off, yeah? And you want to cry because everyone's mad at you and you feel really upset, but still feel kind of sexy like . . .'

He goes on like this (sweating), as he massages and strokes, and the room dips and rises like you're under alcohol anaesthetic, like the tap's gone into the back of your hand and Hooch is replacing blood in your veins. Like in the ward afterwards when you threw up on the blanket, and the Indian lass in the bed next to you pissed on the floor, and in the distance another girl sobbed that she was bleeding. Everyone was an animal, the ward a kennel, the floor a wash of bestial fluids.

He flicks his forefinger over your nipples like he's scratching an itch, then he presses his hand very firmly over your eyes (his palms are wet) and it's causing a six-pack Hooch headache. You're lying in such a way that the stale shirt pulls taut and rips into your diseased flesh, and you know you must lose weight today, ditch the goddess Celeste, drink soup.

'It's a fresh morning, right? You're sitting at the far edge of the school field just happily waiting, hanging around . . .'

Through his fingers you see on top of the wardrobe a box for a 21st-century warrior woman: Silicone Nipple Shields. '. . . It's so hot you pull your skirt right up to tan your legs, exposing the flesh of your thighs, and . . .'

Outside the breeze speaks: fresh flesh fresh flesh fresh flesh fresh flesh. Fish is now floating sideways up, watching. Far off dog is beginning to bark. There in the girl's grim uniform, with the too-tight shirt unbuttoned, you suddenly feel a forgotten emotion; a schoolgirl's piqued concern for the natural world.

'. . . And you see me, your teacher, coming towards you.'

You push at him and he lets you sit up, if you don't you might vomit because the Hooch and the tablet are hotly working. Downstairs, Leo is crying fierce as a car alarm.

'OK,' Jason says, with a disappointed look, 'you tie me up, yeah?'

You turn away from his baggy nudity and peer into the bowl, through the silver flecked with blue. Natalie's orange friend looks like you feel: ill.

You pull the tie from your neck, wrap it round Jason's wrist and over the steel bed-head, and pull tight, till it rubs a red welt in his skin. 'Do the other one, quick,' he says, looking at his watch and pointing at the chest of drawers, where you see Natalie's cotton knickers in rainbow colours, black tights and short socks. At the bottom of the drawer lies a cocktail stirrer drug applicator, the exact same one as your own. Her bra is 38D, her tights' label says Large, and there's a yellow box of Maternity Disposable Briefs. You pick at the box and feel inside. They're slimy and warm against your hot fingertips. It's horrible. On the cover is a pencil drawing of a baby breast-feeding. You close your eyes, sway.

'What've you got?' he demands, seeing your hands in the drawer.

'I've got something so terrible,' you want to say, but instead you turn and put your hands round the warm belly of the bowl like a fortune-teller.

Poor Natalie. Despite your swilling, her fish just floats, bobs deadly on the surface. Lifting him out of his bowl, between finger and thumb, he's no heavier, no plumper, no more living than an oven chip. You lay him in the stretcher of your palm then place him on the dressing table like an earring your mother might wear.

Jason demands, *quick quick*, a pair of black tights secures his other wrist to the bed-frame. You hope, sadly, that in his last moments poor fish bobbed up, glimpsed the hilarious scene unfolding in the world of man and died laughing.

Pulling with that deadly prehistoric strength, your newly found arm muscle arches. You can still feel the rubbery briefs on your fingers and pause to wipe them. Then you do the same tights trick round his ankles till he's spread like a starfish waiting to be wheeled in for an operation. The way your arm pulls is amazing, the perfect levering of it.

'Imagine we're on the school field, imagine you're horny . . .'

You do try but strangely, suddenly, unexpectedly, for the first time in six months, the sight of him makes you want to laugh. You stagger, feel naughty, childish, feel sure there's heavy furniture sliding about in your head. Your stomach begins to shudder with the will of holding in the volcanic giggle. Even thinking of dinosaurs, bird life, vampires, can't keep it down, and silver chuckle flecks explode like fireworks from your lips.

It's as if dark mischief's been left like a sticky sweet in the pocket of the uniform and you're stroking and poking it. It's scary. As if that grimy girl's uniform has taken over and is tainting your sickly, primitive womanhood with a hard, rude, almost-forgotten insolence – which is very close to fun.

Jason's fingers make scrabbling spidery movements, but he's tied firm. A shot of sun is warming your shoulder and misting the windows yellow. Abruptly the laughter blasts through the roof like a rocket, and above your head, for the first time in weeks, is blue sky.

Something very odd is happening.

'OK,' he snaps, 'if you're not gonna play, you might as well take it off.'

'No, I like it.'

'Really?' He beams.

'Yeah, it makes me feel good.'

'Go on, darling, in what way exactly?'

'It reminds me of myself.'

Now that you are fearless and young, he seems scared and old. When he swallows, his dry throat creaks. As you lean back to get a better look at him you fold your arms then assess him, with eyebrows raised, like a young medical student. 'Hmmm,' you say with a shake of the head, a scratch of the chin, 'very, very, worrying.'

He is wriggling, saying things, glistening now, oiled like meat. 'Don't laugh,' he barks, 'don't laugh, you naughty girl.' He's right: rubber pants, sore nipple creams, silicone shields, everything in the bedroom reminds you that, despite the bird life and barmaid's gear, you're seventeen, babyless, unwed, much more a bad schoolgirl than a mother or a wife.

Downstairs, there's a shuffling, coughing. 'What's that?' you ask. Then, a louder screeching. Jason checks his watch and says, 'It'll just be Leo. I'll go when we've finished. Come on.' He looks shabby, older than thirty-two, old as your dad now and, tied up that way, just as helpless.

Outside in the street, kids are coming home from school: bike brakes, rubber, the hiss of slow cars. He pulls at the knots but can't move. Forgetting the butterfly-bra fluttering on the chair, the hipsters scorching the carpet, you button up the blouse, zip up the skirt, pick up the fish and sigh, 'I'm going down to check on him.' And gallop down the stairs in your uniform, sniggering.

Leo smells sour like flat beer. His face is stingingly wet with red tears. The dead fish in your hand feels like a severed finger. Poor Natalie. You lurch out into the street with the stiff, screaming baby in one hand, fish in the other. 'Shut up,' you shout up at the bedroom window. 'Shuddup, shuddup, shuddup!' Then sit there on the step with Leo on your lap, waiting, swaying, bouncing: shipwrecked but safe. You hum a lullaby. You rest your head on the doorframe. Besides you lies the bronze arch of scaly water-life, like an alien's eyebrow or a robot's lip.

Across the road, telly colours are blaring. Leo's warm dribble makes a damp patch on your school shirt. A woman walks past with a baby in a pram and another child walking by her side clutching the buggy's steel frame. The woman's old, about twenty-four, and fat. She sniffs, *fe fi fo fum*, and looks at the upstairs window where the great man noise is coming from, then seeing you sitting on the step in your grubby, ill-fitting school uniform, she grins a ripe smile, moves her head slyly, like you've just reminded her of something wicked.

Then you see her coming. Natalie, down the road towards you, a skip in her step for her son. The sight of her coming closer, saggy, savaged, cracked and sore, similarly diseased but survived, smiling, makes you exhale in relief.

Again and again you blow against Leo's blond hair, so it flies up in the late summer sun like a dandelion clock.

SeaSky

Annie Murray

By the time the health visitor came it was raining again, as hard as it had done in the night. Sam caught herself listening out for her, held the door open as she floundered across from her car in navy wellingtons with white soles, the weighing scale clutched to her chest.

'Would you believe it?' Sliding off her rain-spattered mac, Elizabeth Nolan revealed her tightly fitting grey skirt and royal blue sweater. She looked, Sam thought, like a farmer's wife in school uniform. 'Cats and dogs? God – it's more like elephants out there.'

It was her second visit. She'd called in a few days ago, taking over from the midwife. As she was blessed with the use of a car, she said, Sam needn't go all the way down to the clinic. 'You'd almost want a rowing boat to get there the way things are and you look exhausted enough to drop as it is.'

She consulted her file as Sam put the kettle on.

'How is the little fellow? Are the nights settling down at all?'

'Not . . . really.' Sam spooned coffee, eyes filling against her will in the face of sympathy. 'But I suppose that's how it goes.'

Last night was bloody terrible. Each time she managed to settle Joe it was barely an hour before he was off again. Once more, Sam resorted to moving into the spare bed with him, next to the desk and Andy's computer. Every time she felt herself begin to relax enough to sleep, Joe began snuffling and writhing beside her. Feeding didn't pacify him, so she dragged

149

herself from the bed and walked him up and down, standing at the window jiggling him, only darkness outside, and rain. Several times her rocking sent him to sleep, but as soon as she tried to put him down he woke with a blare of alarm.

'You certainly look weary today,' Elizabeth said.

'Oh, I'll be OK.' Sam let her dark hair fall forward. She wasn't the sort of woman who snivelled. Besides, Elizabeth had already mentioned her own upbringing in Tipperary as the oldest of fourteen children, most of whom she'd had a hand in mothering through her teens. She was not married herself. And who could blame her, Sam thought, after such a childhood? What would Mrs Nolan the elder have made of such heavy weather over one baby? She must have spent most of her life up in the night. Let alone those poor women in slums in India and Latin America: no money, no nappies, no running water . . .

Elizabeth perched large on a kitchen stool. 'To begin with there'll be more bad nights than good, dear. As time goes by there'll be more good than bad.'

Sam carried Joe down and Elizabeth weighed him. The midwife had hung him in a cradle from the spring balance as if from a stork's mouth, but now he lay naked on the chill white scale. His face screwed up. He grizzled.

'Hmm. He hasn't gained this week . . . Has he been feeding all right?'

'Not brilliantly.' Sam wiped her nose, spirits sinking further. *I can't even feed him properly.* 'I think he's getting a bit of a cold.'

'Ah well – that'll be it – nothing to worry about.'

Once Joe was dressed again, she showed Sam the graph, talked percentiles, feeding habits, bowel movements. 'He's fine. Got a thoroughbred for a mother, lucky chappie. So –' She peered into Sam's thin face. 'You're coping all right?'

'Oh, yes. I'm fine.' She dragged her features into a smile, absurdly gratified at being called a thoroughbred when she felt like a carthorse fit for the knacker's. For God's sake, she thought, I'm a project manager. I've set up the online booking systems for Travel Inns – of course I can cope with a *baby*.

'He's doing grand. And I'll drop in again in a couple of days. You just stay inside and keep dry now.'

As Elizabeth headed for the door, Sam narrowly stopped herself saying, Don't go yet – *please*.

Once Elizabeth Nolan's beige Metro had splashed away through the puddles, Sam made Horlicks, cradling Joe on one arm. Exhaustion made her nauseous, so she lived mainly on sweet milk like him, as if their digestive systems were still interdependent.

While the pan warmed, she stared out over the back. The street was on the edge of the town – literally. They'd moved in here midway through her pregnancy. Their house was at the very end, pushing out like the point of a diamond on to the brow of the rise: they'd liked that, the way they could live in both town and country at once. Beyond a low garden wall, the land sloped down towards the fields, bordered by a dark clump of woodland, then the river. Normally it would be pasture, slow-jawed cows dotted about. But the fields were flooded now, and off limits because of foot and mouth. At the bottom of the slope there were still ruts from tractor tyres filled with shining puddles, and then, as far as the woods, brown water. An oak tree to one side of the field stood stranded and a couple of coots drifted side by side, so near she could have thrown bread to them. To her right, where the woods ended at a bend in the river, there should have been a firm rim of land. Instead the water, grey in the distance, melted into grey sky.

With her drink she sat on the sofa, Joe on her lap. She considered phoning Andy to tell him Joe hadn't put on weight, then saw this as small-minded, wifey behaviour. A few months ago, a professional techie herself, she would have laughed at anyone being disturbed at work for such a trifle. Thought it pathetically needy. Now, her home computer had a cover on to keep the dust off, and had done since Joe's birth.

For the first week of his life, Sam and Andy laughed and muddled through the novelty together, as oblivious to the difference between day and night as Joe was. They lay in bed with him between them, staring at him, awed, amused, mimicking his yawns and cloudy-eyed, quizzical expression. They hardly ever got dressed. Andy didn't shave. The first time they ventured out with Joe, new buggy unpacked from its polythene wrappers, they whispered to one another, *We're parents!* Course, Andy didn't stay awake through many of the night feeds. Nor did he experience what Sam thought of as childbirth's 'free samples' – raw nipples, non-stop bleeding and the enduring feeling that she'd been kicked up the arse by a jackboot – but in every other way the experience was shared. Then, the next Monday, he'd become intensely purposeful, shaved, put on his suit and tie, and reverted to twelve-hour absences – *So much to catch up on*.

From then on, Andy went to work every day exactly like he used to: he just happened to be a father as well. Of course, the responsibility of this, the galvanizing realization of fatherhood, drove him to stay at work even longer (perhaps, she thought in resentful moments, providing an excuse to keep out of the sudden anarchy of home under baby occupation). But Andy was ever one to shoulder responsibility, the elder boy, the one with flair, who'd worked his way out of the Clements Lane estate and into a good career. His shiftless brother, Pete, still lived at home with Mum, who'd been nervy since Dad died. Andy's sister, Sue, lived in Suffolk. It was always Andy – uncomplaining – who ended up unblocking the gutter for Mum.

Sam watched Joe as he lay along her thighs. He was dozing with his eyes open a fraction, flinty irises just visible between the lids. He breathed rapid, snuffling breaths, turned his head slightly to one side, winced, squeaked, relaxed. As she eased back he flung his hands out, clown-like. Moro reflex, the midwife had told her. Not, after all, a unique Joe-ism. She smoothed his thin shadowing of hair, slicked down with sweat, stroked his cheek with her thumb. Her capacity to sit and stare astonished her. As she gazed upon Joe's face, she found herself thinking, *Behold, the face of Joe* – closely followed by, *Will you listen to yourself?* She lost all estimation of time. What was it now – eleven?

Andy would be in his office with its clean blue carpets, the warm breath of computers on all sides. Work entailed developing their new program, breaking away for meetings, a team-building lunch down the pub once a week. An ordered, confident world, which had been hers, too: before, in another company. A mouse-clicking world of logical responses, of eliminating bugs with the right commands.

'Lucky old Daddy, eh, Joe?' she said, taken aback by the bitterness in her voice. What I'd give, she thought, for one normal day at work – gossip, stress, whingeing, the lot. Yet she pitied Andy because he wasn't here now, witnessing the fluttering passage of breath in and out of their son, vital feeding of the tiny mauve vessels which forked under his skin. Instead, Andy boarded the 08.25 to Basingstoke, to spend his day dealing with all that . . . nonsense, it now seemed. Who would be so feckless as to give birth to a child? Yet who would be so wanton as to expend time on anything else?

Andy's sister Sue had filled her in about motherhood. Painted it in full gloom. She had one child, six-year-old Rosie. They'd phoned yesterday, and Sam stood in the hall rocking Joe while Rosie told her all about Grace Darling who they were 'doing' at school.

'This lady a long time ago,' Rosie gabbled, barely pausing for breath, 'lived in a lighthouse and she rowed a boat and saved lots of sailors from drowning and because she was *so* brave they wanted to chop all her hair off . . .'

Sue cut in. 'God, I've had bloody Grace Darling up to here. Year Two have been doing her for ever: cutting and sticking storylines, role play, pin the flag on the Farne Islands. Anyway, Sam –' A portentous pause. '*How's it going?*'

'Fine,' Sam said.

'Well, it's always appalling for the first six weeks,' her sister-in-law assured her, with all the optimism of a Greek chorus. 'I remember feeling so *dreadful*. So harassed and *alone*.'

'I'm perfectly all right,' Sam insisted.

'What about Andy – is he helping out, doing his share at night and everything?'

'He's fine too.'

Childbirth had been a heavy-duty experience for Sue. She'd had pre-eclampsia, an elective Caesarean and, probably, concomitant post-natal depression. She wasn't prepared to repeat the experience. But surely, Sam told herself, it didn't mean everyone had to be so doom-ridden? Women the world over gave birth every day, after all, without making all this fuss.

Once they'd rung off, it was the thought of Rosie's chatter which cheered her. Lying Joe on the sofa, hemmed in by a cushion, she went to fetch an atlas. The rain was gentler now, pattering on the window and for a few moments there came beams of strained, buttery sunshine. She found a map of the north of England, the Farne Islands tiny crumbs scattered off the Northumbrian coast. Their encyclopedia had a brief entry on Grace Darling 1815–42. She became a heroine on 8 September 1838, when she rowed through boiling seas to rescue survivors from the ship *Forfarshire*. Her fame, the entry quoted, 'had led to more requests for locks of her hair than nature could reasonably provide.' Sam smiled. So that's what Rosie must have meant.

Andy was much later than usual that evening. It was almost ten when she heard the car pull in. Joe was hot and fretful, had cried most of the evening until Sam felt like nothing but a tangle of screaming nerves herself.

'Sorry . . .' Andy rushed in pulling off his tie, as if this flurry could make up for the intervening hours. 'The earlier train was cancelled.' As he hugged her, it struck her that someone who goes out and arrives back always attains more of an air of importance than the one who stays in. He looked tired. Why the hell should he be tired? He slept through last night.

Andy hung his jacket over the back of the chair and sat at the table. 'So, how's it been? Where's Joe – down?'

It's been fucking, fucking terrible and I hate motherhood and I want to resign.

'He is for the moment.' Sam yanked the oven door open, struggling not to appear pathetic. Joe had slept for the last fifteen minutes, which had helped unknot her nerves. The torment of baby crying seemed, like pain, to fade from memory as soon as it was removed. 'The health visitor came. Said he hasn't put on any weight. I don't think he's very well.' She laid Andy's meal before him, kept warm under foil. Breaded haddock, mashed potatoes, carrots, soggy now and uninviting.

'We should get a microwave.' He sprinkled juice on his fish out of a plastic lemon.

'Sorry.' She wasn't sorry at all. She wanted to go to work, feel like her real self again and come back to find her child safely cared for, not sit marooned here.

'I just meant –' He smiled cautiously at her. 'To make things easier for you.'

When he'd eaten they watched the news: sheep in Devon shovelled into pits like woolly bin-sacks, snapped necks flopping. Joe woke again and sucked half-heartedly at Sam's breast. She felt a raging thirst, then identified it as a craving for some kind of reassurance. Andy fell asleep, a mug of coffee in his hand. When she woke him he looked lost for a second, then anxious, and said, 'Oh God, I haven't checked my email,' and went up to the spare room. Sam took Joe up to bed. She stood on the landing holding him, watching Andy's back as he worked the mouse over the screen, summoning other worlds. She noticed his hair was beginning to thin on top.

That night was little better than the previous one. When the clock's red digits read 02.07 she stood holding Joe's hot body against her own, wondering if she should call a doctor. But

Elizabeth Nolan had said he might be restless. There was nothing they could do for a cold except try to keep him drinking. She shifted her weight from one chilled foot to the other. It was quiet except for the swish of the rain.

Sam wondered if anyone else was up along the street. She barely knew a soul except the woman next door, just to say hello to. Her friends were work friends. A gust of wind spattered water against the window. Like the sea, she thought, and her mind flew to Grace Darling in her father's lighthouse, standing at the window in a white nightgown, surveying the dark water all around. Grace was twenty-seven when she died. The encyclopedia entry said she had visited the mainland on numerous occasions, but always returned 'with such reports of the outer world as deterred her from marriage'. Sam sat down on the bed, rocking Joe. The notion of such a life appalled her, abandoning land for good to live in that unpeopled eyrie, confined in the smudgy elements. But Grace must have found her own kind of clarity. What held her so fast to her lighthouse? Was this solitary life her liberation, the place where her thoughts could fly freest, amid the mingled vapours of sea and sky?

The next night Sam was sleeping – longer than usual for these fractious nights – beside Joe in the spare room. She woke suddenly on an instinct, heart hammering. From a distance she heard her own screams. 'Andy! Andy, something's happened to him! Call an ambulance . . .' And as he reeled on to the landing, punched out of sleep, *'Don't just bloody stand there!'*

Joe was rigid, body curved backwards, strange. Lifeless, she thought, groping for his pulse, trying to give him the kiss of life when the siren howled up the road – lights, voices, tiny oxygen mask and her swimming through all of it because her own heart had stopped, she knew. Starved of oxygen herself, nothing would come back into focus until they were on the ward and they knew Joe was functioning properly again. Andy was the one who asked the right questions, held his arm round her to keep her upright. Febrile convulsions, the doctors said. Not unusual. But they would do tests: perhaps a brain scan to be safe. By the time she and Joe were released twenty-four hours later the doctors told her he would be fine. She didn't believe a word of it.

Every night she lay with Joe in the crook of her arm, the clock pumping out seconds. Very often she jerked, palpitating from sleep, feeling for the tiny prod of his pulse. Her expression became pinched and driven.

'Bring him into our room and sleep with me,' Andy said. 'I don't mind if he wakes.' He added, 'Please, Sam.'

He was coming home earlier, boiling pasta to eat with sauces out of jars. She wasn't cooking. Something in her hardened down to a fine point. The uneasy adjustment to motherhood, envy of Andy's life: all dissolved as frivolous malcontent, women's magazine chatter. She was locked into something more primal: Joe's survival. Nothing else mattered, not sleep, not food, not any other person.

When Elizabeth Nolan called on her again Sam sat crying, unable to release Joe from her arms.

'He nearly died,' she wept. 'I thought he was dead.'

Elizabeth parked herself down and put an arm around Sam's shoulders. 'Oh now, you poor girl – what a fright you've had. And when you were coping so well. Is there no one could come and stay for a while to help you?'

Sam shook her head. 'My mother died . . . when I was fifteen.' She cried even harder. 'And my sister-in-law lives in Suffolk.'

'Dear oh dear, you are a lonely soul.' Elizabeth Nolan squeezed her hand. 'It will get better, dear. But I know it can be a terrible time with little ones. My own mother now – the nuns took my twin sisters for a time after the birth because she wasn't managing. But we'll get you through. You're from good stock.' Sam wept further with gratitude when Elizabeth promised to call in every day.

A week passed, and most of another. She barely slept in her own bed; her every fibre centred on Joe. She had nothing to give Andy. He just didn't seem relevant. One night when she was awake beside Joe at 01.32 she heard a dragging noise, a sob. The dragging came closer and Andy crawled into the room.

'What's the matter?' She felt beyond surprise about anything.

'*Please*, love . . .' Crying, he laid his head on the duvet, over her belly. 'I don't know how to do this either. I just don't know what to do.'

Sam put her hand on his head, stroked his thinning hair, nothing more. Eventually he was calmer. He kissed her, then went back to bed. She lay listening to Joe's breathing. For once it wasn't raining.

The next evening Andy cooked chicken burgers and said, 'It's time we went out. We haven't been anywhere together since Joe was born. That lady next door said she'd sit in if we wanted.'

'Are you mad?' Sam roared. 'I wouldn't leave him with anyone! He could die while you're out stuffing your face.'

'OK –' He came closer and dared to touch her. 'Don't get in a state. But we could go and take Joe with us. How about that?'

'I don't know.' Tears welled up at the thought of anything out of routine, any more change. 'Not yet.'

'Right. OK.' He ate his meal, then sat beside her in the front room. He tried to put his arm around her. She sat stiffly, staring at the TV, then got up to pick up the remote as an excuse to sit down further away.

'Look, Sam – are you all right?'

She wouldn't meet his eyes. Five minutes later he went up to his computer.

The next night he wasn't home by ten. Joe slept for most of the evening. Sam made cheese on toast and tried to eat. Fear seeped through her. At ten-thirty Andy phoned, his voice weary.

'I'm sorry, love, there's been a system failure at ZipSys.' One of the companies using their software. 'We're going to have to stay and fix it overnight. I'm not going to be able to get home.'

'OK,' she said flatly. 'Good luck. See you when we see you.'

Lying next to Joe in their house between the street and the blank water behind, she wondered if there was really a system failure at ZipSys. She pictured Andy curled up for comfort beside his monitor, the screen flashing him reassuring messages. More and more people slept at work these days, she'd heard. Easier to cope with than being at home.

She held Joe close in the cold night and wept wretchedly. In the morning when he was still alive she held him up by the window, laughing, crying in the strengthening light. To the right, beyond the dark woods, water and sky merged.

Andy phoned at nine to say they were close to fixing the problem and he'd be home by lunchtime. But through the awake-all-night staleness in his voice she heard a strain of melancholy which cut right through her.

Sudden ability surfaced and she dressed Joe in his snowsuit, fixed the rainhoods on the buggy and walked down to the shops. In the post office, amid the smell of wet macs, the card arranged in a row of others on a lopsided carousel caught her eye. Bordered by red clamshells and starfish, it showed a lozenge of rock beside a streaky green sea, blue sky crowded with fat cumulus and gulls and, perched on the rock, a sturdy red and white lighthouse. She bought the card and tucked it into the string basket under the buggy. Leaning over, she tickled Joe's tummy.

'Hello, gorgeous boy.'

Joe tipped his head back to look at her and a dimple appeared by his mouth.

The sky was full of moving clouds, and as she pushed the buggy back up the hill the sun broke through for a moment, dazzlingly, just above the houses. The line of roofs stood out dark and sharp.

At home she found a note through the door: *Called in but*

alas no reply! See you Monday without fail. Grand that you've got out now the rain's let up. Fingers crossed the racing'll be back on! Yours, Elizabeth Nolan.

Sam made Horlicks and sat down to feed Joe. Ragged scraps of sunlight drifted across the carpet. Once Joe was content, she played with him, and again the dimple appeared in his cheek.

'Oh Joey – you're smiling – you really are!' She nuzzled against his cheek. 'Almost six weeks old, bang on time.'

Leaving him to kick down on his blanket, she fetched the lighthouse card. She'd bought it to give Andy, but grimaced now at the sight of it. It was wrong. Tacky. Maybe she'd show it to him one day, when they'd gone on far enough to look back and laugh. Hard times and all that. But now she had to leave the lighthouse behind. It had been a refuge, never her proper home: it was only to Grace that it truly belonged. She slipped the card under the dustcover of her computer and sat down to wait for Andy. She felt shy, as if she hadn't seen him for a long time. In truth she probably hadn't. She was the one who needed to move out now towards him, show that the foreign, blurred days of her confinement were ending. To find a look for him when he arrived which could say it all at once, direct and clear: sorrow, new strength, that she was coming to meet him back on the mainland.

Carolina Live

Rachel Bradford

If she turns her head away, she can't see that reduced fat, crinkle-cut oven chip lying just out of reach under the new fridge freezer. The real Christine could never just leave it lying. The real Christine wouldn't even be sitting at the table in the middle of the morning, let alone face down on a woven place mat, crying. The woman from the playgroup will be round in less than three hours to talk about fund-raising. Oscar's banging his beaker on the highchair table. She's turned him round to face the corner, can't let him see her like this, it could affect his primary socialization, even set his reading age back. The real Christine would give a shit.

She can feel the mat digging into her cheek. It'll leave an imprint, big red welts like a tree-trunk slice – you could count them to find out her age. Every other morning she would be a young-looking thirty-one, but this morning, she's back to fourteen again. She can feel the post-sob headache/throatache coming on, and she hasn't even finished crying.

The Marigolds wave on the empty, gleaming milk bottles, beckoning at her to take out the lemon Ajax and resume normal service. Oscar is clucking away now, amusing himself with snot bubbles, but he'll be bored soon, demanding entertainment. But there'll be no glove puppets this morning. Christine has snapped. Hayley Capps from next door called her a piss flap.

*

The day Hayley Capps moved in, Christine had palpitations and had to have a lie down in the afternoon when Oscar took his nap. She'd turned up in a noisy estate car full of kids, dark ones, blond and ginger ones, at least half a dozen, but they didn't stay still long enough to count. Christine would have sworn that not two of those kids shared a father, but they all had Hayley Capps' mouth: wide and turned down at the edges.

Christine stayed behind the venetian blinds all day. Phil couldn't park in his usual place outside the house; they'd had a skip delivered next door. He had to pull right up into the drive. Christine preferred the van out on the road, it kept the shingle even and, besides, it was good advertising. No point in paying all that money to have a signwriter paint *P. R. Scarnell Painter and Decorator: Interior, exterior . . . give me a call, no job too small!* – and then park it out of sight. Phil didn't really see the point. After all, living in All Fellows Close, it wasn't like people drove past. But it was good to let Christine feel involved, and she was a one to take things to heart.

Oscar should have been bathed and fluffy in a clean sleepsuit by the time Phil came in. Hayley Capps had spent the whole day unloading her dirty car and trailer, laughing with her older children as they struggled with boxes and black bags. Stopping every now and then to stand in the garden drinking cans of cheap cola and smoking. Then they'd go off for another load, leaving the little ones with the sullen teenage daughter who sat on a kitchen stool on the path reading magazines, ignoring them as they played pirates in the skip. By teatime, Hayley Capps' T-shirt was nearly as dirty as her car, and the knees in her leggings were down to her shins.

Christine saved every detail to tell Phil over chicken Kievs, new potatoes and fresh garden peas, but he never even made it up the path. She let Oscar down onto the rug to play with his tractor, so he wouldn't have to see his daddy helping the dirty lady next door as she struggled with a wide-screen TV. Then Christine took him up for his bath so she wouldn't have to watch them leaning on the fence, laughing, that Hayley Capps with her pale skin and freckles, laughing with the sun in her hair.

The Kievs had shrunk until they were barely more than chicken nuggets and garlic by the time Phil got away from Hayley. He sat at the table – still in his overalls, when he should've left them in the basket by the back door.

'Poor woman, on her own with all those kids. Seems ever so friendly.' Phil chatted away while Christine struggled to swallow a piece of dry chicken.

'She's got a girl Oscar's age, birthday's in the same week. She said he must go round for his tea one night.'

Christine didn't think this was a good idea. She didn't want her son developing a taste for artificial sweeteners or eating anything that might contain traces of nuts, just in case. But she thought it best not to say this to Phil, he would just laugh and call her his silly kitten. So she just smiled and loaded the dishwasher.

Hayley Capps caught her the next day. She'd wanted to be ready, blow-dried and composed, not red-faced with a damp fringe stuck to her face, struggling with a hungry Oscar and bags full of damp towels and armbands after a hectic morning at Aqua Tots.

'Hiya! Are y'all right? I'm Hayley. I met your old man the other night. It's Crystal, isn't it?'

'Christine.' Rhymes with pristine. Obviously Hayley Capps didn't remember.

Christine grappled with the keys as they slid to the bottom of her handbag. Trying to get a hand free, she put Oscar down on the step, where he crumpled into a heap and started to grizzle.

'Oh dear! Bless him, little chap. Are you tired, little man? Are you hungry, eh?'

Oscar stopped to look where the loud voice came from, then dropped his head back into his anorak and carried on crying.

'God, I remember when I just had the one. Seemed like going

ten rounds with Tyson every single day at the time. When you got three of the little bleeders hanging off you, it makes having one look like a piece of piss!'

She threw her head back and laughed. The sullen daughter came to lean against the doorframe, arms folded, her heavily lined eyes alternating contemptuously between her mother and the sweating woman next door.

In her efforts to hurry to get through the door, Christine dropped the swimming bag, and the 2-in-1 shampoo and conditioner split and oozed out over the talc and hairbrushes.

'Here, love. Why don't you just dump that lot off, come round and I'll get the kettle on and we can have a proper good yarn, eh?'

'Oh, that's very nice of you, but Oscar's hungry so I really should get started on lunch.'

'He'll be all right, won't you, little chap? We can stick him in the pen with little Rosie. Our Nicolette can do him a Pop Tart in the toaster, won't take a minute, it's no trouble.'

'Erm . . . that's very kind of you, really, erm . . . but, actually, Oscar doesn't eat refined sugar.'

'Oh.' Hayley Capps looked disappointed, hurt even.

Christine finally got the door open and hauled Oscar up under one arm.

'Maybe another time then.'

From the other side of her front door, Christine heard the sulky daughter. 'Snotty cow.'

Christine's eyes smarted with held-in tears. That voice sounded so exactly like Hayley when they had been fourteen at St Mary Magdalene's. The voice that had haunted and taunted long after they'd left school. Now that voice was living next door, and it had cloned, like Gremlins. '*Snotty cow, pristine Christine – she thinks her shit don't stink!*'

Out in their garden, Hayley Capps told her daughter not to be so rude, told her to watch her lip and get indoors, to come and help make the kids' lunch.

*

Christine's temples and eyes are throbbing from trying to cry without making a noise. She can't just sit here all day, can she? What will Phil say if he comes in from work to find Oscar in a sopping nappy, hungry and hoarse through crying all day? Will he be angry, will he shout at the back of her head, still stuck to the kitchen table, eyes tightly clamped, shutting out the knowledge of feral chips and dirty breakfast crockery? No. He'll smooth and soothe, then he'll call the doctor out.

Maybe she needs the doctor out. She certainly feels ill enough, that head, that throat, that sickly prickly 'waiting for a teeth shattering crash' feeling in her stomach. She peels her face off the place mat. She'll have to get up now she knows she's ill – she isn't wearing the appropriate clothing, and her flannelette pyjamas and towelling dressing gown are upstairs on the ottoman.

Sick people should be allowed to have the television on during the day.

Christine lies on the sofa under the light duvet from the spare room that has never been used. She can't remember ever having done this before. As children, she and Jacqueline had their illnesses in bed, stayed there until boredom forced them to act as if they were better. The sofa, the whole front room in fact, had been where her mother lived.

Her mother had never been well. Ever. Christine wondered if Mother was, at that moment, lying on her own sofa, with the curtains drawn against the sun. Christine had often doubted her mother's 'troubles', but she would never have dared say so. In any case, she used to hope she was right, she hoped that when they were all out at school, Mother would throw off her shawl and travel rug and dance the tango all day long, even have a fancy man to call in the afternoons. Sometimes she used to call one of the girls in when they got home, to dampen her face cloth, or maybe make her some lemon tea. It was on one of those days that her mother had caught her crying.

'Whatever's the matter with you, child?'

Christine had poured out the whole story before Mother could even ask for her pillows to be rearranged. Choking sobs and gulping air, she told her all about how that Hayley Capps had ruined her peacock picture. The special peacock picture that she'd been working on all term, each piece of every feather painstakingly brushed. The picture was almost perfect when Hayley Capps threw a splat of black and white paint right at the middle of the tail. Miss Middler had tried to get to the bottom of things.

'Weren't me, miss,' said Hayley Capps. 'Looks like bird's mess to me, maybe the peacock did it!' The whole class crowded round to look at the peacock shit. Hayley Capps didn't even get a detention.

'Now then, Christine, don't take on so,' Miss Middler said. 'It's only a bit of paint, you can scrape the worst of it off, then blend it in.'

Christine's nose began to bleed when she tried to explain that it couldn't be blended, it was ruined. 'Peacocks don't have black and white. It was perfect. Perfect!'

Hayley Capps had killed the peacock and nobody seemed the least bit bothered. They'd all laughed on the bus, doing impressions of Christine: 'Perfect!' 'Pristine Christine!' 'Peter Perfect's girlfriend!'

Mother got the vapours just from listening. She could feel one of her heads coming on. Miss Middler was right. Christine shouldn't take on so, why did she always have to make such a fuss? Why did she want to be good at art anyway, that wasn't going to feed a family now, was it?

Christine cried in the kitchen, into the pan of potatoes she'd peeled. She wasn't to use salt, on account of Mother's blood pressure.

Now it's Christine's turn for the sofa.

She reaches past Oscar's farmyard for the remote control, turning up the sound to drown out the memories. *Carolina Live on Five*; fascinated, Christine wonders if Mother ever watches these sort of shows with women whose husbands cheated on them, husbands whose wives nagged.

Carolina is smart and articulate in her green two-piece and court shoes. She knows exactly what to say to get the truth from her guests. She knows when people are lying.

A caption flashes up on the screen at the beginning of each commercial break:

> *Something to say?*
> *Need to be heard?*
> *Call Carolina Live on Five!*

Christine has two weeks to prepare her case. She goes through it all over and over, making lists, memorizing, then tearing them into little pieces and putting them in empty juice cartons in the recycling. Hayley Capps came round just the once. Christine stood in the hall, backed up against the ironing board, as Hayley called through the letter box.

'I know you're in there! Come on, Christine. Don't you think this has gone far enough?'

Christine smiled to herself. She practised smiling in the mirror, and composure. She's going to be appropriately responsive, yet composed. How could the audience not empathize with her? Carolina would have no devil's advocate role to play. It's an open and shut case.

She buys a new suit, a fitted jacket and elegant sweeping trousers, just like Carolina. A new bag and matching shoes, cheap but smart, in peacock blue. She's ready.

'Hi, I'm Amelia, I'm looking after you today.' Amelia's smile covers two-thirds of her face and she has too many teeth. She tries to take Christine's jacket.

'Oh, I'd really rather keep it on, it's part of the ensemble, you see.'

'Right.' Amelia raises her eyebrows. 'It's just that it gets ever so hot under the studio lights. You wouldn't want to be on the telly all shiny, would you?'

Christine looks past her, they are sitting in a small beige room with comfortable chairs; a TV monitor, high in the corner and angled down, showing the *Carolina* logo in black and white.

'I'll go and get some coffee then, all right, Chrissie? The show's just starting. Here, I'll put it on for you.' Amelia flashes her inane grin once more, turns on her chunky wedge-heeled trainers and leaves. Christine practises her composed face. She supposes that Amelia is fairly new to the world of television and public relations. Carolina probably reserves the experienced and perceptive members of her team to look after the less composed guests. The ones she's seen from her sofa, red in the face, wailing, shrieking, half their vocabulary bleeped out by the censors. They were the ones who needed looking after, the guilty ones.

'Only me!' Amelia reverses into the room with a tray. 'Tea for two! I got some cake, it's only cherry though, the audience have eaten all the nice fruit cake. Honestly, they're like a plague of locusts.'

Through the plasterboard walls they can hear the audience cheering and whistling. Christine watches their faces on the monitor. They are smiling, but look quite hard. Still, at least they're not all young and pierced. There are older people there, they would be more reasonable; there's not much room to reason with the young.

Amelia's clipboard is covered in cake crumbs. 'Are you nervous, then?' She gives a practised, sympathetic smile.

Christine ignores her, gazing serenely at the monitors. *Deep breath in . . . composure, hold for the count of two, composing, deep breath out . . . composed.*

'Here, I'll take your bag for you when you go in.' Christine is too composed to argue, nobody will know that the shoes match now. *Deep breath in . . .*

The signature tune starts up. Carolina is introduced, cheers, whistles. *Hold for the count of two . . .* Christine goes to stand up.

'No, not yet.' Amelia tugs at her sleeve like a toddler. 'You go on after.'

'After what?' *Hold for the count of three . . . four . . .*

'After your neighbour from hell, what's her name?' She drags a glittery thumbnail down the clipboard. 'Hayley. Hayley Capps. She goes on first, then you.'

Deep, hard, punctured body slam against the wall-bars, breathe out . . . Christine's left eyelid sets off its familiar old twitch. This is all wrong. She was the one who'd rung in, had things to say. She'd practised, for weeks, years even. This was her say, she'd waited for ever. She feels her composure flaking away like old mottled paint. *Shallow, rapid dog in labour breaths in and out . . .*

Hayley Capps sits smiling on the monitor. She must've spent her family allowance on a fabulous urchin haircut and a vertical fast-tanning session. Christine's suit begins to cut in and stick to her like melting plastic. Hayley Capps is wearing a long, demure, ivory linen dress; she'll probably pull off a button and send it back to the catalogue tomorrow, but how will the audience know that?

Amelia steers Christine towards the corridor. Hayley Capps' smile shines out through the monitors, single mum, six kids, struggle struggle, bleat bleat, butter wouldn't melt. Christine stands in the wings, Amelia pushing at her shoulder like a girl on the edge of a playground fight. The harsh studio light makes her eyes water, her mascara blot, but she can't blink. She's a hare in a poacher's lamp, and she can't even see the lurchers.

Afterwards, Christine hides in the toilets. She doesn't want to run the gauntlet in the foyer, had more than enough feedback already.

Hunched on the bowl, creased, smeared, *breathe in, out, in . . . decomposure, decomposing, decomposed.*

She hadn't stood a chance. All the carefully reasoned arguments, the examples of the broken window, the birthday party clown fiasco, the disturbing additions to Oscar's vocabulary. All had floated away like helium balloons when she'd walked in and somebody booed.

She rubs her knuckles against her temples.

She'd said piss flap on national television. The audience couldn't stop laughing, and she'd said it again. Piss flap. They were doubled over, they couldn't hear a word she said, she'd have to be bleeped out now. And she'd tried to tell them, it wasn't even her word, she couldn't even have thought of a word like that. It was that Hayley Capps' word, she said it first, it was her. And Hayley Capps smiled with the audience, batted her eyes, dabbed at her lip liner, her perfectly glossed mouth; precise. Pristine.

The door of the Ladies swings open, a pair of heels clicks past the cubicle. Carolina and her maroon snakeskin boots. She's talking loudly into a mobile phone.

'What's that? You're breaking up, darling . . . I said you're . . . no, there, that's better.'

Christine thinks she should probably flush out of politeness, but then there was nothing in the bowl to get rid of, and when they sent out the water-shortage flyers and banned hosepipes, Christine would take comfort in knowing they weren't talking to her.

She can smell cigarettes. Smoking is forbidden in all areas of the studio, Christine has seen the signs. Click, click, click. The heels stalk up and down the length of the mirror. Carolina is laughing into the phone, braying and snorting. Christine thinks she should hate to be on the phone to someone who laughs like that, even if they are famous.

'What's that? What! Look, I don't give a damn what you tell wifey, you get your taut little arse round to the Beeches by eight-thirty p.m. or I'll have your fucking job!' Click, click, click, slam.

Christine takes a paper towel and runs it under the tap. A More Menthol butt bobs in the plughole. She dabs at her puffy eyes, her streaky cheeks, soothing and cooling. She doesn't need to reapply. She sets her makeup bag down on the smoked glass shelf, next to a drained miniature Gordon's bottle ringed with claret lipstick.

She takes out the compact, the silver is tarnished, the mirror chipped. Mother gave it to her on her wedding day. Something old. She said Christine would inherit it anyway, no use waiting for the inevitable, and, anyway, she wants to witness the joys brought about by her legacies. Christine gives herself a light dusting for cover, not too much, just enough to walk out with her head up, smile when appropriate, and have nobody ask what's wrong.

Static

Pauline Masurel

One morning she wakes to find herself contained within a live metal box, the shell of the caravan perceptibly humming with electricity.

'It's static, see? That's the joke, pet. The van may be buzzing but it's not going anywhere,' her father had said on just such an occasion, long in the past, when the power lines came down around their home.

Rhiannon eases her father's signet ring from her finger and places it on the pillow, then wriggles out of bed, taking care not to dislodge the ring from its resting place. She slides on a pair of wooden-soled sandals and inches her coat down from the plastic hook. Only just awake, she's alert to the danger of inadvertence, and knows very well by now not to touch the sides of the van.

It's still dark and the wind flutes through the tiniest of gaps in the buckled, aluminium window frame. Later she will rail at the site owner as she did the last time it happened. 'It could have killed me,' she'll say – as if he'd care. As if she cares.

When the wind has dropped, daylight fully set in and the maintenance crew departed, Rhiannon has a short fit of the shakes, then pushes the incident away and tries to make plans for the following hours. She likes, if she can, to go down to the beach as she did almost every day when Ellie was around. The child came to stay for weeks in the summer, or at half term, while her mother, Rhiannon's sister, was working. Ellie could slip effortlessly across the divide between white sheep and black, English sister and Welsh, just as Rhiannon herself had shuttled between parents in her youth. She remembers the battles for approval, the nagging distress of never being fully present in either's attention.

It was a long time before Rhiannon would acknowledge any hint of retardation in Ellie's development but eventually some pang of it broke through. Her niece was too sweet, too innocent, happy with the sand and the sky, willing to run up to any tourist's mutt on the beach and throw her arms round it. Ellie was also too obedient. If you gave her a warm but deeply unfashionable hat then she would wear it, not knowing why other children laughed.

Sarah had patiently tried to convey her daughter's lagging progress. 'She tries, Rhi, she's perfectly willing, but somehow her brain doesn't make connections the same way ours do. They've told me it's a . . . predisposition. Something on her father's side. I always said he was . . .'

When speeches like this began, Rhiannon preferred to leave her sister to it, to let whatever needed saying flow safely away to earth. Sarah almost always ended up telling Rhiannon that if she'd had a man of her own – and, by implication, her own child to sacrifice herself to – then she might understand 'everything' a little better. Rhiannon had tried to 'have' – and even to hold – men. She really had. But, ultimately, if families were shackles then why insist on a new set of chains?

Somehow, though, when it was just her and Ellie and the waves at Abermaw, these 'predispositions' seemed un-important. But Rhiannon recognized that it was Sarah who had to meet a sobbing Ellie at the school gate all through term-time. In five generations of driven developers and climbers it seemed that she and her niece were the ones who'd followed their fathers' routes and opted out.

Rhiannon had followed him literally as well, to join him in the static caravan in North Wales. He'd retired to the van after relinquishing his share in the failing upholstery business along with his family. Now it was her only inheritance apart from his wedding ring.

If you were looking for something to make you feel that your whole life was a mistake, then appearing in the world thirteen years after your sister could easily fit the bill. Sarah was already taking her accountancy exams when their father left. Rhiannon was still at school reading the *Mabinogion* in the original. Whenever she struggled up the hill from the beach at Harlech, both the walk and the statue at the top reminded her of toiling through those stories. It was a grim memorial; Bendigeidfran forever riding motionlessly home with the burden of his nephew Gwern's body bundled in rags on the back of the horse.

'Blood ties, see?' her father would have said. 'Blood ties you in, weighs you down.'

Ellie was no bind. The van itself had never fizzed with electricity when Ellie was there. There was never any need. The child brought her own.

She flashed with laughter as her scrappy hands crept out of mittens to stroke a gull's feather or smuggle seaweed into a bucket. She was a patient but excitable kite-maker. They'd build kites together and then fly them in the fields above the top road, away from all the power lines. Ellie would stand in the wind, pallid cheeks whipped pink by the slap of it, her life running just beneath the skin. Near-translucent strands of hair blustered out in the breeze. Rhiannon felt free up there; the two human animals like interlopers among the ewes.

But now Sarah has taken Ellie to Adelaide. Rhiannon feels that the ocean makes her closer to Ellie somehow, even though she's facing the wrong way: the Irish Sea, Ireland, the Atlantic and North America are all that is out there for thousands of miles.

Occasionally she meets tourists on the beach, or a small walking party brave enough to wrap up and cross the estuary on the iron and wood railway bridge. Sometimes they smile and engage her in conversation. If they ask where she's staying, she often replies, 'I'm residential,' meaning the van, but feeling that it actually describes her self now as well. In the shops she conveys the same thing – encoded differently – by only speaking Welsh to the assistants. Sometimes she's surprised to hear her own voice speak English. It reminds her of visiting her father when she was Ellie's age. It reminds her of Ellie, and so the circle goes – or rather it doesn't.

She can't forgive her sister for this catastrophic emigration. Sarah had consulted their mother. She'd asked Ellie's mostly invisible father, even though she'd once claimed that he had done everything he'd ever been irresponsible for without any kind of warning or consideration. 'His daughter is evidence of one such occasion,' she'd added cruelly.

A man who couldn't be bothered with birthday cards and visited only sporadically was allowed to express an opinion before tickets to the New Life were booked. Aunts, however, have no status in the exclusive mother and daughter loop of blood relations.

Rhiannon still bakes tarts with homemade jam, even though there was never anyone but Ellie to eat them. She cooks cinder toffee; a molten pumice, which sets so hard it needs a hammer and chisel – kept clean in the kitchen for just this purpose. The food might be sweet. It might sicken sometimes with its sentiment but she watches her choice of recipe carefully, from the leaden slabs of gingerbread to Victoria sponges. If she once suspected romance in their baking then she would take the hammer and smash the tokens to pieces, ramming them back into the heat to return them to liquid or to char into ash until their shapes are hidden like the peaks of Rhinog Fawr and Rhinog Fach buried under deep cloud.

Today there's the hot smell of burnt sugar and a tarry slick has erupted onto the baking sheet. She takes the baking tray from the oven and it slips from the pot towel, spills jam across her hands and then clatters directly into the sink. Lemon-scented foam engulfs the food and soaks up through the pastry. The food is no more pointless now that it's ruined.

It remains one of those days of split weather; light and clear now out to sea where the Llyn peninsula is illuminated. Behind her, as she walks away from the site, a dark cloud is chasing the mountains inland, skulking low on its haunches like Jepp, the one-eyed border collie who monotonously haunts the entrance of the van park, barking at everyone before he's taken the time to discover who he's greeting or warding away.

Rhiannon carries her drowned burden of love down to the water's edge, across sand inset with the smashed backs of mussels like acres of shattered Delftware. The blistering kiss of the jam lingers on her fingertips. She wants to hurl the tray out to sea but instead sets down the small parcels of saturated food as offerings, to drift out on the tide.

Two jet-engined shadows, close flying from Mochras, curse at the silence as she bends. Further along the beach a formation of terns is skimming the water's surface, as though driven from their own air space.

She stares out across an opaque greyness, laced white, and watches for any change on the horizon; watches as if Australia might actually be out there to the west, within eyesight, rather than thousands of miles to the south.

She's not looking for love any longer. Blood love is too fierce, too demanding. With her eyes shaded against the brightness, she seeks only something that she would call affection. For all the waterlogged pastries she sends out as lures, she realizes that she is looking in entirely the wrong direction.

Like Rabbits

Penny Feeny

Everything is yellow. The painted cupboard doors, the top of the table, the seats of our two chairs, even the lady's blouse and the cups we're drinking out of. Makes my eyes hurt. She's writing a list, the lady. All the things on the list are yellow: cornflakes, lemon squash, butter, cheese, crisps.

'Twenty Bensons,' I say. My mind isn't working properly. Bensons are gold.

'This is a food list,' she says.

I shrug. I'm not interested in food. I haven't felt hungry for a long time. Probably haven't felt hungry since I found Shelley face down in all that vomit.

The lady isn't what I'm used to. She isn't wearing jeans and dirty trainers and an old parka. She's got leather shoes with high heels and her skirt is leather too. It ripples like melted chocolate and when she moves it squeaks, very softly. I reach out to touch it and she doesn't stop me.

Maybe she's different because she's not a social worker, she's a probation officer. Probably earn more money, probation officers. Probably have wardrobes full of leather.

'It will be easier for you to manage here,' she's saying. 'A fresh start.'

Albert Fletcher Flats they're called, after some dead councillor, and they've just been done up. I been on the waiting list so long I couldn't care less if they got double glazing or not. Of course, the lady never saw the last place. She never saw the black stuff crusted on the cooker, the spongy green mould growing in the fridge; the sink were blocked too. She'll of been told about it, though. Seen the photographs they took. There's nothing about me she don't know. Except Johnny of course. She don't know about Johnny.

'You'll get regular visits,' she says. 'To make sure you're coping.' She has a nice calm voice, a nice smile. 'If you have any problems you should ring this number.'

My hand is still on her skirt. She picks it up and looks at me very straight. 'And you'll keep that doctor's appointment, won't you?'

I fidget a bit. I hate doctors. I hate all that prodding and poking. And what they're going to do to me is worse than that. They want to stick things into me.

'Perhaps I should come with you.' She takes out a little leather book, her diary. 'Next Thursday. I'll get here at ten-thirty. Make sure you're ready.'

'I don't know,' I begin. I've left my hand between hers. It feels safe.

'I promise it won't hurt. You won't feel a thing.' Her voice drops. 'Actually, I've got one too.'

'You?'

'Had it for years. Don't even know it's there.'

IUD. I imagine it like a corkscrew, screwing up your insides.

'You got kids already, then?' I say.

'I've got a son, Arthur.'

Arthur, what a name, I ask you. Bad as Albert frigging Fletcher.

'What you done with him today?'

'He's at school. He's eight.'

'Eight. That's big.'

She lifts up the flap of her bag and puts her diary and her pen neatly in their pockets. She looks at me. 'Do you want to talk about it?'

Of course I don't bloody want to talk about it.

'When you went out that night,' she says, ever so gently.

'Wasn't there anyone who could have come to babysit?'

'She were asleep,' I say.

'Didn't it occur to you she might wake up?'

'It could of happened anyway. If I was in.'

'You'd have heard her choking.'

'Might not.'

It were bad enough finding her like that, leaning over to pick her up, dead eyes popping out of a face like a little stone doll's. I didn't need people telling me she had a sore bum cos her nappy weren't changed, that she should of had a proper cot to sleep in. I didn't need people telling me I shouldn't of gone out with Eddy. You don't argue with Eddy.

The lady has chocolate Malteser eyes, like her skirt. Her boy Arthur is eight and I bet she listens when he tells her things. She seems like a good listener.

'You needn't be frightened of him any more,' she says. As if she can almost see what I'm thinking. 'He won't be out for at least four years.' Then she says, 'Did you love him?'

'Eddy?' I burst out laughing. 'You's joking, int you?'

When I was with Eddy, everything was black. Vicious evil bastard. All he was good for was pulling hair and poking things inside you. I got all me hair cut short so as he couldn't pull it. The ends was breaking off anyway. He said it made me look like a boy. That he didn't fancy me any more. I thought, Thank fuck.

'But he was your baby's father?'

I don't say nothing. I let her think it, doesn't make no difference now. Johnny never knew our Shelley. Had to do a runner afore she was even born. He never felt her skin, all pearly and warm, never saw her smile, never had his finger gripped by her little hand. Never heard her screaming neither, her face all creased up and yelling. Never saw her stiff and blue or smelled that awful pong of piss and vomit.

She hands me the list. I don't want to be left by myself. This place is too bright and too lonely like nobody's ever lived here. But she goes anyway. She's got another appointment.

I take off my shoes and walk around on the carpet. Cheap carpet, but it fits into every corner. I have a bed-sitting room and a shower and the yellow kitchen. There's a single bed with clean sheets; my clothes are folded in the drawers. I don't want to go out and do the shopping. I want to sit and wait for Johnny.

Johnny always treated me good. When he was around, that is. Bit of a one for disappearing tricks was Johnny. But he couldn't half make you feel special. He was the type who, if you said you was starving, wouldn't just nab a pork pie. He'd bring you chocolates and fancy biscuits tied up in ribbon. He'd put his own coat round your shoulders if you said you was cold. He could tell stories and jokes to make you laugh, and the way he played harmonica was like you'd never heard before. He'd give you this deep look and his hands would flap like birds' wings and those long sad notes would make you tingle all over.

He was scared of Eddy, though. He couldn't protect me against Eddy. One night there was Johnny, stroking me with his magic hands, kissing my tits, giving me the baby. The next he was gone. Eddy seen him off. But now he's inside, we got another chance. That's why I'm hoping Johnny will come back for me. Soon.

It's Wednesday. Or maybe Thursday. The doorbell rings. I'm excited. I'm scared. I go slowly to open up.

It's the lady.

'Goodness,' she says. 'Have you only just got out of bed? You're due at the doctor's in half an hour.'

Her voice is not so warm today, but she has a lovely coat on. Thick soft wool with a fur collar that must feel fluffy like rabbits against her cheek.

'You're to have a coil fitted,' she says. 'Remember.'

'I can't.'

'Why can't you? It's the best solution, the only solution really.'

She goes into the kitchen and wrinkles her nose. She looks in the sink and sighs.

'While you get dressed,' she says, 'I'll do the washing-up.' She turns on the tap and lets it run for a bit. 'There's no hot water.'

'No,' I agree.

'And there's no washing-up liquid. Didn't you buy any?'

'It weren't on the list,' I say, though I can't remember what was on the flaming list, because I chucked it down the stairs when I went out for bread and ciggies.

She talks to me like a teacher. 'If you don't wash the dishes,' she says, 'they'll become a breeding ground for bacteria. They'll be difficult to clean thoroughly and then you'll get food poisoning. Possibly that's what happened to Shelley. Possibly that's why she died.'

'You telling me I poisoned me own baby?' I yell.

'Of course not,' she says quickly. Tries to put her arm around me. I want to be held. I want someone to hold me, look after me, but I don't trust her any more.

She sits down, pretends she has all the time in the world, though I catch her sneaking a deck at her watch. Thinking: five minutes to calm down, five minutes' chat, five minutes in the car, and then we'll have her on the operating table like a stuck pig, ramming bits of metal up her fanny.

'What I'm saying is this.' She lifts my hand again but it don't work the same this week. It flops between hers like a limp fish, like I don't care what the hell she does with it. 'Your baby died because you couldn't cope. You didn't have the support to show you what to do. Your social worker will call on you soon and make sure you're eating sensibly and keeping the place clean.' She looks around at the tip it's already become. 'You'll get your life sorted out, get some training, get a job. Maybe you'll meet somebody nice and want to start a family. And then you can go back to the doctor and have the coil taken out.'

I'm thinking, What planet does she reckon we're living on?

She with her leather skirts and her high heels and her fur collars that probably had six baby rabbits killed and sewn together just to make her skin feel cherished.

'I can't today,' I tell her. ''Cos I've got my period.'

She has to decide whether to believe me, though she's not much choice. Civilized types like her, they can't force you into anything you don't want. You need an Eddy for that.

She gets out a neat little mobile phone and makes another appointment for another day. I'm not bothered when.

'If you were to get pregnant and have another child,' she says very slowly and clearly so I'll know what she's on about, 'it will be taken away from you at birth and put into foster care.'

I nod, remembering my Shelley when she was just a podgy little dumpling, the way she gurgled and clapped her hands – before she got all whiny and irritating. And I wonder why in eight years this lady's only had the one kid, Arthur. Why hasn't she had her coil taken out by now? So I ask her.

'The time was never quite right.' Her mouth smiles but her Malteser eyes look sad and she gets up to leave.

I go back to bed, no point in getting dressed really. I doze a bit. I dream I can hear a tapping, a quick regular tapping like a woodpecker, and I know it's him. Johnny. I let him in and he creeps through the doorway so nobody sees him. He's thinner than he used to be and his jacket smells like he's been sleeping rough. I take him with me, back under the warm bedclothes, and he slides his cold hands under my T-shirt.

'Let's make a baby,' he says.

Slow Burn

Hilaire

Robert lies on his back on his nan's spare bed, the hard springs digging into his thin shoulder blades. Dangling his head over the edge, he places his feet high above him on the wall. The Walkman nestles humming into the concave of his belly and he turns the volume up, the high-pitched feedback and whiny vocals ricocheting between his eardrums. It's eleven a.m. and although the mercury in the thermometer on his nan's back porch is nudging thirty, the plaster beneath his feet feels cool. As the blood drains from his legs they go numb. He loves this sensation. More than this, he relishes this position because it is forbidden.

Don't put your feet on the wall, his mum nags, angered by the two dirty oval patches halfway up the wall by his bed at home. He lies like this when he speaks to Blaney on the phone, in the evenings, for hours, the silences longer than any exchange of words, sulking, brooding or listening to each other breathing, unable to hang up, until Robert hears his mum approaching, coming to check up on him. *Don't do this, don't do that. Robert, don't pick your nose, it's a filthy habit.* But she's not yet brought herself to say, *Don't stick your snot on the sheets.*

Lying here, the soles of his feet tingling, eyes shut, his head awash with noise, Robert wonders if this is what freedom might taste like. *School's out for-evah!* Shimmering ahead of him are four weeks of unrestricted, shapeless time, his to do as he pleases, as long as he feeds his nan's cat, Marmalade, and tends to her garden.

– Are you sure you'll be all right? his mum fussed the day before, as his parents dropped him off and collected his nan, like a pre-arranged hostage swap. His mum thrust list after list at him, emergency phone numbers, meal suggestions and a housework regimen: *Change sheets and towels once a week. Put bleach down toilet every night.*

His nan, on the other hand, gave him brief verbal instructions. – Half a tin twice a day. Marmalade does his business in the garden mostly, so don't worry about the dirt tray unless it gets a bit whiffy. And just keep the garden tidy. I'm sure you know what to do.

On the veranda, his dad took him aside. – Don't smoke in your grandmother's house, Robert, he warned, before patting a fold of bills into the back pocket of his shorts.

– OK, Dad. Robert doesn't smoke, but he doesn't want his parents to know. There's always a crushed Camel packet discarded casually in the litter of his bedroom.

Then off they drove – Mum waving her hankie, his little sister Belinda sticking her tongue out – off to the coast and the same cottage near Warrnambool they've rented as long as Robert can remember.

As soon as the station wagon turned the corner at the bottom of the street Robert pulled off his shoes. *Don't walk around barefoot.* Mostly he wears black kung-fu slippers, the thinnest shoes he can find. Now he can go everywhere barefoot, through the house, in the garden, down the street to buy milk.

Which is where he heads once the gnawing in his stomach becomes too pressing, intensifying from a pleasant churning to sharp prods, drilling beyond his music-induced stupor. Outside, the concrete pavement is baking, stinging the soles of his feet. He enjoys the feel of his shorts, hanging loosely from his hips, and his faded grey T-shirt limp against his skin, and his hair falling forward over his eyes, more enigmatic than sunglasses. Moving through the thick heat, he is conscious of feeling unburdened, lightened by his lack of shoes. Then he passes through a doorway of plastic strips into a refrigerated zone, cool and dark, and swimming with the dizzying possibilities of choice. No doubt there is a byelaw that forbids unshod feet in a milk bar, but the shopkeeper doesn't notice or doesn't care. The vinyl flooring is sticky and bouncy; Robert lingers by the freezer cabinets – *Mum, Mum, can I have an icypole?* – hot childhood days of discontent buzzing at the back of his mind. Finally he buys a litre of skimmed milk, a packet of cereal and a banana Paddle Pop.

Back at his nan's, Robert soothes his feet on the plaster walls and slowly demolishes the ice cream. *You don't eat properly.* Ice cream for breakfast, Coco Pops for dinner. He's in seventh heaven. How long can this last? Four weeks? The rest of his life? Not if his dad has anything to do with it. He badgers Robert. *When are you going to apply yourself? What are you going to do with your life? You can't lie around all day. You young people have so many opportunities these days.* Robert's not interested. Actor, rock star, football player; it's all too much hard work. Why can't he just be? Blaney has it sussed somehow. As far as Robert can make out, he just drives around all day. Only Robert doesn't drive; and he prefers to be driven. To keep his dad quiet he's enrolled on a film studies course – an easy option, slouching in the dark all day watching films, pretending to learn something.

Until then, he plans to block everything out, the future, his parents, the hole which widens inside him if he thinks too much. The banana ice cream slithers down into his tummy, curdling, dampening the pangs, so that he drifts off into a sugary, spiky sleep.

Mid-afternoon, Blaney arrives, hooning round the corner into the dead-end street, the heel of his hand glued to the horn. Robert comes out onto the veranda, smearing the sleep from his eyes, embarrassed for his nan though she's not there.

Blaney gets out of the car, puffed up, his tight T-shirt tucked into his black jeans, flaunting himself now Robert's parents aren't around.

Robert unlatches the low wire gate and swings it open for Blaney.

– Cool. Show me around, kid, Blaney says, stalking up the path and into the house ahead of Robert.

Robert hates it when Blaney calls him kid. Reason enough to sulk, and Robert loves a good sulk. In the hallway Marmalade is flaked out on the floorboards and Robert scoops him up, holding the cat against his chest like a child clutching a favourite toy. He follows Blaney prowling proprietarily through his nan's house, picking up knick-knacks and putting them back in the wrong place, running a finger through the motes of dust on the sideboard, poking his nose into drawers, behind curtains. Robert notes each transgression, shoring up his mound of resentment, fuel should the slow burn of his sulking fade.

Up until now it hasn't occurred to Robert to explore. His nan's house is as familiar to him as the family home, part of the unchanging scenery of his life. Out of habit he took the spare bed. Now Blaney has sniffed out his nan's bedroom, a violation too far.

– Don't, Robert says, stopping in the doorway.

Blaney's hands are cupped behind his neck, his stomach taut as he lies back on the sagging mattress. – Come on. I thought the whole point was we could be alone.

– Not in here, Robert says. Marmalade struggles against his hold and lands with a thump on the floor. He scoots between Robert and the doorframe, affronted, darting outside and under the house where it is low and shady and out of human reach.

Robert pouts, shoving his hands in the pockets of his shorts. Can't Blaney tell this is the wrong place? His nan's presence in the room is overpowering, her cornflower-pattern dressing gown draped over the back of a chair, a carafe of stale water on the bedside table, the ghost of his grandfather buried deep in the mattress that Blaney is sprawled upon. Robert has envisioned the laundry as the place where he'll untuck Blaney's shirt, where they'll lock together, grappling with each other, the tang of detergent in their nostrils and the cold granite trough which one of them will be pressed up against. He longs to uncover Blaney's mole again, on his back beneath his left shoulder blade, the dark, raised bump which is the sole imperfection on his groomed and tailored body. For Robert, it is an emblem of hope. If he could penetrate that small chink of vulnerability he might make Blaney love him.

Blaney stares up at him from the bed. – Ro-*bert*. Come to be-*ed*, he singsongs. But Robert withholds his gaze. His body is wedged in the doorframe, all awkward angles, his back rigid, his feet flexed against the opposite jamb. – Ro-*bert*. Blaney draws the syllables out, his voice wavering between enticement and warning. His right hand brushes back and forth across the bedspread, making a sound like windscreen wipers.

Finally Robert breaks away from the door, lurching off towards the laundry. – I have to feed the cat, he announces.

Later they lie together on the living-room floor, the only light coming from the muted TV. *Switch the light on. You'll ruin your eyesight.* Sometimes the silence crackles with tension; at other times, like now, it is tranquil. Robert closes his eyes and listens to Blaney breathing, the insistent ticking of his wristwatch, and outside the rustle of the azalea bushes beneath the window and occasionally the gathering boom of a passing aeroplane. He unties the laces of Blaney's trainers by feel while Blaney begins the slow dance of his fingertips up Robert's bare calves. Each time, still, it's a discovery, learning the wonderment contained in another being, how Blaney remains a mystery to him and yet turns Robert inside out so that he feels raw and exposed. He voices none of this to Blaney. He doesn't want him to know how necessary he is to Robert. Blaney can make his feet walk up the wall. Moments of blissful numbness, when Robert feels drained of everything.

Only it never lasts. Lifting Robert's T-shirt to nuzzle the hollows of his arms, Blaney recoils. – Sheesh, Robert. When d'you last take a shower?

Robert retracts his body like a concertina, knees up against his chest, burrowing his face into the smell of himself: dry and leathery. What's wrong with it? It's the smell of summer heat, of indolence. Whereas Blaney smells strangely of nothing, never sweat, never sex, not even soap. Robert thinks of the thin, pale skin behind his ear. That bit of him must be pure, and he imagines Blaney placing his lips there, hesitantly. But if Blaney loved him he would want to discover Robert's odour on his own skin.

Besides, Blaney sounds like his mum. *When did you last wash? Your nails are filthy. You should use a deodorant at your age.*

– God, Robert, Blaney flares. – If you're going to get the hump with me again I'm out of here. He wrestles his T-shirt on over his shoulders, turning away from Robert.

But Robert snatches the evening back, jumping up from the floor and grabbing the belt hooks on Blaney's jeans. – Let's go for a drive.

This is how his days span out. Spats, reconciliations; the routines of sleep, and feeding Marmalade, and tending his nan's garden; the night drives with Blaney, given up to speed, cruising the highways which bleed out from the suburbs into tracts of nowhere, or careering along the boulevards leading down to the bay, a cassette blasting, cool air streaming in through the windows, Robert hanging out for the brief, heady scent of mimosa.

At the hottest point of the day Robert ventures out to the high street, when the shops will be emptiest, taking a shortcut along the lane which runs from the police barracks to the railway line. The lane is paved with worn bricks, thistles and dry grass sprouting from every crack. On both sides a corrugated iron fence, painted the colour of iodine, bulges and buckles, contorted by the thick trunks of the trees which overhang the lane. Ripples of heat radiate out from the metal and up from the bricks.

The lane is like a corridor of fire; the light so sharp Robert squints through his fringe. He treads gingerly, twigs and splinters of brick nipping at the soles of his feet. The hairs on his arms stand on end, pricked by the heat and Robert's sense of the lane as an illicit place, the scene of a potential encounter, reminds him of the secluded patch of tarmac behind the boy's shelter-shed where the sixth-grade boys and girls played spin the bottle. He stayed away, ashamed and fearful and consumed by curiosity.

Within a few minutes he steps unharmed from the lane to cross the railway line, singeing his feet on the tracks. Beyond, on the high street, he wanders in and out of the few shops, bored as soon as he crosses the threshold, but needing their icy interiors to recover from the heat. Or he lingers under the shop awnings, trickles of perspiration sliding down his spine, down the backs of his legs.

Once the throbbing of his temples has subsided, he heads back to his nan's via the main road. He swings his arms to encourage airflow around him and hugs the edge of the front gardens to make the most of the shade. As a reward for his endurance he promises himself an ice cream from the corner shop. He is working his way determinedly through the full range on the display card above the freezer.

In the late afternoon he waters his nan's garden, holding a finger over the nozzle of the hose so the water fans out, a glorious arc sweeping across the lawn, twisting the spray to a certain angle so it's shot through with a rainbow. Robert loves the smell of damp earth rising through the evening sunshine, and the patter, like a burst of applause, as the water hits the leaves of the trees and shrubs on the periphery of the garden, and the moist, springy feel underfoot when he crosses the lawn. Out the front, he meticulously combs through the honey-suckle, picking off the dead flowers as he has seen his nan do.

At the end of every visit his nan would wave the family off; and as their car pulled away, if Robert glanced back, he'd see his nan tweaking at the plants in her front garden. He has seen her lips move, as if she's talking to the roses and the lavender bushes as she nips them into shape. The gestures she makes recall other gestures, brushing crumbs from the corners of his mouth when he was little, or ruffling his hair as she tidies around him while he watches TV, or adjusting the line of his T-shirt before kissing him goodbye. The longer Robert spends tending her garden, the more he understands it to be an expression of love.

Robert is sweeping the front path one afternoon when he hears the blaring wail of Blaney's horn, and then the screech as his car two-wheels it round the corner.

As the car jolts to a stop Robert spots Blaney's mate, Franco, in the front passenger seat. His place. Blaney leans out of the window, shades pushed back on his head. – Hey, kid. Hop in. We're going for a spin.

Robert swishes the broom across the path, back and forth over the same patch, hoping to ignore Blaney. There's another flourish on the car horn. What will the neighbours think? Robert worries instinctively.

Franco hauls himself halfway out of the car window to jeer at Robert. – Where's your apron, Roberto?

– Shut up, Robert says, tossing the broom aside, about to skulk off into the house.

But Blaney bounds up, placing a hand in the small of his back. – Hey, Robert, come on. Franco called round. We were going to burn up the esplanade. Check out a café. Could be fun. Why don't you come?

An invitation from Blaney. A tribe of tiny men begin a war dance in Robert's chest, drumming furiously on his heart. He tightens the muscles on his face to prevent any trace of glee. – Let me lock up, he mutters with an affected sniff.

Blaney punches the air. – Whoo-hoo! Hooon-adelica!

*

Robert has met Franco two or three times before. He's around Blaney's age, has a semicircular scar beneath his right eye, a shaved and oiled scalp, and a Maltese cross tattooed on the underside of his left wrist. Like Blaney, Franco is of indeterminate means, occupied with nothing more than hanging out with friends. But whereas Blaney's louche demeanour forms part of his appeal, Franco, in Robert's view, is a user. Robert doesn't get what Blaney sees in him. – We go way back, Blaney explained once with a shrug.

Robert resents being consigned to the back seat of the coupé. He resents the pitch of hysteria which builds between Blaney and Franco, the two friends egging each other on to giddy heights of silliness and obscenity while Blaney swerves round traffic islands and accelerates through amber lights. By the time Blaney finds a tight, illegal space to park in a cul-de-sac off the main drag, Robert's earlier euphoria has evaporated.

He lags behind as Blaney and Franco wade into the swarm of promenaders thronging the esplanade.

– Jeez, every man and his dog must be here this afternoon, Blaney observes.

– And what dogs they are, Franco titters, eyeing up the platinum and bronze female accessories dangling on the arms of the local lads.

It's rude to stare, Robert thinks, an echo of his mum's reproof the first time he saw a man dressed as a woman, on the train into town when he was seven, transfixed by the bold strokes of makeup and the chunky hands crossed primly in his – or was it her? – lap, the stubby, work-worn nails defiant in cherry red.

After the quiet of the deserted suburban streets, the bustle and noise of the esplanade come as a shock to Robert. His feet take a battering, broken glass and bottle caps littering the pavement. Why did he jump at Blaney's invitation? Why is he tagging along now like a panting, faithful, unwanted dog?

While Blaney and Franco forge ahead, bitching and sniggering, looking for all the world like lovers.

He bobs along in Blaney's wake. What else is there for him to do? He doesn't have to think, he doesn't have to make choices, he can just coast along in neutral.

Blaney cajoles him. – Pick your feet up! We're dying of thirst here.

Robert catches up a step or two, closer, glaring at Blaney's sculpted backside. He follows Blaney and Franco into a café. A rainbow flag flutters over the doorway. The interior is wooden and air conditioned; a welcome respite from the close afternoon. And it's empty, much to Robert's relief, just the waitress leaning on the bar studying the form guide. They sit at a table with a view of the bay, Blaney and Franco opposite each other, Robert at the end, tilting back in his seat to indicate his detachment.

The waitress bounces over to take their order. – Hi, guys. What can I get you?

Blaney considers. – I'll have a Becks.

– Ditto, Franco says.

Robert mulls over the possibilities, the opportunity to choose whatever he wants glittering before him like the surface of the bay, vast and tantalizing. – I'd like a caramel milkshake. Please, he adds as an afterthought.

– Great! The waitress seems thrilled to have something to do at last, her long single plait swinging as she trips back to the bar. She even sticks on some rapid-fire techno to drown out the hum of the air conditioning.

– Bit of an eager beaver, Franco comments, and he and Blaney crack up, spluttering, cheeks puffed with suppressed giggles while the waitress deftly uncaps their beers.

Then she places a tall, frosted glass spiked with a black plastic straw in front of Robert. The milkshake is a creamy golden colour, glossy bubbles slowly bursting on top. Robert purses his lips round the straw and begins to suck. He drinks the milkshake in one go, ignoring Blaney and Franco, giving himself up to that fleeting moment of bliss. The milkshake is thick and sweet and teeth-achingly cold. Robert imagines it flowing through his body, right down to the tips of his toes, and he tingles all over. When he has drunk it all he continues to suck air through the straw, making the satisfied rasping sound which always aggravates his mum. *Robert! Stop it! That's enough now.*

Blaney and Franco drain their bottles at the same time. Franco winks at Robert and shows him a tiny sachet containing a disc like his nan's hearing-aid battery. – I got this in a joke shop. We're going to let it off when we leave.

Robert doesn't respond, but Blaney is eager. – Come on, let's do it. Let's go. How much was your milkshake, kid? He throws some coins on the table.

Franco squeezes the disc and hides it under a scrunched up serviette. – We've got thirty seconds. Act cool.

Blaney and Franco saunter past the bar, Robert trailing after them.

– Ciao, Franco says.

– OK. Thanks, guys! the waitress says, looking up from her form guide.

As soon as they are out the door Blaney and Franco sprint off, whooping like larrikins, dodging through the crowd, racing each other back to the car. When Robert trudges round the corner into the cul-de-sac they are bent double, clutching their thighs, catching their breath. Franco straightens up. – I bet it *stinks* in there right now. And he and Blaney break into uncontrolled laughter again.

Robert stares at the ground, at his blistered, dirty feet.

– What's the matter with you? Blaney challenges.

– It's dumb, Robert says, as he clambers into the car and lies down on the back seat. *It's dumb. Stoopid.* He could argue with Blaney, but what's the point? Robert has just consumed the best milkshake of his whole entire life and now Blaney has ruined it. But his discontent goes deeper. All the way back to his nan's house Robert lies with his eyes shut, thinking about the cheerful waitress and how calm the café had felt when they first entered. That, too, has been tainted. Not only dumb, but wrong.

The following afternoon they start to bicker as soon as Blaney arrives.

– Don't blast your horn outside. I've asked you before, Robert says.

– I don't have to come round, you know, Blaney counters.

– Don't then. Robert sucks in his lower lip, raking his teeth over the shredded skin. They're on the veranda; they haven't even got inside yet. He chips cracked paint off one of the weatherboards.

Blaney flips. – I've had it, Robert. I've had it up to here. He storms back to his car and stands with the door open, shouting at Robert. – I'm sick of you, Robert, sick to death.

A gust of hot wind scuttles through the treetops and rattles a can back and forth in the gutter. All the other houses in the street are closed against the heat, but they're listening, Robert knows.

– I don't ever want to see you again. Blaney slams the door, grinds the car into gear and tears off down the road, his fist punched into the horn.

Robert waits until he can no longer distinguish Blaney's car in the distant rumble of traffic, and then he marches down the front path and out towards the main road. There is a coil of anger wound tight inside him and his feet carry him on, walking fast, his mind rushing with everything he has never said to Blaney.

He walks beyond his usual boundaries, past the high street with its parade of shops and on further, only vaguely aware that he is treading new territory. His T-shirt clings to him, plastered with sweat. He is afraid that if he stops walking his anger will snap into something like despair. It is clear to Robert that this is the big bust-up he has been expecting for some time. It is not yet clear to him which way he will go.

Eventually he slows a little and cuts in down a side road. He begins to take back streets that lead roughly in the direction of his nan's house. His surroundings come into focus, the clipped lawns and neat suburban houses, all the evidence of life – parked cars, dog mess, scraps of litter worried by the wind – but no one about, every living thing seeking refuge from the searing heat. Down by the coast, his family will be waiting for sundown to take a dip in the sea, Belinda dropping ice cubes down his dad's shirt, his nan preparing jugs of iced tea, his mum worrying whether Robert will remember to put sunblock on before going out.

Tomorrow he will be burnt, the skin on his feet swollen and shiny red. Tomorrow there will be no visit from Blaney, nor the day after. For the first time since they left, Robert wonders how long it is until his family returns.

He passes a squat block of flats. The smell of grilled chops drifts out from one flat, the sound of a baby crying from another. Shortly afterwards he comes out onto the high street. Blinking in the glare of sunlight, it's several seconds before he recognizes where he is. Then he crosses the road and heads for the lane which will take him home.

As he enters the lane he is assailed by a stench of stale urine, intensified by the heat, but undercut by the crisp scent of dried grass. As he nears the end of the lane, Robert notices a slight movement in the weeds to his left. Sometimes skinks have darted across his path, but this is different. When he steps closer there, in a nest of grass, is a tiny, panting ball of black fur.

Robert squats down and gingerly picks up the kitten. It lies in the palm of his hand: hot, seemingly blind, quivering, the little mouth pink and ajar. – Oh, where's your mum? Robert whispers before he can stop himself.

Already, as he carries the kitten back to his nan's, cradling it under his T-shirt to protect it from the sun, Robert understands that this is what he will rescue from the summer.

'Tutto Bene?'
Polly Wright

Does everyone start to look like tortoises as they get older? I thought. I had moved fast, but as I turned my head – there it was. In the mirror. The thickened neck. The straight line from collarbone to chin. I looked at Clare as she bent over the map. She whispered Italian place names to herself as she traced today's walk with her index finger. Her neck still curved. Not quite like a swan, but not bad. For forty-six.

'You've still got a young neck,' I said.

'Mmm,' she said as she held the map up like a newspaper and folded it in a new place. She took her glasses off to study it close up. She looked even younger without her glasses.

'Is this bread stale or do the Italians like it like this?' I said.

Clare was measuring the walk with her fingers. 'Five miles,' she muttered.

'Coffee's not even fresh. I mean, you'd have thought, in the morning. Wouldn't be that much trouble.'

I looked around the room. We were surrounded by tables. Each one covered in lace and heavy brocade, like Victorian ladies. The shutters kept out most of the sun. The wall lights and fringed side lamps were still on. We might as well have been in Bournemouth.

Only table number 9 was still at breakfast. She was probably in her seventies, and huge. Accidentally my eyes met hers. This was a mistake.

'*Buon giorno!*' she yelled at us over the sea of lace and cruets.

We *buon giorno*ed back, hoping it would do.

It didn't. The woman pulled herself up on her elephant legs and shifted her weight from side to side as she made for our table. She was wearing a shocking pink chiffon blouse, through which you could see every detail of her black lacy bra. She stopped beside us. My eyes were dangerously close to bra level.

'*Sorelles?*' was the only word we could make out from the whole paragraph of Italian she directed at us.

'Oh no, no . . . we're not sisters . . . we're friends . . . *amiche*,' Clare explained.

'*Amiche! Amiche!*' She hooted and snorted with laughter, and the lacy cups and their contents danced happily as she rolled off to share the joke with the other hotel residents who'd settled in for their card games in the conservatory next door. We heard them laugh too.

'Clare, are you sure *amiche* doesn't mean "lovers"?' I asked.

We were lovers, of course, but unlike some of our younger friends, we weren't in the habit of broadcasting it. We'd been together now for twelve years, and spent our modest salaries on house, garden and holidays abroad, once, sometimes even twice, a year.

And here we were on our – what was it? – thirteenth or fourteenth foreign holiday. Later that morning I counted them, as I slogged up yet another hot hillside, rising above yet another part of the Mediterranean. Sweat was dripping down my face and into my eyes, like teardrops going backwards, clouding my contact lenses.

'Means you're healthy,' Clare said. 'Your body's learnt to sweat.' She'd said that before, on one of our more adventurous holidays in Nicaragua. I was starting to feel irritated. Maybe my period was due. Yesterday as we tried to cross a racetrack – called a road in Italy – Clare said, 'Every woman for herself.' She'd said that in Nicaragua, too.

We stopped for a rest and sat on a large rock. Clare rested her arms on her knees and drew in air in great gulps and gasps like an asthmatic. I looked at a bush whose succulent leaves were as pale as sage. Its violet flowers with yellow hearts were like anemones.

Why do I always forget to bring the *Flora and Fauna of the Mediterranean* book? I thought.

'We forgot that book,' I said.

'*Flora and Fauna?*'

'Yes.'

And how many coastal walks had we done? I continued my list: Dorset, Wales, Kent, Crete, Spain, California. And all smelling roughly the same: heavy and woody, with a hint of salt. In Wales, though, there had been damp wild orchids; while here, dried thyme came and went. And in Wales there was always the same confusion of blackberry bushes, their delicate white flowers threaded through with convolvulus. But here, the convolvulus was exotic. Violet horns with bright pink veins, like raspberry ripple ice cream.

And wherever you were, coastal paths were always narrow, so you had to walk behind each other, sometimes stepping high to avoid the brambles. Especially when you were wearing shorts. But I always follow *her*. Always behind *her*, I thought. Following my bloody leader, I thought.

I went on counting. No, it couldn't have been fourteen *foreign* holidays, because we couldn't afford them at first. No, when we first got together we went to Wales and Devon. Places like that. Some friends of ours gave us this book called *SisterTravel*. An inventory of Women's Bed and Breakfasts in Britain.

The last one we went to was in Lyme Regis. All the rooms were named after Great Women, some of whom, of course, no one had ever heard of (but doesn't that just prove our point: *hidden from history*). We stayed in the Mistress Bedroom – the Vita Sackville-West room. They'd just done it up. A four-poster bed with maroon drapes, and sepia photos on the walls.

The effort of all the home improvements had obviously taken its toll on the landladies. The meals were often late, the customers left waiting in the draughty dining room. Although there weren't many of us, we were always seated together at the same table. Perhaps it saved on the washing-up.

Our fellow residents were a couple from Germany. I sat opposite Greta whose orange hair sat, like a hat, on top of her pinched, grey face. Clare faced Greta's lover – we never did catch her name – who was dark and glamorous and never spoke a word.

For a while we all sat in awkward silence, listening to the rows from behind the kitchen door and staring at a lurid painting called *Dorset View*. Its azure sky and emerald fields contrasted with our own view of Boots the Chemist, which was blurred with rain. Eventually, Greta addressed me in an effort to drown out the shouting. Maybe she had seen me squinting at *Dorset View*.

'Are you short sighted?'

'Yes . . . very.'

'*And you fancy Stacey, don't deny it, you* flirt *with her under my bloody nose!*' The oven door slammed.

'Why do you not wear glasses?'

'I wear contact lenses,' I replied.

'*Well at least Stacey makes some bloody effort to be interested in me – you never even* look *at me.*'

'Are *you* short sighted?' I shouted back to the thunk of a pan on the stove.

'Only when I was a child,' Greta bellowed.

'Pardon?' said Clare.

'*Why don't you just* piss *off?*'

'I was short sighted when I was a child because I didn't like what I saw of the world.'

There was suddenly a terrible silence behind the kitchen door. Greta warmed to her subject.

'Now I like my life, I don't need to wear glasses. You should try it. Take out your contact lenses.'

'Are you saying that short sight is psychological?' I could see that Clare was about to challenge Greta's theoretical position.

It was the silence that was worrying me, though. After all, there are knives in kitchens. A door swung and banged. I looked round, as one of the landladies advanced towards me, her horsey face pink with anger and cooking.

'Avocado?' she snarled.

'Thank you,' I whispered.

After that we booked a holiday in Spain.

I stopped behind Clare and waited while she studied the map. She turned it upside down, put her head on one side to orientate herself, swivelled the map round, looked out at the sea and up at the hillside, made decisions and finally led us down steep paths to the beach below. I didn't acknowledge her map-reading skills, and went straight into a café and up to the old man behind the bar.

'*Servicio?*'

He looked up and appraised me with distaste, and didn't answer. I saw myself as he must see me: a sweaty, dirty foreigner dressed in shorts and a singlet like a schoolboy. Women didn't look like that in his country. I became irrationally angry.

'*Toletta?*'

Pause.

'*Dov'e la toletta?*' I added, for clarification.

He lifted his hand and pointed to a door, not looking at me at all this time. I felt dizzy. I leant across the counter and hissed: '*Grazie!*'

He looked away from me and up at the football match on the huge TV which hung from the ceiling.

The beach was divided into narrow strips by wire fences, like a battlefield. Every hotel in the village owned a section. Only the large rocks jutting out into the sea were public, and people covered them like birds. We gave our ticket to a bored-looking girl who sat beside our hotel sign. I tried to ask if it entitled us to an umbrella. I pointed to a picture of a grinning family with orange tans under a scarlet umbrella and then back at my ticket. The girl looked blank. Clare walked away from me.

'It doesn't matter, Jenny. Leave it.'

'We'll get sunstroke.'

'We've got hats.'

I gave up and followed her down to a tiny piece of sand on the edge of the sea. Clare stood and wrapped her towel round her waist, wriggled off her knickers and stepped into her bathing costume. It was one of those M&S ones with legs, so you don't have to worry about your bikini line.

I sat down and looked out to sea. An old man stood at the end of one of the public rocks, fishing. He had a huge head, and his knock knees stuck out like those on a cartoon character of a weedy schoolkid. His chest was sunk into his body and his hands were disproportionately large, like a baby's. Most of his face had shrunk into his nose. The focus of his whole frail being was his fishing line.

I looked around at the people on the beach. Some were sitting in deckchairs in lines, like an audience watching the sea's performance. Others were splayed out like starfish in the sun. At the edge of the sea, a young couple played with their baby. She screamed at the foamy waves; her fat rubbery legs stuck out from under her white frilly dress and her arms went into spasms of excitement.

'Silly old sea . . . you can't catch me . . .' I said.

'What?'

'Something Dad used to say to me when I was little. We used to shout it and run away from waves coming in.'

'Have you seen how yellow the foam is? Means the sea's polluted,' said Clare.

The sun went in. Large grey clouds blotted out the blue. An Italian beach without the sun is all wrong, I thought. The starfish sat up; their backs rounded, their glamour lost in the grey. Rain began to spit. I suddenly longed for the great, deserted beaches of home. I remembered holidays in Wales when we were kids. The silver sea and sky, no line dividing them. The donkey-brown sand pitted with shining puddles. Where it was dry, the sand was like riddled ash.

Clare and I trailed up the path back to our hotel in the rain. We walked through the conservatory, where the hotel's residents were sitting waiting for their evening meal. A few of the old women stood round a scrawny young girl. One wound a piece of cloth around her arm, another waved a tube of rubber about and they all shouted and gesticulated. It had been the same every night we'd been there. Blood-pressure-taking was the evening's entertainment.

A father and daughter sat on a garden two-seater swinging seat, upholstered in a drab pattern of yellow and beige. The father pushed one of his feet on the ground to make the seat swing. The daughter sat very close to him, her right thigh seemingly attached to his left. They both stared grimly ahead.

We slowly mounted the stairs. Past the painting of a little girl exposing her bum, looking coyly through enormous fringed eyes over her shoulder at the viewer; past the fire extinguisher and the embroidered, Latin-inscribed scenes of the adventures of Marco Polo, and into our room.

We unrolled our damp gritty towels, chucked our swimming costumes in the basin, emptied sand out of our trainers, took books and Boots SolTan Factors 8 and 15 out of the rucksack (8 for me; 15 for her), emptied the rucksack of sand on the balcony, showered, put on loose cotton trousers and shirts and went out again. All without speaking.

'Have you got the key?' asked Clare. I held up the pink plastic slab and looked past her into a mirror shaped like a standing-up ironing board. I avoided my profile this time, but I still looked old. The sunburn emphasized it somehow.

In the dining room we sat at our usual table and drank last night's wine. They re-corked the bottle for us every night after our meal, labelled it and kept it in the fridge. On the table, beside our starters, were two copies of tomorrow's menu. Mario, the manageress's son, used his English dictionary to translate. We were offered a choice between Without Spines

Trout or Salmon Aggrieved with Sauce. We ticked our boxes and Mario bowed and smiled and we all made circling and shrugging gestures to indicate friendship.

The dining room was very empty tonight.

'Business is bad,' I said. Clare didn't reply.

The father and daughter from the swing seat came in with the rest of their family. The father was very handsome – blond hair, a heavy tan and a stylishly sulky mouth. His wife wore a wrap-round flowery skirt and strappy gold sandals. She fussed over her younger daughter, who was messing with her food. Eventually, when the child started screaming, the mother yanked her up from the table and dragged her out. The father and older daughter remained aloof from this struggle, and sat, not eating, not talking, just staring, staring ahead. The coy picture on the first-floor landing came into my head. I got up quickly.

'Let's go,' I said.

On our way upstairs, Theresa, the hotel manageress, jumped out from her office and accosted us. We stood by a desk light: a huge wrought-iron model of St Mark's Cathedral. Theresa was like a pretty rat – thin, anxious face and strained eyes. She could speak no more English than we could Italian and she mimed at us with her long, elegant hands.

'*Tutto bene?*' she asked, searching our faces for truth.

'*Si, tutto bene.*'

I thought it was about time I asked the sentence I had prepared earlier, about whether umbrellas were included in the price of the beach ticket. The Signora looked worried. I repeated my sentence, confident that I had checked every single word in the dictionary, and still Theresa looked uncomprehending. Clare took over and Theresa understood perfectly.

I felt dizzy with anger. I didn't give a damn about the bloody umbrella; I'd just wanted to communicate, independently, like a grown-up. I was fed up with being an inadequate Brownie to Clare's Brown Owl. I was forty-five, for God's sake. Some people were *grandmothers* at my age and I couldn't even make myself understood on the simplest level without bloody Clare intervening.

Upstairs, in our tiny, twin-bedded room, which was far from *tutto bene*, I threw the Italian dictionary at Clare and screamed, 'I'm not a child!' – knowing that at that moment I was on shaky ground. Clare took off her shirt and hung it up.

'What are you doing?' I shouted at her.

'Going to bed,' she said. She put on a T-shirt which someone had given me for Christmas. It had a picture of a woman crying cartoon tears, a bubble coming out of her mouth, saying: *Oh no, I forgot to have children.*

'That's my T-shirt,' I said and opened my book.

Clare curved her back towards me and opened hers.

I pretended to read until I was sure she was asleep. Then I lay and stared at the shutters and listened to the shouting and slamming of car doors outside. Eventually, I got up and sat on the tiny balcony. *Sea Views*, the hotel publicity boasted. Well, you could just about see it in the daytime – a blue triangle between blocks of flats and a building site. But at night all you could see were towerblocks and lights from the bars.

A light snapped on in the apartment opposite. A young woman in high heels clicked out onto the balcony. She started unpegging a bikini and a pair of boxer shorts from her nylon washing line. A man called from inside the rectangle of light. After a moment he came out and put his arms round her waist and nuzzled her neck. I watched them kiss and giggle. They didn't notice me.

I remembered staying with my grandmother one time in Wales. When she discovered me ticking off the days on a calendar till going home time, she looked at me, hurt.

'We do it at school,' I'd said. 'We tick off the days till the holidays.'

'But you *are* on holiday, now,' she'd said. 'You're meant to be enjoying yourself.'

I pictured the pages in my diary. Every year was the same.

Each page packed with instructions in different coloured inks and types of scrawl – sometimes big and hurried, other times cramped and meticulous. And then – two weeks in August. White, a diagonal line across the whole two pages. Sometimes I'd write *holiday* or the place I was going. But still, underneath the line, there would always be boxes of nothingness. Perhaps it would help if I went on writing in them: *11.00 a.m. Go up Mountain. 3.00 p.m. Have coffee. 7.30 p.m. Try Fish Place by Harbour.*

And when I got home people always asked, 'How was it? Did you enjoy yourself?'

And I'd have to look dreamy and say, 'Yes. Really great, thank you.' It would be disloyal to Clare to say anything else. A wrong sort of ticking-off.

If we had children, I thought, there *would* be some point. We could be teaching them things – introducing them to new bits of life. Showing them the sea for the first time. *Oh no. I forgot to have children.* Somebody gave me that T-shirt as a joke. Some joke. I forgot to have children and now it's too late. *Silly old sea, you can't catch me.* The best years of my life, gone, in a flash. I started to cry cramped, tight sobs.

After the tears stopped, I sat for a while in the warm night, listening to the ebb and flow of traffic and voices. The couple opposite were still outside, laughing and getting drunk. They couldn't have heard me crying. And if they had, what would they have made of it? Some incomprehensible, foreign grief.

A light came on in our stifling room.

'Are you all right?' Clare called.

I went back inside and lay down, with my back to her on her narrow bed. She curved round me: her hand on mine, her mouth on my neck.

'Why didn't we have a baby, Clare? I mean, we could have done. Like Liz and Karen. One of us could have gone off and had a fuck. Or the turkey-baster.'

'Is that why you were crying out there? Because we haven't got a baby?'

'Yes,' I said. Sort of, I thought.

'Oh, Jenny,' she said and hugged me tighter.

The next day we skipped the hotel breakfast, and went instead to a café and dunked croissants into fresh cappuccinos. We bought bags of fat maroon cherries and sweet tomatoes, and goat's cheese and bread baked in olive oil.

We left the village and headed for the hills. We passed the farm we passed every day, where vine-leaves were woven through a trellis roof into an arbour. As always, an old man sat in the shade on an upturned crate, staring at rows of emerald green lettuces and a haze of fennel.

'Perhaps he's waiting to catch slugs,' I said.

We ate our picnic under an olive tree. Afterwards we lay, heads on our rucksacks, gazing up at the thin chalky-green leaves and the tiny khaki fruit. The cicada chorus came and went like shakes of a tambourine.

'Clare, why do they stick bottles on some of the branches?' I asked sleepily.

'To fend off ivy, I think,' she said. She was right. The ivy was stopped from winding itself round trees wherever there were old green bottles. I squeezed her hand, and felt her skin, clammy with sweat. I loved her for knowing things.

After lunch, I followed Clare up the hill again, and watched her walk, leaning forward and slowly shifting her weight from side to side. Every now and then we both stopped and stood looking down the valley, wiping the sweat off our faces with our T-shirts and swigging from the water bottle. The hillside looked as it must have done for centuries, I thought, with the furry ridges of the terraces and the roofs with terracotta tiles like flower pots on their sides.

At last we hauled ourselves to a café in a derelict church at the top of a hill. The old bell had been taken down and a fence put round it, as if it were a sapling or a special plant. We ordered a bottle of wine and sat with our books, the valley stretched out before us.

The peace was broken by screams. The young couple we'd

seen on the beach the day before were determinedly pushing a buggy towards the café. The husband almost ran inside, leaving his wife to wrestle their crying baby out of the pushchair. When at last she'd pulled her child free of the straps, she sat, disconsolately jogging her up and down on her knee to no effect. The young man didn't emerge from the café. From where I was sitting, I could dimly see him inside, leaning on the bar and drinking a beer.

'We could ring up that place when we get home,' Clare said.

'What place?' I asked.

'The Women's Reproductive thingy. That place in London.'

'Too late, my love, too late.'

'Never too late.'

'The saddest two words in the English language.'

'Who said that?'

'Enid Blyton.'

I watched the young mother's face as she rested her chin on her child's lacy sunhat and stared ahead without focusing. You couldn't tell whether she was looking at us or at the caged bell. The baby was whimpering, exhausted by her own crying.

'Seriously. It's not too late. I read this article in the *New Scientist* . . .' Clare tailed off as I put my arm round her and kissed her coarse hair. The mother stared at us with sudden interest. Clare sat up straight and pushed me off.

'Time to go home,' she said.

'Time to go home. Andy and Teddy are waving goodbye.' I poured myself another glass of wine and raised it to mother and child. The girl stared for a moment and then smiled.

'Jenny . . .' Clare stood up.

'I know. Behave. Lead me home, Cap'n. Take the bottle.'

We finished it off on the way back and even Clare had difficulty in finding the path.

That night, as we came downstairs for dinner at the hotel, we could hear raised voices and laughter and, when we opened the door, the room was full. A group of Germans, big and loud and smoothly brown, replaced the sinister father and his family. Black Lacy Bra had been moved from table number 9 to a table in the corner, with lots of other Italian people to talk to.

Everyone was shouting and clinking glasses and drinking. It was Friday night.

And Saturday's menu was ready for ticking. As we tucked into our trout fillets, we anticipated tomorrow's feast. I caught Mario's proud eye as I read: 'Squids and Sardinians.'

End of Story
Ali Smith

I know a good one, the woman says. It's a really horrible one, but it's good. Does it matter if it's horrible?

I am out for the evening at a Turkish restaurant in a part of the city I don't know, with my friend Anthony and two apparently very old friends of his. Anthony is my old friend. These old friends of his are people who, though I've known him for years, Anthony has never mentioned to me.

No, he is saying. The horribler the better. He rubs his hands together.

So long as it's true, the woman's husband says. His name is Bob.

We are halfway through the starters and supposed to be taking turns at telling stories to each other. The stories have to be true. It isn't my turn yet. I can't imagine what I'm going to say when it is. I can't think of a single thing and I am already panicking about it. I also can't remember the woman's name. I think it's Linda, but I'm not sure. I am hoping someone will call her by her name again soon. So far I've managed to avoid using it.

Right, she says. A famous mountaineer goes to stay at a rich lady's house.

Everybody looks animated. I try to look it too; I widen my eyes and nod. But for the past few days I've been in a kind of a fog where I can't seem to hear or see properly, and whenever I try to think all I'm able to think about is the dreams I've had, two different dreams. I had them last weekend. I had them one after the other, one one night then one the next, and they were both about my first love and in one she was young and sharp and happy-looking, like she was when we were fifteen, and in the other she was the age we are now, and a drunkard.

He doesn't know the lady but they have friends in common or something, and she invites him for supper, and it's a huge old manor house out in the country, out in the middle of nowhere, somewhere he's never been before, and it's the kind of place you can't get back from easily so he's going to have to stay there overnight.

Which mountaineer is it? my friend Anthony asks.

I can't remember his name, the woman says. You'd know it, he's famous, he had, what's it called, in his toes, when they, you know, freeze and fall off.

Is it Bonington? Is it Scott? Bob asks. Is it Ratcliffe?

I don't think so, the woman says.

Is it Fiennes? my friend Anthony asks.

No, the woman says. It's something else.

She looks blank. They look blank. I look blank too, though right now the version that's inside my head is the drunk version, where she is raddled and shouting, her face is alcohol-red, lined like a homeless person's, her clothes are all filthy and she's sitting on the pavement kerb and slurrily pointing at me and shouting, *I know you, I'm sure I do, who are you again?*

Anyway, the woman says. He gets to the house and the lady welcomes him in and it's this beautiful house, centuries old and all antique furniture and chairs, with tapestries on the walls, and paintings of the lady's ancestors on their horses. And it's the middle of winter and stormy outside, the lights are flickery, the walls and floors are all wood so that when people walk everything around them creaks. And there's a butler and a cook and maids, there's a maid who takes his coat when he comes in.

So the lady leads him through to the dining room and they have their supper at one of those long tables, with the local dignitaries or whatever, who've all been invited to meet the mountaineer.

I know you, I'm sure I do, who are you again? I poke at the vine leaves on my plate. One has unravelled and I can see the broken bits of rice and mint stuck together randomly and waiting to be eaten.

It's really delicious, she says, one of the best meals he's ever had, and they drink a lot of old wine from the lady's wine cellar and then after supper, after the last guest has gone home, the lady says now she'll show him upstairs. So. They're going up the stairs, and the lady tells the mountaineer that there's no electricity in the guest bedroom and would he like a torch or a candle, and he says, no, he'll be fine –

Why is there no electricity? Bob says.

I don't know, the woman says. Probably because it's an old house. Because of the fittings.

This isn't a true story, Bob says. He sits back, folds his arms. The woman's face darkens.

It *is*, she says. I read it in the *Guardian*. I'm not making this up. No, I tell a lie, actually I saw him, I saw him on TV. It was on a documentary. Well, I'm not going to bother telling it if nobody's going to listen.

Bob is looking around him now in a bored way at the other people in the restaurant.

Go on, Lynn, my friend Anthony says.

My friend Anthony. I always think of him as that, never just as Anthony, I always have. This is the first time I've seen him in nearly a year. He's sitting next to me; he smells comfortingly like he always does, even in a strange restaurant, of cigarette smoke and of his flat.

It *is* true, Lynn is saying. She sounds angry.

Come on. They're going up the stairs, my friend Anthony says.

I nod at her and make an encouraging noise in my throat. We need to know what happens, I say. I'm surprised at the sound of my voice. It's the only thing I've said all evening, apart from saying hello when I arrived. Also I don't want her story to stop in case it makes it my turn to tell one. I am getting edgy. I still haven't thought of a story that's true and we haven't even finished the starters yet.

Well, Lynn says, as long as someone needs to. So. Right. They're going up the stairs. And she says the thing about the light and the torch, and he tells her he doesn't mind being in the dark or anything because, you know, of being a mountaineer and how they don't mind extremes and aren't afraid of anything and spend half their lives in the dark scraping for footholds on some rockface. And then the rich lady says to him is he afraid of ghosts, because people who've stayed in this room have told her it's haunted, and the mountaineer laughs –

Stupid ghost story, Bob says.

Actually it isn't, Lynn says. She looks at him with venom. Wait and see, she says. It isn't a stupid ghost story at all, and the whole point of it is that it isn't one. And that it's true.

And how can he get up the stairs if his toes have fallen off? Bob says. He must be disabled. He must be in a wheelchair, or on crutches. You can't walk without toes, never mind get upstairs, never mind climb up a bloody rockface.

I didn't say *his* toes had fallen off, did I? Lynn says. I just said he had the thing that sometimes *makes* them fall off. And the mountaineer says he doesn't believe in ghosts. So it's no problem for him. And the rich lady smiles and opens this small wooden door in a wall, with one of those old-fashioned latches that you have to lift, like in National Trust properties, and he has to bend down to get in, he's quite tall, on the programme he stood up, I saw, so there was nothing wrong with his legs, and showed us how he went in.

So, he's in the room, and there's a four-poster bed that takes up most of it, and he turns to say goodnight to the lady but she's suddenly put the landing light out and just disappeared, and he's completely in the dark.

It is so dark that he can't see his own hand. He holds it out.

He can't see anything. So. He feels his way over to the bed, and it has these thick curtains all round it and it's quite high off the ground. He feels for the gap in the curtains and swings up on to the bed. It's even darker in there, with the curtains and everything. He takes his clothes off, he gets in under the covers, and he goes to sleep.

In the middle of the night he wakes up. The bed is moving. The curtains are swaying. The whole frame of it is moving, back and fore, back and fore. There's a creaking noise coming from somewhere, creak-creak, creak-creak, like that. And at first he thinks he's drunk too much. He thinks he's imagining it. But it goes on, and on, and on, the moving bed, the creaking noise, the moving bed, the creaking. He's terrified. He realizes he's never been this terrified in his life. He's too terrified to look. He's too terrified to move. He's too terrified to do anything. All he can do is lie in the pitch black in the bed, creaking, like the bed is a boat on water, and keep his eyes shut.

Lynn stops. We all look at her. She looks at Bob.

And? Bob says.

Lynn raises her eyebrow.

Eventually, she says, the noise stops. The bed settles down and stops moving. The mountaineer falls asleep again. But in the morning, when he wakes up –

A waiter comes and clears our plates. We sit back to let him, then all lean forward again.

What? I say.

What? my friend Anthony says.

Lynn waits.

Well, what? Bob says.

What do you think? she says.

What do you mean, what do we think? Bob says.

What do you think happens? she says. What do you think he sees?

Oh, I know, Bob says, I bet I know. He wakes up and now that there's light he can see that there's a couple in the bed beside him, the rich woman and a dignitary, or her and the butler, or a dignitary and a maid, and they're asleep.

You mean, like the creaking and the moving was them having sex? Lynn says.

Absolutely, Bob says.

Lynn smiles. She looks pleased. Nope, she says.

No? Bob says. Are you sure?

What do you mean, am I sure? Lynn says.

There's nothing else it could be, Bob says. It is. I've guessed it. You're just changing it to suit yourself.

He gets a cigar out of his pocket, pulls the cellophane off and crumples it in his hand, then throws it into the ashtray on the table where it slowly opens itself out again as if it is daring itself to be insolent to him.

I'm not changing it, Lynn says, nonplussed. She looks at us. Tony? she says.

I've got it, my friend Anthony says. How about this? He wakes up, and there are cobwebs everywhere, all over the moth-eaten curtains, all over him too. He wipes them off his face onto his clothes, the clothes he took off last night. They're covered in cobwebs too. He pushes back the curtains – they're so old now that they fall apart in his hands. He finds himself in a ruined room, dust everywhere, ceiling rafters all collapsed and broken bits on the floor. He opens the door. It falls off its hinge – rotten. He goes downstairs. He has to be careful where he puts his feet on the stairs because they're rotten too. When he gets downstairs, he knows. He ate the food of the dead last night. He's in a house that hasn't been inhabited for years.

No, Bob says. It can't be. She said it wasn't a ghost story. Or if he's right and I'm wrong, then you're lying, Lynn, and it *is* a stupid ghost story.

You're both wrong, Lynn says. And it isn't a ghost story. And I said it was horrible, remember?

That's pretty horrible, waking up covered in cobwebs, my friend Anthony says.

Lynn shakes her head.

Well, *I* think that's horrible, he says.

Lynn is looking at me. What do you think, eh, –

I know you. I'm sure I do. Who are you again?

I tell her my name again, and shrug. I don't know, I've no idea, I say. I haven't a clue.

The clues are: horrible, and true, Bob says. Those are the clues. Come on.

They are all looking at me. They look angry and impatient, even my friend Anthony.

Maybe he wakes up, I say, the mountaineer, and finds that instead of in a bed in a bedroom, he's just lying in the wet grass in the middle of a field. The whole house has disappeared. Maybe there never was a house at all. Maybe he's spent the night in a place that doesn't exist any more, or a place that never actually existed. Maybe he can't remember who he is or why he's there, and there's nothing anywhere around him to tell him these things.

Lynn's eyes grow large and round. Bob makes an exasperated noise. The waiter comes back with our main courses, four plates balanced on his arms and in his hands. He places them one in front of each of us. He gets it right, and asks if we want anything else. Then he goes to fetch the beers.

Oh my God, Lynn says after he's gone, nodding at me. That would be really horrible, what you said.

Just the same thing, the ghost story thing, Bob says. It can't be what happens. Is it? She didn't get it, did she?

No, Lynn says, that's not the end. But it would . . . oh God, imagine, imagine how creepy.

So what *is* it? Bob says.

Imagine, Lynn is saying, if we all thought we were sitting somewhere and then we woke up and we weren't sitting there at all, it hadn't existed. Like if we thought we were eating at a Turkish restaurant, like, telling stories like this, with people we knew, and then it turned out that none of it had ever even happened.

Bob starts to swear and the people sitting at the next tables turn and stare at us.

No, this is all definitely happening, my friend Anthony says as Bob bangs our table with his fist and the glasses and plates jump. The people sitting near our table jump.

What's the fucking end? Bob shouts. Three men with their wives at the table closest to us look at us, annoyed and muttering. Bob glares at them. All I'm saying, he says, is I want to *know*. I just fucking well want to *know*. What's the problem with that?

He is standing up now, threatening to punch the nearest of the men at the other table. What's your problem? he says. The man stands up. His wife pulls at his sleeve. Lynn stands up. A waiter comes over. Bob asks the waiter what his problem is too. More waiters come and stand behind our waiter.

It's shortly after this that we are asked to leave the restaurant.

The mountaineer's story ends like this:

When he opened his eyes and pushed back the curtain he saw that one of the rich lady's maids had choked herself to death on a rope tied on to the end of the bed. That's why the bed was moving; that was the source of the creaking noise. For the mountaineer, though, this was a gruesome find, it wasn't just an end, it was also a beginning. Fear makes you powerless, that's what he learned when he woke up in the rich lady's house that morning, he says. He didn't recognize the maid, he didn't know her, and he had no idea why she would want to do this to herself, or to him, or in his room, but those things are irrelevant. They don't matter. What matters is that at the crucial moment he chose not to look. He tells the camera he will never not look again, the incident has opened his eyes. He nods his head at the camera. The credits roll.

The story of the dreams about the first lover ends like this:

I go home and get undressed and washed and brush my teeth. I sit on the edge of my bed. I tell myself that if I dream that she is her pure young self tonight, and the dream-self tries to kiss me, I will kiss her back in my dream with all my heart, and if I dream that she is drunk and out of it and sitting on the pavement asking who I am, even if I am terrified to, I will go across the road in my dream and tell her, and sit down beside her, and I will do it with all my heart too. I have no idea what I will dream. It could be anything. It probably won't be about her at all.

I get into bed and stare upwards in the dark. I think about the first time she touched me so that touch mattered, which was the first time anyone did. We were in the school corridor. We were fifteen. We were late for different classes; there was no time. She didn't say anything. She looked me in the eye. She put her hand on my shoulder, gripped it tight. The touch said: we're comrades. It said: see you.

I close my eyes and nothing is over.

I wonder what will happen.

The story about the four people telling true stories while they're out for a meal ends like this:

Getting thrown out of the restaurant makes all four of us into old friends. Since we haven't eaten properly yet we go to McDonald's and queue up at the counter. Bob asks for a Big Mac. Lynn has a McChicken Burger. Anthony has a Happy Meal and I have Chicken McNuggets and fries. We ask for drinks, the names of which also have a Mc stuck on the front. For a while we stick Mcs on the front of random words to each other, as if we've invented a language.

Everything smells sweet and tastes sweet. We eat sitting in a line on the castle wall, laughing about how we got thrown out of the Turkish restaurant. Then Bob and Lynn say goodnight. They both hug me before they go; Lynn kisses my cheek, Bob kisses the top of my head. We all agree to go out together another time. They leave arm in arm, waving goodbye.

Anthony says he'll walk me home. I tell him I'm going to the all-night supermarket for a pint of milk and some toothpaste. He says all right, he'll walk me there instead. He says he could do with some excitement. He says he's not ready for the evening to end just yet.

It's only Wednesday and it's only about ten o'clock, but it's warm and the streets are full of people shouting. There are groups of girls in their teens and their twenties squealing and yelling, and groups of nearly-men boys bellowing and snarling. Occasionally the groups are mixed, and when they are the laughter and shouting is a mix of deep and high, nervous and sexual. Across from the bus station the taxi drivers sit sullen by themselves in their cars. A girl, about eighteen, pushes past us; her mascara has run so that her face in the light of the supermarket front looks damaged, as if someone has stamped it.

In the shop light I catch sight of Anthony, my friend. I haven't noticed till now. He looks dreadful. He is dishevelled. His hair needs cut. He brushes with his hand at his face like he can't see properly. He looks, in this light, as if he's been through something terrible. I can't imagine what it is. I realize I don't know anything about him. We've been friends for years. He is standing in his jacket by the tins of meat like a man standing after an earthquake. He squints upwards to read the words above the aisles telling us where and what everything is. Suddenly he turns to me and smiles.

Toothpaste, he says, triumphant, and points the way.

We buy the toothpaste and the milk. He lends me three pounds so I don't have to break a twenty pound note. I buy him a bar of chocolate with his own change. Outside the supermarket he breaks the chocolate bar in half and gives me half. He says it's the food of explorers and tells me to eat it slowly. I say I will if he will. Then we say goodnight, and promise to be in touch with each other, and he goes one way, and I go the other.

Biographical Notes

Naylah Ahmed was born in Birmingham in 1976. Her passion for writing began with poetry (*Red Red Tears*, Jaru Publications), and now includes radio drama (*Mrs Parker*, *The Happy Gathering*: BBC Radio 4), television (*Kismet Road*), and short fiction (*Whispers in the Walls*, Tindal Street Press). She is currently developing her first stage play with the Birmingham Rep's Writer's Attachment Scheme. One of her next ambitions is to write for the big screen.

Gaynor Arnold was born and brought up in Cardiff, but has spent over half her life in Birmingham. She works in foster care and adoption. A member of Tindal Street Fiction Group, she has had short stories published in *Nutshell*, *Raw Edge*, *The New Writer* and the Tindal Street anthology, *Mouth*. She has also written a novel. 'Hospitality' was shortlisted for both the Asham Award, 1999, and the Fish Prize (Ireland) in 2000. Gaynor is married with two grown-up children.

A widely published poet, **Rachel Bentham**'s stories and dramas have been broadcast on BBC Radio 4. Her first screenplay won the Picture This prize. She is presently writing a novel set in the twelfth century, in which her heroine can make such hideous faces she is taken on as a gargoyle model – but she's also used to model the Virgin Mary. Rachel lives in Bristol, teaches scriptwriting and knits odd things. She has four children.

25-year-old **Gemma Blackshaw** grew up in Chelmsford, Essex. 'Girlfriend' is the third story to be published from her collection in progress, *The Promised Land*, which is strongly located in the Essex landscape. Gemma joined Tindal Street Fiction Group in 1998, after receiving the Audrey Pipe Creative Writing Fellowship from the University of Birmingham. She now lives in London's East End, where she spends her days in the British Library, writing up a PhD thesis.

Rachel Bradford was born in 1971. She studied English Literature at UEA. She is currently living in North London and working on a collection of extremely short stories that she calls *Chips & Scraps*.

Liza Cody grew up in London. She has worked as a painter, furniture designer, photographer, graphic designer, basketball coach and hair-inserter. Her first novel, *Dupe*, won the John Creasey Memorial Prize for Crime Fiction. In 1992 she won the Crime Writers' Association Silver Dagger Award for *Bucket Nut*, the first in a trilogy which included *Monkey Wrench* and *Musclebound*. *Gimme More* is her latest novel.

Myra Connell, an acupuncturist and Zero Balancer, has been a writer all her life. Her work has been published in *Spinster* and *Writing Women*. She was a founder member of Women and Words, a Birmingham group which published *Don't Come Looking Here* and *And another thing . . .*, and of Bleak House Books, a publishing co-operative that published *Birmingham for the Under Fives* and *Getting on in Birmingham*. She has two teenage sons and travels frequently to New York.

Helen Cross was born and brought up in the village of Newbald, East Yorkshire. Her stories have appeared in several magazines and anthologies. Her first novel, *My Summer of Love*, was published by Bloomsbury in 2001. She lives in Birmingham.

Donna Daley-Clarke is British and lives in London. Her parents are from the Eastern Caribbean island of Montseratt. She graduated in October 2001 from the Creative Writing MA at the University of East Anglia, and she read at the Hay Festival in 2001. Donna is currently working on a novel called *A Lazy Eye*. 'Saturday Soup' is her first published story.

Penny Feeny, a former copywriter, editor and freelance broadcaster, now concentrates on fiction. Her first successful story was produced on BBC Radio 4 in 1997. Since then, her stories have won prizes, been broadcast, or published in, for example, *Atlantic Monthly*, *Mslexia*, *QWF*, *World Wide Writers* and *Northern Stories 8*. Born in Cambridge, Penny came – via London and Rome – to Liverpool, where she has long been settled with her partner and their five children.

Jackie Gay is a writer and editor. Her first novel *Scapegrace* was published by Tindal Street Press in 2000. *Her Majesty* is the third anthology that she has co-edited, following the prize-winning *Hard Shoulder* (Tindal Street Press, 1999) and *England Calling* (Weidenfeld & Nicolson, 2001).

Emma Hargrave lives in Birmingham. *Her Majesty* is the first anthology she has co-edited.

Hilaire was born and brought up in Melbourne, but has lived in London since 1986. Her stories have been published in various magazines, and the anthologies *5 Uneasy Pieces* (Pulp Faction, 1998), *The Ex Files* (Quartet, 1998), *Suspect Device* (Serpent's Tail, 1998) and *Neonlit: The Time Out Book of New Writing Vol. 1* (Quartet, 1998). Her novel *Hearts on Ice* was published by Serpent's Tail in 2000.

Tina Jackson is a journalist and writer. After working as features editor for Leeds' now-defunct independent magazine, *The Northern Star*, she became arts editor of the London-based *Big Issue*, and has written for newspapers and magazines, including the *Guardian*, the *Independent* and *Hello!*. Her short stories have been widely anthologized, most recently in *England Calling*.

Pauline Masurel has spent most of her life within walking distance of one tributary or another of the Thames. Her short fiction has been published by *London Magazine* and *Writing Women*, and broadcast on Radio 4. In 1995 she was a winner in the BBC's First Bite competition for young writers. Much of her recent writing has involved online collaboration; see http://www.northpoint.org.uk/writing.html. A short-story collection is currently with an agent.

Annie Murray has published stories in *SHE*, in two *London Magazine* anthologies, *Signals 1* and *Signals 3*, and six historical novels with Pan Macmillan, among them *Birmingham Rose* and *The Narrowboat Girl*. She comes originally from Berkshire and after a long spell in Birmingham now lives in Reading, with her husband and four children. In her free time she likes swimming, walking and conversation.

Kwa'mboka is half Kisii and half Kikuyu. An economist, curator, broadcaster, author and producer of performing arts, she is currently launching a web-based process, 'Jua-Kali' (Fierce Sun), exploring creativity in and out of Europe. A nomad, she lives in a large tent pitched on the plains of the West Midlands. Her short story 'Secret Life' was published in *Whispers in the Walls* (Tindal Street Press, 2000).

Ifemu Omari has written three stage plays, *Edge of the Circle* (1989), *Ruby* (1991) and *Dream Circus for Hire* (1993). Her short story 'Chrysalis' was published in *Whispers in the Walls* (Tindal Street Press, 2000). Ifemu is a freelance lecturer, who specializes in African and Caribbean literature, and she is also a freelance worker in research and development.

Sadie Plant is a writer based in Birmingham. She has taught at the University of Birmingham and the University of Warwick, and now writes full-time. Her most recent book is *Writing on Drugs*, published in paperback by Faber and Faber in 2000.

Amy Prior has edited two themed fiction anthologies for Serpent's Tail. Her own stories have appeared in several literary journals and anthologies. She runs writing workshops at universities in London, programmes multi-arts events and occasionally contributes to US and UK magazines. Amy recently received an Oppenheim-John Downes Memorial Trust Award to complete her own short-fiction collection.

Penny Simpson's short stories have appeared in anthologies published by Bloomsbury, Virago, the Bridport Prize and in *Myslexia*. She received an Arts Council of Wales New Writers Bursary to complete her first novel. A former TMA Theatre Critic of the Year, her play, *Knuckle Down*, was presented by Sgript Cymru at Theatr Clwyd Cymru in 2001. Brought up in Sussex, she now lives in Wales and earns a crust working for touring theatre companies across the UK.

Ali Smith was born in Inverness in 1962 and lives in Cambridge. She has published two collections of short stories, *Free Love* (Virago 1995) and *Other stories and other stories* (Granta 1999) and two novels, *Like* (Virago 1997) and *Hotel World* (2001), and co-edited *Brilliant Careers, The Virago Book of Twentieth Century Fiction* (2000).

Polly Wright, born in London in 1950, is a lecturer, writer and actress. A founder member of the Birmingham-based theatre company, Women and Theatre, she has co-written and performed in many plays and cabaret sketches. In 1999 she joined Tindal Street Fiction Group, and started to write short stories. Polly now runs the Arts and Creative Studies department at Fircroft College of Adult Education.